EVERNIGHT PUBLISHING ®

www.evernightpublishing.com

Copyright© 2016

Evernight Publishing

Editor: Katelyn Uplinger

Cover Artist: Jay Aheer

ISBN: 978-1-77339-046-8

DARK CAPTIVE ANTHOLOGY

Everyone has a dark side...

Take Me by Jenika Snow

Sinful by Lily Harlem

One Last Job by Alexa Sinclaire

Captive Artist by N.J. Young

The Shadow by Elena Kincaid

Godsend by Jocelyn Dex

TAKE ME

Jenika Snow

Copyright © 2016

Chapter One

The music was loud, the bodies crammed together, but Holly felt free, felt like nothing could touch her. With her life, and the restraints her father put on her, she couldn't help but just let go, even if it was just for this one moment.

"Let's get you another drink."

Holly looked over at her friend, Rachel, and nodded. Yeah, another drink sounded good right about now, especially since her buzz was wearing off. Holly didn't even want to think about having to go back to the house, not when she knew she'd get the third degree from her father for not being home at the time he set, and because she'd been drinking.

I'm twenty-one years old. I shouldn't have to be set with such high restrictions.

Of course, she'd never say those words out loud, not when she knew things had been so tough around the house.

Breathing out to calm and center herself, she watched Rachel move through the bodies crammed inside the club, and walk up to the bar. Rachel held up two fingers to the bartender, but Holly turned her back to her and scanned the dance floor. They'd been dancing together, a trick that usually kept the creepers away, but of course, tonight they were in full force as they ground their bodies against them.

"Fresh from the bottle," Rachel's voice came from behind, and Holly turned, smiling.

"That was quick."

Rachel winked and held out a glass filled with something pink.

"What is it?"

"It's fun in a plastic cup, Holly."

Good enough answer for me.

With Rachel being the DD, and Holly hardly getting to go out, she took the opportunity to enjoy tonight, and that meant finishing off the evening with a fresh drink. When the cup was empty, they both grinned.

"That'll put hair on your chest," Rachel said.

"My father will kill me when he knows I'm getting wasted." A sympathetic look covered Rachel's face.

"You need to leave every once in a while. Your mom will understand."

Holly nodded and looked down at the ground. That's easier said than done. "My mom needs me, Rachel." She looked up at her friend and the sympathy on Rachel's face evident.

"I know, honey. I just hate that you have to live in that house with that asshole while your poor mom is sick."

Holly nodded. Her father *was* an asshole, that was true, but her mother was an angel. Her mother was sweet, sincere, and always thought about others before herself. But her mother was sick, and Holly knew it was only a matter of time before the illness claimed her.

"I'm going to go to the bathroom," Holly said, needing to escape for a second. If she didn't, she'd start crying, and she didn't want to ruin the night.

"I'll go with you."

They pushed through the throng of people, Rachel holding her hand and leading the way. They came to a stop in front of the hallway that led to the bathrooms. Holly turned her head, and saw a row of tables off to the side, one of them partially obscured by the poor lighting, but nonetheless she still saw the man sitting there, watching her. His focus was on her. He had one thick and muscular arm on the table, appearing relaxed, although he looked ready to move into action if need be. He wore a shirt that was rolled up his arm, with dark ink covering his flesh in a grisly display of dark lines and intricate detail. She could see it all as if she stood right before him, as if she were running her fingers over those tattoos right now. The longer she stood there the more she felt this tightness fill her, the more heat encompassed her. She couldn't even describe it, couldn't stop herself from breathing faster, trying to suck air into her lungs.

And then he leaned forward, the act slow, calculated, and his focus still on her. His dark hair was short, his eyes the same color, seeming bleak, emotionless ... frightening.

I know him.

You don't.

He seems so familiar.

He watched her like he was a predator about to pounce and he'd just found his prey—her—and that had her entire body lighting up.

Fight or flight.

Fear was strong in her and she couldn't understand why she felt this emotion. It was a little unnerving and creepy the way he watched her, but the fear she felt still sent arousal moving through her.

"Come on," Rachel said, unaware of the exchange Holly had with this mystery man … this dangerous man.

They went into the bathroom, and Holly found an empty stall. After using the facilities she stood there, the stall door still shut. She tried to catch her breath, the intensity from the man still so strong inside of her. She looked at her arms, the ones currently covered by the sleeves she wore. It wasn't hot outside, but going to a club usually had people dressing in less clothing because of the heat and sweat. But here Holly was in a long sleeved t-shirt, hot and sweaty, but needing those sleeves to hide what her father did to her.

Pushing the material up her arms, she looked at the black and blue bruising. They were in the shape of her father's fingers, a result of his drunken outbursts that he seemed to reserve for her on the best of days. But she was glad he put his anger toward her and not her mother anymore. The only solace Holly found was the knowledge that when her mother passed her father wouldn't be able to cause her pain anymore, that her mom would be in a better place and finally have the peace she deserved.

The sound of her cell going off had her grabbing it from her purse and looking down at the screen.

Darra: Your father is pretty upset, and I have to go to work soon, honey. I don't want to leave your mom here alone when he's been drinking.

She was so thankful to have Darra in her life. Darra, an older woman who lived next door and watched over Holly's mother when Holly couldn't be there, was a saint and savior.

I'm on my way now.

She shoved her cell back in her purse, made sure her sleeves were completely down, and left the stall. Rachel was waiting for her by the door, and once they left and managed to move out from the hallway, Holly leaned in close to Rachel.

"I have to go. Darra's leaving, and I don't want my dad there alone with my mom when he's been drinking."

Rachel nodded. "Yeah, I understand. Come on."

Holly looked toward the tables once they were close enough, searching for that man, but he was gone. She didn't know why she felt this slight disappointment over that fact.

When they were only a few feet from the front door, someone grabbed her around the waist, spun her around, and pressed her back to the wall. A guy instantly started grinding on her, the scent of sweat and alcohol slamming into her like a slap to the face.

"You smell good," he said right beside her ear, his voice slurred, and his breath rancid. She felt him run his tongue along the shell and this sickening feeling filled her.

"Get the hell off," she said loud enough she knew he'd be able to hear, and pushed at him. He stumbled back, but was grinning. Thankfully he turned and moved back into the fray of bodies pressed shoulder-to-shoulder.

She saw Rachel stuck between a group of people, but Holly was so over this scene that she shoved her way through. She grabbed Rachel's hand, and together they left the club.

Once outside, Holly took a deep breath, not realizing how claustrophobic it had been in there.

"Shit," Rachel said.

"What?"

Rachel pointed down the alleyway that was only lit by a flickering lamp.

"Shit."

"Yeah," Rachel said. "It was barely dark when we arrived, and it was the only parking spot at the time, that or we would have had to walk a hell of a long way. I'm regretting this paring spot now." Rachel looked at Holy and grimaced. "It looks like a scene from a movie about girls about to get jumped.

"God, please don't say shit like that."

Rachel started rifling through her purse and retrieved her keys. She held them up. "Mace on my key ring, courtesy of my dad. And…" She dug into her bag again and pulled out this big square bag. "A Taser courtesy of Timothy." She grinned after she said her boyfriend's name. "Anyone fucks with us I'll shock them in the nuts with this bad boy." She held up the Taser. They made their way quickly toward the car, which was all the way at the end of the alley. Other vehicles lined both sides of them, the feeling of being a sardine in a can strong.

Of course.

There was a set of dumpsters right before the car, and when they were about to reach it, the scent cigarettes and the sight of smoke coming from behind the dumpster had Holly stopping and grabbing onto Rachel's arm. She shook her head and placed a finger to her mouth for her friend to be quiet.

"Let's go back, now," Holly whispered, and they backed up a few steps. The Taser and pepper spray were all good, but having someone there, not knowing if there was more than one, or what would happen, had a lot of things changing, a lot of emotions filling Holly.

Use the Taser, Rachel.

But Holly was just as frozen, just as frightened as Rachel was. Just as they turned around they both slammed into something behind them. Holly turned and looked up at a big guy, the baseball cap on his head pulled down low, his expression hard.

"Hey, pretty girls," he said in a low voice.

"Got something, Bobby?"

Holly looked over her shoulder at a man stepping out from behind the dumpsters. He flicked his cigarette away, and although she heard them, it was muffled by the sound of her heart beating in her ears. Tightening her hand on Rachel's, she wanted to run so badly, but she knew the big asshole blocking them would easily get them.

The sound of gravel crunching behind them told her the other guy was moving toward them.

"I want this one," the one named Bobby said, tilting his chin in her direction. His face was still hard and expressionless as he stared right into Holly's eyes.

"Listen, we don't want any trouble," Holly said, holding her hands out, feeling pretty damn scared right about now. A plethora of thoughts went through her mind, ones that questioned why she agreed to come out tonight, why they hadn't been smarter when parking the car, and how in the hell she was going to get away from these assholes.

"We don't want any trouble either," Bobby said, showing no expression as he focused on her. And then he reached out, gripped a chunk of her hair behind her head, and yanked her forward. She cried out as pain assaulted her. The sound of Rachel making the same sound, of her purse and the Taser dropping to the ground, had Holly's fear rising, as if that were even possible. Bobby twisted her around and pushed her up against the dumpster, and as Holly looked at Rachel, she saw the other guy had her in the same position. Holly knew unless a miracle happened she wouldn't get out of this unscathed.

"Stop," she cried out, and lifted her knee to kick him in the balls, but he was a lot bigger than her, and easily used his weight to make her submit. The tears were right there on the surface, but she didn't want to cry, didn't want to give him that satisfaction.

"You smell so damn good," Bobby said right beside her ear, and the sound of him inhaling made her stomach roil.

Twisting, turning, and trying to get enough leverage to fight back was harder said than done, especially since Bobby used all of his weight to keep her pinned. But then there was the faintest sound in the darkened corner of the alley, and as she stared at the shadowy spot, tried to see what was there, the feeling of being watched filled her. It was as if everything stood still as if this situation wasn't happening. She couldn't even describe it, not with how much it consumed her, but it was real, and it scared her.

And then, coming out of the darkness looking massive in size, like a vision of what danger and violence personified resembled, was the man she'd seen sitting at that table in the club. He moved like a wild animal toward them, stealthy, intently, the expression on his face calm, but his gaze took in everything. Bobby and his friend didn't even realize they weren't alone, not until the mystery man reached out, grabbed Bobby's head as if it were nothing but an apple in his grasp, and slammed it against the dumpster, right beside her. The sound and vibrations seemed loud as if reality finally crashed forward. Bobby loosened his hold on her and groaned, but he was big, and didn't collapse to the ground right away.

"Hey, motherfucker," Bobby's friend said, but the mystery man turned and cold-cocked him right in the side of the head, knocking the asshole out. He fell to the ground, groaning, and the sight of blood coming from his ear looking like spilled ink.

The man turned and faced Bobby again, who was righting himself, but holding onto the front of his head, clearly in pain.

"You, fucker," Bobby gritted out.

In the next few seconds, it was like everything happened in slow motion. Holly moved over to Rachel, and although they should have run off, gone to a populated area, it was as if they were both transfixed by what was happening. The man gripped Bobby around the neck with a hand, and lifted him easily off the ground before slamming him back against the dumpster. This whole time he hadn't said anything, and his face had kept that calm demeanor. This man that had come out of the shadows like the very devil himself, was saving them for whatever reason. But even though he'd stopped them from getting raped, a tingling in the back of Holly's neck told her he was far more dangerous than Bobby and his friend.

He started punching Bobby in the face repeatedly, so much, and with so much force, that she gasped when blood covered every inch of her would-be attacker.

"We need to go," Rachel whispered, her voice strained, frightened. She bent down, her focus on the mystery man, and grabbed her purse. The pepper spray was far too close to the man's feet, and no way in hell was either of them going to get it.

The mystery man dropped an unconscious Bobby to the ground, and for a second just stared at where his body lay at his feet. He then lifted and turned his head in their direction; his focus trained on Holly.

God, it feels like I know him. How do I know him?

And then he reached down, picked up the Taser, and while staring at Holly for a long moment, turned to the asshole on the ground and gave him a shock that lasted several seconds. He still stayed emotionless, but she could see the sadistic pleasure in his eyes as he hurt the men.

They took a step back, the intensity of that stare spearing right into Holly. Rachel tugged on Holly's hand, moving backward, away from the man, and toward the car.

"Thank you," Holly whispered.

"Thank you," Rachel repeated.

Holly looked into his bottomless, black eyes, and felt a tingle cover her flesh. She knew whatever was happening wasn't the end. She had no clue how she knew that, but she felt it as clearly as she'd felt Bobby's warm, disgusting breath on her face. This mystery man was looking at her like he wanted to take her for himself, and she should have been more frightened at that than she felt.

Chapter Two

Two weeks later

There wasn't anything holding her back anymore, nothing and no one making her stay at home, and Holly had no intentions of prolonging the inevitable of leaving her father behind, or trying to forget about the shitty moments spent under this roof. Her mother had passed two weeks ago, and Holly had finished finalizing everything. Her father, the drunken bastard that he was, hadn't done shit. It had been all Holly that planned everything: the funeral, her mother's property, everything. But truth be told she was glad she'd been able to do that, to be the one that took care of her mother during her last days, and after she passed.

But she'd finished everything, and planned on leaving tonight. Her father had gotten worse with his anger and drinking since her mother's passing. It was time for her to get out of here, to leave this shithole and the horrible memories she had, and leave with the sweet remembrance of her mother to keep her going.

The sun was starting to set. Holly turned from the window to grab her bag. She had a few more things to stuff in there before she left all this behind. With her father gone for another couple of hours, she thought she should have felt bad that she'd be leaving without saying goodbye, but the note she wrote was what he deserved. He was a bastard, selfish, and hadn't been a good father. Her poor mother had to go through it all, as well, and she wished she'd been here to be that rock. But things couldn't be changed, her mother was free, and Holly was leaving.

Going over to the bed, she looked at the envelope that held the note to her father, telling him she was leaving and not coming back, telling him what a worthless father and husband he'd been. Hell, she didn't owe that asshole anything, especially not an explanation on why she was leaving. But writing the letter had been a sort of therapy for her. It let her vent, to get emotions off of her chest. Holly couldn't face him, couldn't say those things to him, not with fear, disappointment, and an array of other suffocating emotions holding her back.

She picked up the picture of her and her mother when Holly was only a child, and smiled. She ran her finger over the image of her mom when she was healthy, happy. Putting the frame in her bag, she zipped it up, and just as she was about to head out, the sound of tires on the gravel driveway had her freezing. Her heart started racing, and she walked over to the window, seeing the tailgate of her father's old truck peeking out from behind the corner of the house. He wasn't supposed to be home for another couple of hours, and facing him when she was about to leave wasn't an ideal situation. But her room was on the second floor, and climbing out the window like some adolescent school rebel sneaking out wasn't an option.

"Holly," her father bellowed out from downstairs, and she felt her heart stall before it started beating fast and hard again.

"Dammit." Well, she'd have to get this over with eventually. Grabbing her bag and the envelope, she headed downstairs. She wouldn't be the emotional or physical punching bag for him anymore. Stepping on the landing, she heard him in the kitchen getting a bottle out of the freezer. She glanced at the front door, which was only a few feet away, set the envelope on the stairs, and decided to just go.

"Where do you think you're going?"

Holly looked over her shoulder at her father. His eyes were already bloodshot, and he held a bottle of vodka.

"I'm leaving." She didn't wait for his response, or to elaborate, and just opened the front door and stepped out onto the patio. But before she could take the steps her father grabbed her shoulder and yanked her back with enough force that she dropped her bag and stumbled backward.

"You think you're going to just up and leave me now that your mom is gone?" He turned her to face him, and she clenched her teeth, so tired of being pushed around, of feeling less than what she was.

"I'm done with this, with you. You weren't there for us, for mom when she was sick." The words just came out, but she was glad, and wouldn't have taken them back.

"You've always been ungrateful. You had a roof over your head and food in your gut. You had it good—"

"You call this having it good?" she kept her voice down, so the neighbors didn't hear, but pushed her sleeves up, showing the cigarette burn scars. "You think getting burned by cigarettes because your dad's drunk and doesn't give a shit about you, a good time?" She shook her head and pushed her sleeves back down. "You think having bruises covering my body, having to make sure no one saw, was what a child should have to go through? Truth is you were a horrible, piece of shit father and an even worse husband." The slap came swift and strong, her head cocked to the side, and she instantly tasted blood on the inside of her mouth.

"Watch it, little girl." He brought the bottle up to his mouth and took a long drink from it.

She shook her head, reached down to grab her bag, and felt strength rise in her. "That was the last time you ever lay your hands on me again."

"The last fucking time."

The deep voice that came from behind her had Holly spinning around. Standing in the shadows partially hidden was a huge man, but even if she couldn't see his face very well, she knew exactly who it was. Her heart stopped, her palms started to sweat, and she took a step to the side. He was here? But why? *How did he know where to find me?*

He took a step forward, the porch light casting a harsh glow across his stern expression. He seemed bigger than the last time she saw him. He looked dangerous, still had that aura around him that had the flight or fight instinct rising, and she knew she was stuck in a very dangerous spot.

"Who the fuck are you?" her father said in a slurred, angry voice.

The man didn't speak but moved closer. Holly was frozen in her spot as she watched him take the few steps up to the porch, slowly move past her with his focus trained right on her, and stop a few inches from where her father stood. He kept his body in front of her, as if shielding her from her father.

"It doesn't matter who I am," he said in a steely, thick and deep voice.

"What the fuck does that mean?" her father responded. "Get the hell off my property."

But the man didn't say anything in return, and instead, let out a dangerous growl in the back of his throat. Before Holly could even react, her father lifted the bottle of vodka and went to slam it on the side of the mystery man's head. But the glass didn't connect with his skull. The man lifted his hand, gripped her father's wrist, stopping him from making contact, and made another low sound in his throat. The position he was in now allowed Holy to see him fully. His face remained emotionless, and Holly thought that was the most frightening part of him. He seemed so detached, so cold and apathetic.

The man slammed his fist into her father's face. His palm connected with her dad's nose and the sound of bone crunching was a disgusting cacophony of sound. She dry heaved as blood started to pour out of her dad's nose. Her father howled about and started fighting back, but he was drunk, sloppy, and the mystery man was coordinated, concentrated, and clearly knew what he was doing. With one final punch to the face her father spun around, hit the front door, and slid to the ground. He groaned before freezing, and although he was still breathing and had just gotten the shit kicked out of him, a part of Holly wished he'd been put out of his miserable existence.

She stood there for a second, looking at her father, and then lifted her gaze to the mystery man. God, he stood there watching her, blood on his knuckles, his face stoic, hard. She took a step back, stumbled off the step, and fell hard on her ass on the landing. Her bag slipped off her shoulder, but Holly grabbed it, stood, and all but ran to her car. He still stood on the patio as she climbed in and shut the door, her hands shaking, her mind a jumbled mess of thoughts. As she put the keys in the ignition, her heart pounding, her body screaming she needed to run, another part of her was … aroused. Her nipples were hard, and her body felt like it was on fire. It was all so misplaced, and she was confused, so damn confused that she was crying from her turbulent emotions.

She turned her key, but the engine wouldn't turn over. She tried several times, cursing at herself and the damn car, but then sucked in a breath when she saw the man was now standing right beside her driver's side door. He reached for the handle, and she realized because of her fear and confusion she'd forgotten to lock it. She grabbed the handle, trying to close it as he tried to open it. But because he was so much stronger than she was, he opened it easily, overpowering her. She scrambled onto the passenger seat, but he grabbed her leg and pulled her toward him. His touch was like fire on her skin. Heating her even further, having her heart skip a beat, and making her scream out. He leaned inside the car, and before she knew what he was doing, he had a rag covering her mouth and nose. She gasped, breathing harder from her fear, and smelling the sweet scent from the rag move into her lungs.

Only seconds had passed before she felt a drug-like sensation move over her until her limbs felt like they were filled with lead, and the realization that she might never wake up slammed into her. The man's stoic face close to hers was the last thing she saw before darkness took her away.

Chapter Three

Sound came back to her first, and then the memories of what had happened. But despite not knowing if her father was dead or alive, she didn't feel remorse for the man, didn't have that guilt, that worry that she felt she should have. The truth was her father had gotten had been what he deserved. But that didn't mean her current situation didn't frighten her, especially since she'd been drugged.

Slowly she opened her eyes and blinking back the double vision, the grogginess, and the feeling to throw up, Holly finally felt herself level out. She didn't move, but the feeling of softness beneath her told her she was probably on a bed. Looking around told her she was clearly in a bedroom, scarcely decorated, but the things that were in the room appeared expensive. Holly closed her eyes again, breathing in and out slowly, trying to get herself feeling "normal" again before she tackled what in the hell she was going to do. When she opened her eyes, a cry left her at the sight of the man standing right across from her, the shadows covering him partially, but his focus right on her.

Pushing back all of the sudden queasiness, she scrambled away from him and ended up finding herself on the floor as she'd fallen off the bed. The sudden drop had the air rushing out of her, but she kept moving away, scrambling on the floor, trying to get further from the man until the wall finally stopped her retreat. He didn't move from his spot on the bed between them, and he continued staring at her like he was waiting for the right moment to attack.

The seconds ticked by with neither speaking, neither moving. Finally, he walked from around the bed and stopped a few feet from her. "You must be hungry, thirsty?" he asked, his voice deep, scratchy.

She shook her head, the very thought of consuming something abhorrent at the moment. "Where am I? Why am I here?" Of course, she had a load of other questions, but she was feeling around, not sure what his intentions were. Holly didn't think he meant to hurt her, not when he'd saved her at the club, and then hurt her father, but she knew nothing about him.

"Come into the living room with me and we can talk." He looked at her for just a second before speaking again. "You're safe." He held her gaze for a suspended second. "I'm not going to talk to you as you cower before me, Holly."

Okay, so he knew her name, and he'd clearly been watching her. She should have felt something more than numbness. Holly should have screamed, kicked, fought for escape, but instead, she sat there staring up at him.

After a moment, he turned and left her alone in the room. The door was open, but there was no window, locking her in, making her feel like she was in a coffin, a prison. She stood, knowing she should be scared shitless right now, but she didn't feel that freezing sensation, that flight or fight response she felt when she ran to her car. It was strange, irrational, and she didn't know if she was still in shock.

Looking around the room for another few seconds, she slowly made her way toward the door. She stayed in the doorway for longer than she normally would have, but she was nervous, not sure what was going on, and confused by what she felt.

"You have nothing to be afraid of," the man said from somewhere out of the bedroom, but his voice made her feel the opposite. "I could have hurt you a hundred times over by now, Holly." He let a moment of silence pass. "But I've saved you, twice, and that alone should tell you, or at least have you feeling, a semblance of safety."

His voice was deep, sharp, like a whip, moving over her flesh and causing this sting of pain to encompass her entire frame. She stepped out of the room, her hands shaking, her palms sweating.

Like he said, if he wanted to hurt you, he could have.

She told herself that over and over again as she moved further into the living room. There was a window that came into view, a wide, massive window that showed a cityscape. She stopped, everything in her stilling even further. She was in the city? And clearly high up given the view she was looking at. Tearing her gaze away from the buildings separated from her only by the glass, she scanned the living room, and saw it was sparsely decorated, only holding the essentials, but was still expensive in appearance.

"Where am I?" she asked again, her voice shaking, her entire body tense. She didn't see him, but heard noise around the corner. She moved closer, tentative, hesitant, her nerves making her heart beat so fast it was painful. When she finally saw him, it was to see him in a modern, stainless steel adorned kitchen, and his back to her.

"You're here because you were running." He didn't bother looking at her as he spoke. When he finally turned around, he held a glass of water in one hand and a plate of food in the other. He tipped his chin to the table, and she found herself moving toward it and taking a seat, even if she should be fighting him on this, fighting for her freedom. He set the plate and glass in front of her and took the seat across from her. She wasn't hungry, and the sight of it had her stomach clenching.

"Did you kill him?" she asked, her focus on the sandwich and carrots on the plate, a nutritious meal that could have had her laughing because it was something a child might eat, but her situation tightened her throat too much.

"No, but I should have."

She lifted her head and looked at him. "Why didn't you?" her throat was so tight, her voice so low.

He didn't answer for what seemed like forever, but he finally leaned back in his chair. The cityscape was his backdrop, the light on in the kitchen dim. Everything was covered in shadows, seeming ominous, foreboding.

"Are you asking because you wanted me to, or because I seem like the type of man to do something like that?"

She shook her head, but she didn't know what she was responding to.

You know. A part of you wanted your father dead.

"You look like a man that would kill someone that crossed you."

He didn't move, didn't speak, and just continued to stare at her.

She shifted on the seat, looking at the food, and then lifting he gaze back to him. "Why am I here? Who are you?" He was like stone, hard, unyielding, and seemingly indestructible.

She had her hands clenched tightly in her lap, her nails digging into her palms.

"You're here because I wanted you here, Holly. You're here because you're mine."

Everything around her stilled at his words, and she felt a droplet of sweat start to fall down her temple. But it wasn't just about her fear of the situation, the unknown of what was happening, but the fact her body felt drawn to him. It was all so confusing and irrational, and the way she felt toward him, that arousal she felt that was a slow simmer inside of her, made no fucking sense.

"Who *are* you?" she whispered the question again, knowing her eyes were wide, her emotion evident in her expression.

He leaned forward, the slash of light coming from the kitchen washing over his face as he looked right into her eyes. "You know me, Holly." He passed for a moment. "You belong with me, to me, and I'll show you that no matter what it takes."

Chapter Four

As she stared in his eyes, really thought about how he knew him, it suddenly clicked.

Kline.

That name moved through her mind repeatedly. She knew this man, had heard his name before, but it had been years ago. Her stomach knotted up as she placed in, remembered the times she saw him. It left her breathless, like she'd been hit with a ton of bricks.

Alex Kline.

It was like this light going off inside of her, this epiphany of the twisted kind. As she stared at the man that had taken her, claimed she'd be his, and saved her on more than one occasion, remembrance hit her entire body over and over again.

"You know who I am," he said without phrasing it as a question.

She slowly nodded. Yes, she knew who he was. She'd first met him when she was only eighteen years old. He'd been the attorney to give her mother advice on legal matters concerning the end of life issues, a Will, and Power of Attorney. That seemed like a lifetime ago now, but she remembered him, and it seemed so clear now.

How had I not recognized him right away?

"Yes, I do know you," she whispered, but confusion still filled her. She tried to recall that meeting she'd gone on with her mother. Her father had been a deadbeat for as long as Holly could remember, and Holly had gone for moral support for her mother who had just been diagnosed with cancer. But after that first visit with Alex Kline her mother hadn't gone back to him. Maybe it was because her mother didn't want to fully take in what she'd been told about her health—which Holly couldn't blame her—or maybe she'd seen the darkness in Alex? Either way no papers had been signed and filed.

They didn't speak, didn't even look away from each other for long moments. It was like this man could see into her soul with his piercing, dark and cold expression. She remembered that visit, how he'd stared right into her eyes. She'd shifted in her seat, squirmed from the intensity in which he held her focus. And when she'd left she'd felt his gaze on her, only to have it affirmed when she'd looked at him once more over her shoulder before she left.

"I don't understand any of this," she said again, shaking her head. He was leaning back in the seat again, one arm outstretched on the table, the other over the back of the chair. She felt her pulse beat in the center of her throat, an almost choking feeling that had her lightheaded.

He still didn't answer, just stared at her.

"Why?" was all she could ask because it seemed to sum up everything that had happened.

"You were running, right?" he asked, but his tone suggested he already knew the answer. She stayed silent, though. "You lost everything," he said again, his voice so intense, so distant, yet genuine. "And now you have nothing."

She felt her eyes start to water, felt the tears threaten to fall as she looked at this man that spoke the truth.

"You have no right," Holly said, referring to the fact he thought he *knew* her, knew what her life was like. "How dare you think to presume you know what my life has been like, what it is like."

He didn't move and still showed no emotions.

"But I do know you and your life, Holly." His voice got harder, if possible, and he leaned forward once more, both arms on the table.

She glanced down, looked at the tattoos that had been hidden all those years ago by his expensive suit. She wiped away the tears that fell and finally drew her gaze away from his muscular body, inked up forearms, and looked in his dark, bottomless eyes.

"What are you thinking right now?"

She swallowed, not afraid of Alex, even if she should be. She didn't worry about the fact he might hurt her—that he could—but she was afraid of the situation she was in, and how she'd handle it when it was all said and done. Holly shook her head, but she wasn't sure what she was saying no to.

"Tell me what you're thinking," he said with a little push in his voice, that hardness having chills race up her spine.

"You had no right to take me away."

"You were running," he said without apology. "I didn't take you away from anything." He stood and walked over to the kitchen, opened the freezer, and grabbed a bottle of alcohol out. He took two glasses next and came back to the table. Nothing was said as he poured clear liquid into those glasses. He pushed one to her, took the other for himself, and while looking at her, tossed it back, drinking it in one swallow.

She looked down at the alcohol, and without thinking, because this was so fucked up, she grabbed the glass and drank it, as well. It burned going down, and made her already teary eyes water even more, but she welcomed the flash of heat it caused in her veins.

"I may have been running, but you had no right to take me, to think you knew what I wanted." She was the one to hold her ground now. "You took me to satisfy things on your end."

Where is this strength coming from? He's dangerous. Just look at him, and you can see it.

She saw the way his jaw clenched, the tightness of his body, and knew she might have crossed the line with her words. Holly knew nothing about him, or what he was capable of.

He's capable of stalking me, of taking me away. He's capable of hurting people and clearly having no remorse. I have no doubts he would have no trouble killing someone that crossed his path.

"Watch it, Holly." His voice had gone cold, steely.

She swallowed, a shiver working its way throughout her whole body. She wanted to say "or what," but kept her mouth shut, being smart.

"Or I might throw you over my knee and spank that pretty ass until it's purple and your pussy is wet."

She felt her mouth go slack at his words. But the most surprising, if not traitorous thing her body did, was react to his words by heating, her pussy becoming wet, and her nipples hardening.

"You're insane," she said and stood. She glanced around the room, but didn't know if she was running from him or what she felt. She turned and saw the front door, ran toward it, but realized it had some state of the art lock on it that was activated by fingerprints. He had his hands on her waist only seconds later, the hold unforgiving. There was a little bit of pain associated with his touch, but she found it arousing.

She hated that fact, loathed herself for getting turned on by this man when she should be screaming.

"You can scream, but no one can hear you, Holly." He let those words sink in before continuing. She heard him inhale right by her hair, and she found herself closing her eyes.

She was still breathing hard, but the need to pass out had subsided. He turned her around but kept his body pressed right up against hers. The feel of his erection against her belly was clear, and her fear heightened that he may rape her.

But would it be rape if you want it, if your body is aroused right now?

Shut up.

He leaned in close and she held her breath, waiting to see what he would do. When their lips were only an inch apart she turned her head, but he must have anticipated the move because he gripped her chin and forced her to look at him.

"I'm not going to rape you. I don't forcefully take from an unwilling woman." He was silent for a second. "But then again you're not so unwilling, are you?"

She didn't answer; her throat closed tight, her emotions turbulent.

He ground his erection into her, and she hated that her body started to warm, that this small sound left her. Why did she have this reaction to him?

"You did take an unwilling woman."

He shook his head and pulled back so inches separated their faces.

Before she knew what she was doing she had her hand up and brought her palm across his cheek. The sound of skin slapping skin was loud, and her whole body tensed, her heart beating faster. His head was to the side, and she could see how clenched his jaw was. He slowly turned his head toward her, grabbed her wrist in a slightly painful, firm hold, and stared at her right in the eyes.

"Don't fucking do that again, Holly."

She felt her eyes widen at the tone of his voice.

"Just listen to me, and understand what I'm saying."

She shook her head but didn't speak.

"You know what's moving between us is what's supposed to happen, the chemistry, the fact it feels right." He still sounded angry, still looked intense. His cock was still a hard rod between them, pressed right to her belly.

What the hell is happening?

Even with layers of clothing separating them she could feel how big and long his erection was.

"I don't want this. I don't want you," she whispered.

He ground himself harder into her. Hot tears spilled out of her eyes, and rolled down her cheeks. "A part of you wants me. I saw it when you looked at me at the club, when I nearly killed that fucker in the alley for touching you." He leaned in an inch closer. "You were scared, but you were also turned on."

She hated he was right.

He pulled back just enough to look down at her chest. Her nipples stabbed through the thin material of her bra and top. She was humiliated, horrified, and started crying harder because her pussy grew wetter at the gentle yet persistent pressure of his cock against her belly.

"I don't know you." She swallowed. "You drugged and kidnapped me." Holly sucked in a lungful of air. "I don't want this. I don't want you."

"You're a fucking liar." He leaned in another inch so that their lips were almost touching. "How can I take you away from what you don't have?" He was stoic in his expression. "How can I take you away when you were running, Holly?"

His reasoning was fucked up.

"Where did you plan on going when you left?"

She couldn't answer because she didn't have a plan when she left her father's house. She didn't know where she was going to go, just that she was going to leave. She had no friends aside from Rachel and Darra. But she planned on keeping in contact with Rachel, and Darra was older, had her own life, and had been a lot of help while Holly's mom had been sick.

"You had nowhere to run. You left because you wanted to get away from everything, because you were done living the life you were dealt."

She shook her head even though he was right.

"I can give you that escape, that nothingness, Holly."

She stared into his dark eyes.

"All you have to do is give yourself to me. All you have to do is be mine, and I can give you as much or as little of the world as you want."

"I can't do this," she whispered, but he was right; she'd been running, escaping into the nothingness.

"I know if I touched your cunt right now you'd be so damn wet for me." He slowly lifted his gaze from her breasts to her face again.

She opened her mouth to say something, anything, but instead a small escaped her instead. He pulled away from her, taking several steps back, and she finally sucked in a lungful of air.

"I can't let you leave, not until you realize you belong with me, to me."

He's insane, a psychopath. How can he think a person belongs to him?

"I'm not a piece of property. I can't be owned."

"How is it owning you when you want me as much as I want you?" He smoothed his hand over her cheek, and she couldn't deny the warmth that filled her despite the darkness of this situation.

"I've wanted you, craved you for a long fucking time."

Shock resonated through her.

And then just like that, he stepped away, breaking contact. "You need to eat what I made you. Once you're done you can shower and rest. I'll give you the time you need to understand what's happening, but I can't let you go, Holly." He'd gone from intense to concerned, and she felt whiplash from it all. "I've been waiting a long fucking time for this moment, and I won't let anything or anyone, not even you, ruin this for us."

Before she could say anything he turned, leaving her pressed up against the door, shaking, aroused, and even more confused than she'd ever been.

Chapter Five

Two days later

Forty-eight hours had passed with Holly being in Alex's apartment. He'd given her clothing, all the necessities for her stay, and that made this even more insane. He'd planned for this, clearly.

He had a balcony off the living room, and she'd gone out there to think, to get fresh air, to just escape the lavish surroundings that were also a prison. The thing that confused her most, the part she hated the most, was the fact she didn't feel trapped, despite the fact she was.

She stood on the balcony, her hands on the banister, her focus down below. They were twenty stories up, the wind sometimes vicious as it whipped by, as if trying to carry her away. She did a lot of thinking these last few days, and although Alex keeping her here was wrong on so many levels, this strange part of her felt … alive because of it. She felt free, in a sense, and it was fucking crazy. She hadn't seen Alex since the night he'd pressed her to the door, and told her that she did want him. He'd frozen her out, maybe as a mental thing, or to make her see, feel, what was going on?

But there was no phone, not that she could find, and she couldn't leave the apartment because of the locked front door. She was trapped in the most elemental of senses, but for the first time in her life, she didn't feel like she was living in a constrained hellhole.

Even when her mother had been alive Holly had felt like she was detached, living in a life that wasn't meant to be hers. It had only gotten worse once her mom had died, and that darkness crept up, like an old friend waiting to suck her back into the world of pain and emptiness.

Can you do this? Can you see what he has to offer?

She closed her eyes as the wind moved her hair along her shoulders.

Can you even imagine a life where you give in to the man that drugged and kidnapped you?

She opened her eyes and stared at the twinkling lights of the city.

What is out there for you?

She had a shitty waitressing job, well, *had* being the word since she didn't call off and it had been two days. But it didn't matter because she'd been planning on running anyway, just taking the minuscule amount of money she had to her name, that she'd saved, and leave everything behind.

What's the worse that could happen if you saw where this went?

That was a loaded question, and she knew that giving into Alex, to his twisted way of thinking, might very well put her in the same box she'd been in her whole life. But then there were the "what ifs." She did feel something strong when she looked at him. It had been instant when she'd seen him in his fancy three-piece suit all those years ago, but he was much older than her, easily in his late thirties or early forties. She'd pushed him out of her mind, forgot about the man that made her feel things she'd never experienced before with just a look. And then she'd felt that connection, that pull, again at the club.

She turned from the city view and looked into the apartment. The lights were on, and there, standing right on the other side of the glass, was Alex in the same three-piece-suit she'd just been envisioning him in. He stood there like a dangerous man, controlled, powerful, not showing how he felt. What kind of man could go to these kinds of lengths to make a woman his? Surely he didn't need help in that department, not with his looks and money. Fear and disgust should have been the only things she felt when she looked at him, but maybe she was just as damaged and twisted as he clearly was?

She left the patio, and once the sliding door was shut behind her she took in a deep breath. He didn't move, didn't speak, and she was afraid to say anything.

"Have you eaten?" he asked, his voice gruff. He started to undo the button of his jacket as he looked at her.

She nodded.

He took it off and slung it over the dining room chair, and then went for his vest. Once that was done, he undid the buttons of his shirt, rolled up the sleeves, and loosened his tie. She couldn't help but appreciate the view. His forearms were covered in tattoos, the ink hidden behind his businessman persona.

This is crazy. You're crazy.

And she was, but her life had already been so out of control, that she didn't know if she was coming or going most of the time. No, she couldn't do this with him, couldn't allow herself to get sucked into some twisted fairytale where the "hero" told her this was what was right, that he was her Prince Charming.

He's the anti-hero.

"I'm ready to go, to leave," she managed to say and swallowed when this dark look crossed his face. Before he could react, she was moving around him and to the bedroom. She had her purse on the edge of the bed, and although she didn't know what she'd do when she left—if she left—she knew she had to figure this out on her own.

She grabbed her purse, turned around, and a cry of surprise left her when she saw Alex standing a front from her, his expression turbulent. This was the first time she'd seen a sliver of emotion cross his face.

It frightened her.

"Where do you plan on going, Holly?" He took another step toward her.

"I don't know, but I have to go, have to make my own way." She moved back a step as well, but the bed stopped her retreat.

"Your way? And how do you plan on doing that?" he crossed his big arms over his chest, his muscles bulging, his strength evident. You have a couple thousand to your name. Going back to your piece of shit father's house isn't an option, and the only thing you want to do is escape." He moved another inch closer, and the scent of his cologne engulfed her. "I can help you escape. I can help your pain about losing your mother and get rid of the memories of your abusive father. I want to be the man that helps you, that brings you to the surface."

Her throat tightened at the mention of her mom.

"This is fucking insane," she whispered, not meaning to say the words out loud.

"No, it's fucking right, and you know it."

She shook her head. "I don't know it." And she didn't. It didn't matter that her body was aroused, that she wanted Alex, remembered him. This was wrong. What he'd done was wrong.

Holly noticed he glanced at her breasts. She looked down and saw how hard her nipples were, her body revealing what she wanted. Covering her chest with her forearm, trying to hide herself from him, even though she was aroused, she knew it was pointless.

"You don't hide yourself from me. Never from me." He pulled her arm away, and she gasped out, not just from the shock that he'd done so, but because the electricity she felt from his touch consumed her. He then lifted her arm, turning her forearm up, and while holding her gaze with his, ran his tongue over the scars. It was a passionate act, one that had her heart skipping a beat.

"You said you wouldn't force yourself on me," she whispered, pulling her arm away.

"And I won't." He smirked, the first time she'd ever seen him do the act. But it was far from pleasant. "You're mine, and I'd never touch you if you didn't want me to, but Holly, tell me your pussy isn't wet for me. Tell me you don't want me. Lie to me, if you dare."

Her chest heaved, but could never quite get enough into her lungs. Every erogenous zone in her body tingled as he looked at her. When he took a step toward her the heat in her body intensified, her pussy became wetter, and her nipples ached for how hard they were.

"Tell me you're not wet, Holly." There was a challenge in his voice, and she physically shivered from it.

"I am," she whispered again, knowing she should have lied, but couldn't help the truth that came out.

He clenched his hands at his sides; his nostrils flared, and he looked down at her breasts again. "Take the shirt off. Let me see you."

She should have said no, should have screamed, fought him, and told him to fuck off. But something in her shifted, snapped … changed. Instead of being smart about this she gave into her desires, seeing where this took her, where the darkness led. Holly gripped the edge of her shirt and pulled it up and off her head. The air was cool, and her skin puckered with goose bumps. She was scared, of course, but the way he looked at her as if he truly did own her, as if he wanted to possess every inch of her, had a drugged feeling consuming her.

Holly felt intoxicated, as if her need, arousal, was a living, breathing entity inside of her. His gaze was penetrating, like he reached out and stroked her skin, touched every part of her until she was a shaking, needy mess. There had to be something wrong with her that she desired this—desired him.

"The bra, and then the rest, Holly. Take it all off."

"And if I said no?" She didn't know why she was pushing this, testing him, but something rose up in her, this desire that was unlike anything she'd ever experienced.

"Then I'll take them off of you, and I won't be gentle about it." His voice dropped an octave, and a chill raced up her spine.

But she found herself getting undressed, and when she stood totally naked, letting him see every part of her, she knew what she was doing would forever change her.

"So fucking hot." Holly could tell in his voice alone that he was barely holding on. She was so cold all of a sudden, but then a blast of heat filled her at the way he looked at her, at the sight of him running his hand over his mouth, as if he was starved for her. Beads of sweat covered her flesh, and only got worse when he took that last step toward her.

"If only you could see yourself right now." His voice was a husky growl. "If only you could see yourself the way I see you. How much I need you, how much I care about you."

He cares about me in his own twisted, fucked-up way.

"Never have I needed a woman the way I need you, Holly." He looked right in her eyes. We can both be free … together."

Alex frightened her on one level, but her arousal, her curiosity for him, overrode everything else. This was wrong on so many levels, but it also felt good … freeing. It was a twisted situation, but her body reacted to Alex in a way it had never reacted to a man before, even though the situation was fucked. But this surge of excitement left her, as if she were standing on a ledge, about to fall over, and not knowing what was at the bottom.

He reached out and cupped her chin, his hold firm, controlled. The air stirred briefly, and she smelled the dark and spicy scent of Alex. A fresh wave of pleasure moved through her.

Just one touch from him and she felt overpowered, but it was the good kind of feeling, the kind she wanted more of.

"You're mine."

Right away she wanted to say she wasn't, but the words got lodged in her throat. Instead, she didn't say anything, just breathed in and out, trying to calm herself.

He slid his hands up her outer thighs, and a tingling sensation settled even more fiercely between her legs, right in the center of her. He moved his hands in slow but demanding movements, digging his nails slightly into her flesh, and causing a gasp to leave her. The urge to fight, but to also give in at the same time rode her hard. He was meticulous and controlled as he touched every part of her, ran his fingers over her belly, her ribs, and finally stopped on her chest.

"Tell me you want this," he demanded.

For long seconds, she didn't speak, didn't even breathe, as she processed what he said, no, demanded.

But then, as she looked at him, watched as he scanned her body with his gaze, she knew this was the most intense and real situation she'd ever experience. "I want this," she murmured.

He made this deep, gruff sound, like an animal getting ready to attack. "No going back."

*There was never a chance for me to go back,
because I had nothing anymore.*

"Lie back and put your arms above your head," he said and moved away from her.

It took Holly a lot of control on her part to keep her composure, but a dark, twisted part of her wanted this, and she wanted to see what would happen at the end. Once she was on the bed, and in the position he wanted her in, she clenched and relaxed her hands around the headboard. She wasn't a virgin, but this sexual experience was unlike anything she ever could have imagined doing.

He came back toward her and finished removing his shirt. The sight of his exposed abdomen of the power that were pronounced, the strength that was clear, had Holly's inner muscles clenching, needing something big and long inside of her.

"I've watched, waited until the right moment to bring you here, to make you mine," he said, his voice like a knife sliding over her flesh. "I waited until you were ready to accept what I want to give you." He lifted his gaze to hers, the dark slashes of light and shadows coming through the living room from the open doorway making him almost sinister in appearance.

"You stalked me," she whispered, her heart thundering harder with each passing second.

He didn't speak for several seconds, but still touched her, smoothing his fingers lightly over her flesh.

"Yes, I did. I make no apologies for doing what I did, not when the end result is you in my bed, about to be mine." He added pressure to his touch, his nails now scraping along her flesh hard enough there was a flash of pain. "And you will be mine, every fucking part of you, Holly. Make no mistakes about that."

A tremor worked its way through her at his words, at the way he touched her. And although she wanted this, was wet for him, a part of her wanted to push him away, to tell him no, that this wasn't right. Before she could contemplate any of those thoughts, he was leaning over her. His breath was warm as it moved along her nipple, his mouth perilously close. She made a soft sound. The peak hardened painfully, but pleasure also filled her. Holly involuntarily arched her back, causing her aching nipple to brush along his lips. Alex groaned deeply, and she swore she felt the vibrations all the way through her body before the noise settled in her clit.

A mixture of self-hatred, disgust, and searing pleasure filled her to the point that she gripped the headboard so hard her nails dug into the wood.

"I knew you'd be like this, so receptive to my touch, so primed for me." He moved lower and murmured against her chest right before he sucked her nipple into his mouth. Over and over he moved his tongue over the peak, and then gently tugged it and ran his teeth over it.

I should stop this. It isn't right. I'm not right for enjoying this.

But she didn't speak those words out loud, because the pleasure he caused her, the freedom she felt, had everything else going to the backburner.

"You want this just as badly as I do," he said, but it was clear he spoke to himself, as if trying to convince himself that this entire situation was right.

No, he knows this is right because this is what he's wanted. He has no remorse for what he did.

He sucked on her nipple more furiously, adding little bites, until arcs of pleasure and pain coursed through her body like lightning bolts.

She was going to come, and a part of her thought that made this so much darker, a touch more wrong. "Wait," she whispered, but she ended up moaning again when he groaned against her nipple, the vibrations going through her entire body.

He sucked harder and faster.

"Oh God."

He moved a hand between her legs, and she knew she was wet, embarrassingly so. He smoothed his fingers between her pussy folds, and she bowed her back, the sensations incredible.

"You're so fucking soaked, Holly." He moved his lips up her chest and settled at the crook of her neck. Alex panted against her throat, his hand still between her legs, his fingers rubbing at her clit. "You want more. Tell me you want more."

She shook her head, but she didn't know why she did the act. A low, desperate sound left her when he applied even more pressure to her clit.

"Tell me what I want to hear," he demanded.

"God," she cried out as the pleasure continued to climb. "I want more." The words left her on their own accord.

"Come for me, Holly," he groaned the words out. "I want to see you let go."

A gasp left her. She opened her eyes wide as pleasure stole her breath. "Wait. Oh. God." Holly's back arched on its own again, and she placed her hands on Alex's wide, strong shoulders. She pushed at him, but it was a feeble attempt. The pleasure was too intense, too mind-numbing that deep down she didn't want it to end.

He didn't stop rubbing his fingers against her clit, and over and over he tormented her, giving her pleasure mixed with pain. Alex bit at her throat, groaning as if this was all too much for him. But she knew better. This man was controlled, calculated, and he knew what he was doing. Holly felt like she was spiraling out of control, but it was a strange kind of feeling, one she didn't want to end just yet.

When the pleasure started to dim she ached, every part of her felt worn out even if it was just from him rubbing her clit and getting her off. She felt tender and exposed in such a way it was as if her very soul was on display.

Before she said anything, Alex pressed the weight of his body down on her, his chest to hers, and lowered his face, so it was inches from her own.

"Stop fucking struggling with yourself and what feels good," he growled out the words and everything stilled in her. "I can see the war inside of you. Just let go, let me make you feel good. Let me fucking take care of you." Alex ground his erection into her belly, and a gasp left her.

"A part of me knows this is wrong."

He ground himself against her again. "Does this fucking feel wrong?" he said in a hard tone and reached between them to touch her wet pussy. "Or this?" He challenged. "You feel how hard you make me, how much I want you?" His strength was immense, his desire like a tank ready to destroy anything that stood in his way. Grabbing her behind the knee and pulling it up and out, he took advantage of her surrender and nestled his waist between her legs, his cock now pressed right up against her pussy.

He was so big, so massive everywhere that she felt insignificant, small in comparison. She felt fragile, but not in the way she'd felt her whole life. This type of fragility made her feel ... strong. Holly wanted to escape, and wasn't this experience, wasn't giving herself over to Alex, that in every sense of the word?

Chapter Six

Holly's thoughts were a jumbled mess, her need and common sense raging war with each other. Being kidnapped and held captive by Alex was not what she had envisioned as being "free," but she'd be lying if she didn't admit a part of herself liked having the power taken from her. It was a type of freedom she would have never expressed before, didn't even know existed.

"Give in to me," he said in his husky voice against her neck. He continued to thrust his cock against her pussy, over and over again, his pants still on, but his cock hard, huge. "Just give in to me, Holy," he said with a more demanding voice, the tone sharp, serrated.

With his mouth at her neck, and him running his teeth and tongue along her overly sensitive skin, Holly could have envisioned herself in a different scenario. She could see herself willingly under this man, and these turbulent emotions swirling within her vanishing as if they meant nothing.

She could see herself free with Alex, and that scared her so damn badly.

"Just enjoy it, let yourself realize this is what you want, that being with me, being mine, is where you're supposed to be." He spoke harshly, and she could tell that his anger, passion, and need to make sure all of this happened the way he wanted was what fueled him the most. He moved away and the chilled air slammed into her.

In a few quick moves, he removed his pants. Clenching her thighs together to try and stop the pulsing need that had settled between them, she shook her head, not knowing exactly why. But a dark look crossed his face, and everything in her heated further. His body was hard, strong, his cock huge.

"Once my cock is deep in your pussy you'll finally accept that you're mine, finally understand what it means when I said this is supposed to be." With that long, thick hardness between his thighs, pointing right at her, she knew there was no stopping this.

You do want it. Be honest with yourself.

"Tell me what I want to hear, Holly. Fucking tell me." He gripped the base of his shaft and started stroking himself as he stared at her.

"I want it, want you." There, the words were out, unable to be taken back. She wet her lips and took a deep, steadying breath. "But you know taking me the way you did wasn't right." She didn't know why she said that last part, but it was too late to take it away.

"I don't feel sorry for taking you. I wanted you, and now I have you. I have shown more patience with you than I ever have with anyone else in my life." And then he was touching her again, rubbing his fingers up and down the lips of her pussy, and having her bite her lip hard enough she tasted blood.

"You don't have to run, don't have to live a lie." His voice got harder, and he moved a finger lower, plunging it into her body.

She opened her mouth wide on a silent cry. It felt good, but it also was sudden in its intensity. Holly was going to come, could feel it starting to build at the base of her spine.

He moved his mouth to her ear and whispered, "Say you'll give yourself to me fully." He thrust his finger harder into her. Involuntarily her pussy clenched around his digit, and he groaned hard against the shell of her ear. "That's it." He added another finger. "Let me help you become free."

And as if his words had been the trigger, she came for him. She felt suffocated, but it was the good kind of discomfort, the pleasurable kind of tightness in her chest and throat.

The bed was moving slightly, and she realized Alex was pressing his hips into the mattress, dry-humping it because he was just as lost in this as she was.

"Fuck," he said in a deep voice. "Spread your legs wider for me. Let me see your pussy."

She curled her nails into her palms until pain lanced through her, but did as he asked. He pulled back slightly and his gaze stayed on her face. And then only seconds later he looked down between her thighs. Her heart thundered behind her sternum with each passing second. She kept her gaze on him, watching for any clue as to what he might be thinking, but found none. He kept his composure on a leash, and that made her feel ten times as affected.

He placed his thumb and finger on her labia, smoothing them up and down on her flesh right before he pulled them apart. The cool air circulated throughout the room, chilling her overheated flesh. With his fingers still spreading her wide, he continued to watch her for what seemed like forever.

Alex shifted so his face was right between her legs now, and his warm breath teased her folds. A dark mask covered his face, and he placed a hand on each of her inner thighs, stilling her, holding her in place. And then he had his mouth on her pussy. He worked his tongue around her clit and then moved it along her inner lips. His hot breath moved along her cleft, sending her spiraling closer to oblivion. How was it possible to desperately need more?

"God." She hated that she sounded desperate for him. The sound of sucking flesh had her on the brink of completion, but just as quickly as he'd started, he stopped.

"You're so fucking sweet." When he pulled away, she felt bereft and disappointed, but she knew he wasn't about to end this.

She squirmed on the bed; her breasts thrust out, her nipples hard as rocks. He leaned forward and dragged his tongue over one of them. She arched into his mouth, his touch like fire along her body. While he sucked and licked at her, he continued to stroke his cock between them. That realization was like gasoline being thrown onto a roaring fire.

He latched his mouth onto hers, making her taste herself on him. He kissed her for several seconds, thrusting his tongue in and out of her mouth, fucking her like she knew he'd do between her legs. But Alex pulled away from her too soon. They looked at each other for a second, and then he lowered his gaze to her pussy, grabbed his cock again, and aligned the tip of his dick with the entrance of her cunt.

"Tell me you're ready."

"I'm ready," she whispered right away.

He started to push inside, and she felt the stretch and burn from the size of his dick.

"It's so fucking good, Holly. *Christ*."

Holly didn't want it slow. She wanted this hard and fast, making her forget about her shitty life and what she'd lost.

He placed a hand on each of her thighs and continued to push deep into her. Tears came, but not because it hurt or she was afraid, but because for the first time in her life she didn't feel like she was trapped. It was like an oxymoron in the most fucked up of ways.

She moaned and thrashed her head back and forth, but she never told him to stop. Holly wouldn't. And then he let loose and fucked her with long, hard strokes. Over and over he plowed into her; the sounds coming from both of them crazed, animalistic. He was sweating, and the beads of wetness slid down the length of his chest and dripped onto her belly.

Seeing the expressions on his face as he took her was like watching an animal becoming free. He thrust especially hard into her and her eyes rolled back into her head. She bunched the sheets in her hands, but only a second of doing that and she was grabbing onto his biceps and digging her nails into his flesh.

Alex pulled out only long enough to take hold of her hips, flip her onto her belly, and push her legs apart again with his knee. She was at his mercy, and although this was the opposite of being free, Holly felt like she was finally there, experiencing that freedom she'd ben lacking in her life.

Looking over her shoulder showed Alex's gaze trained on her ass. He slipped his finger through her slit, gathered her moisture, and used his other hand to spread her ass apart. Holly knew what was to come, and her throat tightened. He got her anus wet with her pussy cream.

"I'm going to claim your ass, Holly," he said without making it a question or asking permission. With only one glance at her before focusing on her ass again, Holly braced herself for what was to come. To her surprise, he placed the tip of his cock back at her pussy instead of her ass, held onto her waist, and thrust into her in one deep, hard move. Her cry was slightly muffled from being pressed against the mattress.

Pumping into her fast and hard, he grabbed her hands and placed them on her lower back, keeping them bound together by one of his. He squeezed his fingers around her wrists, taking control, dominating her with his strength. She turned her head to the side even more, opened her mouth, and sucked in air. He slammed into her, held his position for a second, and then pulled out slowly again.

"Yes," she hissed out.

He gathered more of her arousal and brought it to her ass again, and slipping the soaked digit over her anus again. He teased the hole, and then slipped it inside. Involuntarily her inner muscles clenched around his finger, and this strangled groan left him. He pumped into her pussy with his cock at the same time he thrust his finger in and out of her ass. He stilled after a few seconds of doing this, spread her ass as far as it would go, and leaned forward. She looked at him and watched as he let a string of saliva slide off the top of his tongue. His saliva landed on her asshole, hot, searing, and erotic.

"Tell me you want me to fuck your ass."

She nodded, not able to speak, hell, not even able to think clearly right now.

When he pulled out of her body, he immediately gathered more of her wetness and smoothed it over her anus, mixing it with his saliva until she knew her back hole was nice and lubed.

"Yes," he hissed out. Alex slipped his finger inside of her ass again until he was deep in her body. The groan that came from him was long and deep, and she moaned, as well, unable to stop herself. "Seeing my finger fucking you makes my cock ready to fucking explode." After several seconds, he removed the digit and replaced it with the thick crown of his cock at her back hole. Every part of her was stretched out and on display. She was nervous, never actually having anal before, but at the moment not caring. She felt too wild to stop this.

He started pushing into her, and she bit her lip and closed her eyes, the stretch and burn filling her. He pushed through the tight ring of muscle at her ass, and then he was fully in her, sliding all the way in until his balls were pressed right against her. He only gave her a few seconds to adjust to his size before he started moving in and out, slowly at first.

"So. Fucking. Good."

After several moments, he picked up his speed and fucked her with long, powerful strokes. His balls slapped her moist pussy, the sound erotic, dirty good in nature.

"I own you, Holly, and I'll make you so fucking free."

He does own you right now, every part of you.

He used his other hand to grip a chunk of her hair, pulled her head back until her throat was arched, and groaned out. Everything in her tightened to the point she knew she'd come again. Alex growled low, thrusting several more times into her before pulling out right at the last minute. He took hold of the base of his dick and stroked himself feverishly until white arcs of cum came out of the tip of his cock and covered her ass. She could only watch him over her shoulder, knowing her eyes were wide, her mouth parted. His pleasure was tangible as he groaned, his whole body tensed.

His orgasm went on and on, and she felt his cum slide down the crease of her ass and along her pussy. When his orgasm receded, Alex moved back on his haunches and looked at her ass, clearly taking in the fact she was covered in his seed.

Holly panted and collapsed fully on her belly, closed her eyes, and just let the post-euphoric haze wash over her. He lay next to her, and for several minutes neither spoke nor moved. She opened her eyes, only to see Alex was already staring at her. He reached out and brushed a piece of hair from her face, the act sweet almost.

"This is what it means to own you," he said and rubbed his cum into her skin, along her ass. "This is what it means to be mine."

He pulled her close to his body, held her like he was afraid she'd disappear, and she let him. Holly relaxed against him, closed her eyes, and thought about how she'd ended up here and where this path would lead.

She opened her eyes again and stared into his dark, turbulent ones, knowing this man could have crushed her without breaking a sweat. He was an animal in human flesh, a machine with a living heartbeat, and she was his, in all senses of the word. There was no going back, not from any of this, but even if there was she wouldn't have wanted to be anywhere. This was her life, and this feeling of being free was something she'd never experienced before. Her mother would have wanted her to live her life the way she wanted to, and right now, right here, this was what she wanted.

"You're mine, Holly."

As fucked as this all was, she felt this blossoming of something darker rise in her. But the feeling wasn't trying to suck her in, but make her whole.

"You want freedom, you have it, but it comes with a price. It comes with being with me, with being mine."

She looked at Alex, seeing the hardness in his face, that determination covering every part of him.

"You want to do this together," she said without stating it as a question. Before he could answer, she spoke again. "I'm tired of being alone, of drifting."

He cupped her cheek, and the hold was firm, almost painful. But she liked that stability, needed it.

"You're not drifting anymore."

And she wasn't. He made her feel stable, and it was a bittersweet feeling. It might be confusing on so many levels, and she might have been thrown into this situation, but right now this was Holly's happily ever after … for now, and slightly twisted.

Epilogue

Several months later

Holly wrapped the blanket around her tighter and stared at the city. It had been months since she'd first been brought to Alex's home, and although the circumstances had been fucked-up, to say the least, in that time she'd *found* herself.

She spoke to Rachel often, but her friend had moved out of town with her boyfriend. It seemed everyone was finding their way. Her bastard of a father was alive, but in prison for a drunken hit and run—one that had thankfully not gotten the other driver too hurt. She was glad he was behind bars, glad he could get the same kind of abusive treatment locked up as he'd delivered to Holly and her mother for years.

The sun had set hours ago, the weather was chilled, and she felt good, happy. It may be only a few of months that she'd been living with Alex, and although to others ... society, this was fast, insane, and she probably suffered from some mental disorder because she wanted to stay with her "captor," Holly didn't care about any of that. They weren't hurting anyone, and this life they shared worked for them.

She was happy, she made Alex happy, and that's what mattered. He wasn't the type of man that brought flowers and chocolate to make her smile, but he let her talk, listened, and was there for her. He'd always be hard and have an unforgiving personality, but that's what drew her to him. He made her feel alive when she'd been trapped in her own skin. Holly wasn't forced to be a prisoner in this apartment, in this life she'd chosen with Alex. In this short time they'd traveled, explored places together, and having him near her gave her this strange, yet intoxicating strength.

The sound of the front door opening and closing had her turning around. She'd left the patio doors open, and watched as Alex entered. He set his briefcase down, took off his jacket, and all the while watched her. That intensity and connection she'd felt that first time hadn't dimmed. In fact, it had grown, and she knew it always would.

He crooked his finger for her to come to him, his expression dark, and full of promise. She felt her strength rise. Holly held control over him, as well, held the power that had his composure cracking, the wall he held around himself coming down, but only for her. It was that strength that made this different, made this right. In her eyes this was where she was meant to be, where her life was meant to go. It wasn't conventional, maybe not even sane to some, but she didn't care. Holly was happy, Alex made her happy, and that was what mattered. She'd never give this up, not now that she knew what living could be like.

The End

www.jenikasnow.com

SINFUL

Lily Harlem

Copyright© 2016

Chapter One

A coil of fear wrapped around my body. It squeezed my chest, rolled in my guts, and pumped my muscles full of adrenaline.

Fight or flight?

The wet cobblestones underfoot were cruel to the high heels on my boots, but I ignored that and carried on. I'd chosen flight. Behind me the sounds of the riot faded—the East London street being burned and looted retreating into the distance. The cries and bangs were thankfully becoming quiet and muted.

Sadly the footsteps that trailed me were still there. Hard. Mean. Persistent. I thought I'd made my escape from the peaceful protest that had turned into a full on revolt, but that wasn't the case.

I glanced over my shoulder, my hair whipping my cheek before the wind caught it.

Darkness and shadows greeted me. There was movement there too, against the wall.

Bile bit at my gullet. How the hell had I gone from protesting against the war to being stalked in the back alleys of King's Cross? My parents had always warned me away from this area. And I'd watched more movies than I could recall of women getting caught out like this. Stupid, risk taking girls! Yet here I was.

An attacker on my tail.

A creepy, dark street.

I sped up.

So did the footsteps.

I suppressed a whimper and let my handbag strap fall from my shoulder and caught it in my hand. The bag was hard leather, full of my usual heavy odds and ends as well. Would it be a good weapon to hit him with?

Presuming it was a *him*.

Of course it was.

It was always a man.

The cold air seemed to fizz on my hot cheeks. My thighs, bare in my short skirt, were tense as I forged forward. My heart rattled and my pulse thudded in my ears, competing with the echo of my footsteps on the uneven stones.

Again I looked behind.

Yes.

There he was. No longer bothering to hide.

Terror gripped me. He was tall. He wore a hoodie. His legs were long and his boots clipped the ground.

I broke into a run. I had to get the hell out of this place. I looked left and right. Dark doorways, shuttered windows. No one to ask for help. The end of the street a lifetime away, and even then it wasn't exactly buzzing with activity.

I ran faster, upping the pace to a sprint when I went past the solitary lamp post. Rain drizzle floated in the halo of light it created.

Damn, what I needed now was a guardian angel.

I sent a quick prayer heavenward.

Please. Don't kill me. I'm not ready to die.

He was running now. There was no pretense that he wasn't after me. Wasn't getting ready to attack me. Rape me. Kill me.

I squealed as he drew level, his speed no match for mine.

He was in front of me.

My only option was to draw to a halt. It was that or barge into him.

"Hey, little girl," he said, his voice deep, gravelly, full of menace. He was breathing hard, as though excited that he'd cornered me.

"What do you want?" I retreated a few steps.

"Just making sure you're okay. It's getting nasty back there."

Yeah right.

"Please, leave me alone." I searched for my most confident, commanding voice. "I have a cab. Just up ahead." I pointed over his shoulder. "The driver is waiting for me."

"Really?"

"Yes." Of course it was a lie. I was scrapping the bottom of the barrel here. I just wanted him to piss off and leave me alone.

I glanced left and right, praying that a doorway would have light coming from beneath, or a window would show signs of life behind the curtains.

Nothing—darkness surrounding a heavy, arch-shaped door to one side and a shuttered up shop to the other.

He took a step closer, his shoulders rounded, his arms reaching out, as though to grab me.

Fuck it.

I dropped my bag to the floor. It landed with a *whump*. Something inside it smashed.

It was time for desperate measures.

I set one foot behind the other and glared at him.

He was white, perhaps late thirties, early forties. A heavy dusting of stubble, and thin mean eyes half hidden by greasy hair.

I concentrated, amid my horror, in case I had to describe his ugly face to a police artist.

He laughed.

Actually laughed.

But it held no humor. It was triumphant. A predator who'd captured his prey.

"I have to warn you of something," I said, tilting my chin. "By law."

"Oh yeah?" He was leaning closer. "What do you have to warn me about, little girl?" The sneer on his face matched that in his tone.

I resisted the urge to turn and run. That would get me nowhere. It was clear he could out pace me. My three years at drama college was all I had left. "Yes. I have to warn you that I'm a lethal weapon. By law, before I kill or maim you, you should know that I'm a fourth dan. I'm registered as such with the police and martial art authorities." I raised my hands like a boxer would, though I kept my fingers stretched out, the way I'd done in the two karate classes I'd attended at the local gym.

"Fourth dan?" He looked bemused.

"Yes." I pulled in a breath. "Just going for fifth actually."

"What the fuck does that mean?" Some of the bravado had left his voice.

"Think of a black belt, times it by five." I laughed. "I've taken men your size down with my little finger."

"Yeah right."

"Yeah right." From somewhere within I harnessed the courage to step nearer to him. "Are those really going

to be your last words before you're on a ventilator …
yeah right?"

"You can't do that."

"I can do what the fuck I want." I moved my
hands in what I hoped was a karate-type move. "You're a
big man, it's a dark alley. Who the fuck is going to
believe you're not out to attack me."

Which you are you cunt.

He stared at me.

"Self-defense will stand up in court no matter
what condition I leave you in." I nodded to the end of the
alley, where my fictitious cab waited. "Now get the fuck
out of here." I paused and laughed. "Or not. I missed
class with my *sensei* this afternoon. This would keep my
training for the internationals right on track."

He took a step backward.

I tipped my head. Grinned.

What an asshole.

"Jesus. You're one fucked up chick."

"Yeah." I shrugged. "One fucked up chick who
likes to fight. So come here."

"Shit." He stooped and grabbed my bag. Then he
turned. Ran. His footsteps banging around the walls like
bullets.

Jesus? Really?

Had he bought my spin?

It seemed he had.

"Hey, come back here," I yelled then swallowed,
the fluid in my mouth was thick with fear. I'd lost my
bag, bummer, but I was still in one piece, the relief of that
was a potent drug.

Suddenly more deep voices accompanied by
footsteps and banging, came from behind me.

Men. All men,

Drunk. Angry. Wound up. Looking for a fight.

I had to get the hell out of there.

Suddenly I noticed a golden light shining from the huge keyhole of the large arched door. Someone was in there.

What was it? Not a home.

I ducked from the openness of the street. I might have had the luck of the devil getting rid of one loser, but a gang of them. I didn't fancy my chances.

There was a sign, next to the door.

St Peter's. Holy Cross Parish. Father R Duncan. All Welcome.

Fuck. It was a church.

I banged on the door with the side of my hand. "Let me in."

It opened instantly. Before my fist was able to whack down a second time.

The man that stood before me seemed surprised to have a visitor.

"Can I come in?" I asked, looking over my shoulder. "It's dangerous out here. I need to shelter."

"Er…" He glanced behind himself, and clutched a black rucksack to his chest.

"Please."

He wore a white collar, he was a priest or vicar. He appeared to have had a rough day, too. His dark hair was mussed up and he had a thick layer of stubble.

The tinkle of glass breaking made me jump. The men were throwing bottles.

"Quick." I took control of the situation and pushed past the man before me and into the warmth of the church.

"But?" He frowned.

"I'm not going to survive if I stay out there." I pointed at the door. "I've just fought off one attacker.

There's more. Quick, shut it. I'm not sure if even you'd be okay."

He glanced at the dark alley.

"Hurry," I said, shifting from one foot to the other, and twisting my hands together.

To my relief he pressed his hand on the dark polished wood and clicked the door shut. As he slid two heavy wrought iron bolts into place I noticed he had tattoos over his knuckles, I couldn't read what they said from where I stood.

The keyhole dragged my attention from his unorthodox body art, and I glanced around wondering where the key was. I couldn't see it on the nearby shiny table stacked with church leaflets, nor was it on the first pew of a row of several to my right.

"You can't stay here." He frowned.

"Father, please. I need to. Just for a while." What the hell? Wasn't a church supposed to be a place of refuge?

"It's not safe," he said, scanning me head to toe and apparently taking in my long boots and short red skirt. "In here."

So he was a priest, he hadn't corrected my assumption.

"I'm better off in here than out there. I've already had my bag stolen and fought off a murdering rapist, I'd like to keep hold of my life." I spotted a box of Kleenex tissues. "We need to block up that keyhole. It's how I knew you were in here. The light."

Quickly, I grabbed a few of the tissues. I squeezed them into a tube shape then stepped past the priest. I set about shoving them into the gap. As I did so sharp, snapping sounds, like firecrackers, rattled around the street outside. There was more shouting, banging, hysterical, manic jeering and laughing. Another bottle broke, I wondered if it were more petrol bombs.

I tried to stay calm even though my hands were shaking. Thank God I'd made it in here.

Once my task was complete I turned to him.

He stood there, stock-still, clutching his rucksack. There were several large cream candles lit on the shelf by the door, and the light from their flames shivered over his black robes and caught in his dark hair.

"Are you okay?" I asked.

His wide shoulders appeared tense and a small tendon flexed and un-flexed in his jaw.

"Hopefully they'll keep moving," I said quietly. "But there will be more. It's crazy out there. The police have lost all control."

"I know." He glanced over his shoulder.

I followed his line of sight toward the altar. A large, golden colored Jesus Christ hung from a cross, his head lowered and wearing a thorny crown. Behind him was a small round, stained-glass window. Before the effigy of Jesus a plinth, draped in white material, held more candles and what I guessed was a Bible on a book holder shaped like an eagle.

"What's back there?" I asked, noticing a door to the right of the altar. "Can anyone get in?"

"No. It's a locked room, beyond that a small courtyard. No one will get in from that way."

"So this is the only entrance?" I nodded at the door.

"Yes."

I blew out a breath. Part of me was glad there was only one entrance to guard, but equally if it were breached, we were trapped.

"Where did you come from?" he asked.

"Brick Lane." I touched my brow, noticing it was clammy. "I was marching with a friend, but a knife fight kicked off next to us. We got separated when riot police intervened. Then I was pushed over." I held out my palms, they were scraped and gritty. "I thought I was going to get trampled but managed to get up."

He nodded slowly.

"And just as I thought I'd be okay, someone threw a petrol bomb, it landed right near me. Scared the fuck out of me..." I paused. "Sorry, the *life* out of me."

His expression didn't change.

"The smoke stung my eyes, and the heat caught in my throat. It smelled so bad. But I found myself in an alley, it was quiet, and I had no idea where I was. I'd lost my bearings. But I stumbled on, I just wanted to get away."

"Did you find your friend?"

"No. I hope she's okay. But I think she went the right way. I got caught up in the wave of violence that went down the street." I shook my head, nausea sweeping over me. "I tried to hurry, but it was hard going. I wished I hadn't worn these fucking heels... I mean ... heels, Father."

He glanced once more at my high-heeled black boots. They came just over my knee and were suede. As a rule they were very comfortable. But today, they'd slowed me down.

There was another loud bang from outside.

I jumped. My heart felt as though it had skipped a beat. What the hell was going on?

The priest didn't seem perturbed by the noise. As though he were used to it. I wondered if he'd been in war zones, perhaps done missionary work in dangerous places around the world. He certainly looked big and tough enough to hold his own.

"I don't know what that was," I said, pressing my hand over my chest. "But I'm so glad I'm in here, with you."

Chapter Two

One side of his mouth twitched.

"I'm Cheryl by the way." I held out my hand. "Nice to meet you, Father…"

He hesitated for a second then took my hand. His palm was hot, his fingers strong. I got to see the letters on the knuckles on his right hand. *L.O.V.E.*

"And you are…?" I prompted.

"Steve."

"Nice to meet you, Father Steve." I recalled the sign outside. It had said Father R Duncan. "Are you just passing through? Where is Father Duncan?"

"He's not here, obviously." He had a familiar accent, East End. "I was standing in for him. Listening to confessions, lighting candles, stuff like that."

"Oh. Okay."

Another loud bang, right near the door this time.

"Perhaps we should move away." I stepped down the aisle as I'd spoken. "Just in case."

"In case what?"

"I dread to think."

When I reached the pew one back from the front, I sat and looked up at the image of Christ. I'd never been particularly religious though I'd gone to a Christian school, and my parents had me christened when I was born. My godparents' had been crap, though, one had run off with her father-in-law and was never seen again, and the other had ended up behind bars in Wormwood Scrubs.

I turned.

Father Steve was still standing where I'd left him.

I rubbed my hands together, gingerly wiping away the grit. "Do you have any water?"

"What?"

"Water, you know, to drink." Fear was bitter and I needed to get rid of the taste.

He glanced at the door again. "Er. Yeah, hang on." He turned to a large stone font. "Here."

I laughed. A silly high-pitched giggle born of surprise and lingering fear. "I don't think it's appropriate to drink holy water."

He frowned and glanced about. "Yeah. Hang on a minute."

Still holding the bag to his chest, he walked past me to a curtain. He pulled it back revealing a shelf holding a cut-glass jug of red wine, a stack of books, and several bottles of water. He scooped one up then strode toward me, his robes swinging and catching around what appeared to be a fine, strong set of thighs.

Damn it. He was actually pretty hot for a priest. I tutted to myself. What was I thinking? Sure I had a high libido, was happy to have fun on a Saturday night out when a guy in a club took my fancy, but...

"Here." He handed the water to me.

"Thanks. I appreciate it." I unscrewed the top. "If I'd had my purse I'd have put some money in the collection."

"Don't worry about it." He tightened his hold on his bag and looked down at me. Jesus was hovering behind him, his thin body and bony shoulders a direct contrast to Father Steve's wide torso.

"What you got in there?" I asked, nodding at his bag. "A million quid of church money? Saving it from looters, are you?"

"Er, yeah, something like that." Again his mouth twitched into a smile.

Fuck, he was handsome as they came in a complete lack of vanity and weary-with-the-day look.

"Well you're better off in here with money. Let's hope the mob passes, or the police get the situation under control soon."

"Were you here for the riots, last time?"

"No, thank goodness. I was on holiday, Portugal. Looked awful on the news though."

"Yeah, bad shit happened."

Bad shit?

I opened my mouth then shut it again. It wasn't as if I could reprimand him. He spoke to God. God would lay judgement. Not that I had an issue with cursing, hell, I could turn the air blue when the mood struck me.

"So do you live around here?" I asked. "In a rectory or convent or something?"

He shook his head. "Regular place."

I took a sip of water. It was cool and refreshing and I was glad of it.

"What about you?" he asked. "I guess by your accent you're from around here, too."

"Yeah, down near Houndsditch."

"Ahh, a favorite haunt of Jack the Ripper."

I raised my eyebrows. He knew that? "Yeah, so they say. Usually quiet enough these days." I sighed. "Wish I was there now. Tucked up in bed."

He turned and walked up to the altar. He set down the rucksack.

I admired his grace of movement, his wide shoulders, the way his black hair tapered into a comma at his nape, just above the dog collar.

It was a damn waste he was off limits to women. His brooding good looks and clearly muscular body ticked a lot of my boxes.

I wondered if he'd ever had sex. Or if his calling to the church had come at a young age and he was a virgin.

A small tremor went through me. Blimey, imagine that—a hot, sexy, virgin priest. I could do bad things with him. Dirty, sinful things that would pass a cold, dark night holed up in here.

I glanced up at Jesus's face.

A wave of shame washed through me. What was I thinking? Lusting after a man of the cloth. A man who was married to Christ. Sexy or not, I shouldn't be thinking that way.

A siren screeched past outside. I wondered if it were a riot van.

He turned to me, his shadow stretching over the two steps up to the altar. "Are you scared?"

"Yes."

"I think that's wise."

I swallowed. "You do?" Wasn't his job to be supportive and caring?

"Yes. You're not completely safe in here."

"Well no, but better than I would be out there." I jerked my thumb over my shoulder, toward the door. "That would get me raped and murdered."

"So you think all men are bad?"

"I didn't say that." I paused as he stepped down and came toward me.

He slid onto the pew I was on, right up close, so his leg touched mine. "So what *are* you saying?"

"That a crowd, when riled up, looking for blood, is not a good place for a woman on her own."

"You're very sensible." He tipped his head, as though studying me, trying to see into the depths of my eyes, my soul.

His eyes were so dark, black, and impossible to tell where his irises stopped and his pupils began. His lashes were thick and his eyelids a little hooded. He swept his tongue out and stroked it over his bottom lip leaving a gentle sheen there.

I tore my attention from what was a very kissable mouth, and looked up at Jesus on his cross again. "I'm not really sensible. I should have stayed home, like my father told me. He said the war wasn't my concern and I wouldn't make a difference by joining in a march."

"You live with your father?"

"Yes, he'll be worried about me."

"And with good reason." He reached for my hand and turned it, palm up, in his. "London is a dangerous place tonight."

His touch sent a wave of sensation up my arm. "I know."

"Mmm..." He pressed his finger to the curved line on the inner side of my hand. "You have a long life line."

I swallowed. "I have?"

"Yes." He bowed his head lower, as though studying my hand.

I could smell him he was so close, faded cologne, tobacco, perhaps coffee lacing his breath. Mostly it was a manly, sexy smell.

Are priests allowed to smoke?

I had no idea. And I didn't really care. He was drawing little circles on my palm and after the horrendous evening I'd had I found it soothing.

"You also have a long sex line."

I coughed. "I beg your pardon."

"Here." He ran the tip of his nail, on his index finger, over one of the grooves in my skin that ran from my wrist to the life line. "Very long, and deep."

"I didn't know there was a sex line. Not that I've ever had my palm read."

"Oh, yes, there's a sex line." He looked at me again. "You're not married, are you?"

"No. Not even close to it."

"Yet you've had lots of sex." He frowned.

"What is this? A confession?"

He shook his head. "No, just a man asking a woman questions."

"Why do you want to know?" I asked.

"I just do." His gaze drifted down my neck, to my chest.

I was aware of my breathing picking up, my nipples tightening. I wore an old denim jacket and a thin white sweater. Beneath that my favorite comfy bra. Right now I felt as though he could see the bra's faded blue-gray lace, and the tattered cotton in the center where a tiny fabric flower used to be.

"I didn't think priests were interested in sex."

He shrugged. "Celibacy doesn't equate to not having an interest."

A loud bang seemed to shake the whole building. Fireworks? A rocket perhaps?

I glanced at the door.

"The roof of this church is made of stone and slate. It won't burn," he said, not taking his attention from me.

"I hope not."

He released my hand and hooked his finger beneath my chin. "So, are you going to confess, Cheryl?"

"Confess what?"

"Who you've been having sex with outside of wedlock."

"No one." It was an instinctual answer, though of course not true.

"A hunky boyfriend, a drunk one-night stand who has turned into a friend with benefits?" He raised his eyebrows questioningly.

"No, neither."

"So what's your poison? A vibrator … no that would be a waste. A woman like you should be adored by a man, not be seeking pleasure on her own."

"A vibrator?" So much of what he'd just said had made my head spin. Sure, I wasn't accustomed to chatting with priests or hanging out in churches, but still … I didn't think the guys down at the local would have asked me any of that.

He chuckled. "I've shocked you, haven't I?"

"No … well yes, a bit."

"Don't be shocked. Tonight is unusual." He reached out and took a lock of my hair between his fingers. He rubbed it, spreading out the blonde strands. "I think God has thrown us together. To take care of one another."

"You do?"

"Yeah." He looked up and smiled.

It was a filthy, dirty smile. The sort I'd seen on boyfriends when we'd been drinking, flirting, having fun and about to start satisfying some seriously carnal urges. "Father," I whispered.

"Yes?"

"What … what are you doing?"

"Sitting with a member of my flock who appears very scared." He shifted on the narrow pew.

"Yes. I am scared. Of what's out there."

"Not what's of in here?"

"Should I be?"

"Not if you have God in your heart."

"I'm not very good at going to church." There, I'd said it.

"I think you're probably good at other things."

"Like what?" My heart rate was tripping along.

"Other things that make you feel good. Things that make the person you're with feel good."

Damn if he didn't have that white collar sitting around his neck, I'd think he was being suggestive. Actually, no, even with that white collar I thought he was being suggestive.

"Feel good?" I repeated.

"Yes." He leaned closer, his lips only a whisper from mine.

Damn the instinct to kiss him was almost overwhelming. Sure he was a stranger, but he was a good man, a man of morals and beliefs.

Which was exactly why I couldn't kiss him.

But what if I died tonight? What if this was it? Surely I should have one last moment of passion. I loved sex, and it was one of my favorite things to do.

"What do you want to ask me?" he asked, his breath washing over my mouth.

"I don't know."

"I know you do." He paused. "One thing. Ask me one thing. I'll be truthful."

One thing. There were so many. He was the most unusual priest I'd ever met. Not that I'd met many. Not only was he handsome in a rugged kind of way, he also oozed sex appeal. It seemed to roll off him in waves. Had we been in a club I'd have gone for him, and had a one-night stand just to see how a guy like him did it.

"You don't have anything you want to ask me?"

"Yes. I do."

"Go on then…"

What was really in the bag? Why was he here at night alone? Where did he live exactly? Did he look at all women the way he was looking at me—as if he were undressing them with his eyes?

"Have you ever had sex?" I blurted. It was the answer I really wanted after all.

"No." He shook his head. "Bonafide virgin."

"Oh." Damn it. If I'd been turned on before, now I was in white-hot ready-to-go mode. The things I could teach him given the chance. What I could do with his naive, inexperienced, gorgeous body. The delights of the flesh I could introduce him to.

"But I bet you've had lots of propositions," I said, wondering if I should sit on my hands to stop myself reaching out for him.

"Yes. But I've always turned them down." His voice was low now, husky too. "Do you want to know why?"

"Yes," I said quietly.

"Two reasons."

"Which are?"

He glanced at Jesus. "I made my promises to the Lord."

"Of course. Yes."

"But lately…"

"What…?"

He shook his head and glanced at his lap.

"Lately what? Tell me." Had he been questioning his faith? Was that it? Was that why he was looking at me as though he had only one thing on his mind—and it wasn't the riot outside.

"Lately my faith has been tested. The evil in the world, including here. It's hard to stay focused."

"I'm sure." It was my turn to take his hand. I gave it a squeeze and looked at the way the hairs fanned over the back and disappeared into the black sleeve. I ran my fingers over the letters on his knuckles. *Love* was clearly a moto he lived by. "And what's the other reason?"

"I told you I'd had propositions."

I nodded.

"And always turned them down."

"Because you'd made promises and you love God." I paused. "Very noble. Very commendable."

"Yes." He tipped his head. "But the thing is, Cheryl."

"What?"

"No one like you, no one as sexy as you, has ever propositioned me."

Chapter Three

"Like me?"

"Yes, you…" He curled his hand around my waist, and the spread of his hand in my back held me firm.

His chest touched my breasts through my jacket. He filled my vision.

Suddenly his mouth hit down on mine, hard. He pushed his tongue between my lips, my teeth and stroked around.

I gasped, the sound muffled, and gripped his cassock; the material was warm and soft.

What the hell?

I pulled back, panting, and looked up at him. "Father?"

"I want you."

"But…"

"I've been waiting years to be with a woman." He too was breathing hard. "Tonight is the night."

"Have you really thought about this?"

"I've thought of nothing else since you stepped in here."

"Really?"

"Yes. My faith is wavering. I need a woman. You are beyond beautiful."

I wasn't, I was fairly average, but I appreciated his sentiment. "But I hardly know you, and … and you hardly know me."

"Have you known every man you've slept with?" He raised his eyebrows, and slid his hand down my back.

"Is that a trick question?"

"No, I want the truth."

"I've always known their name."

"And you know mine." He slid his other hand up my leg, from the top of my boot, over my bare thigh, and onto my short skirt. "Maybe this is the way it should be for me. One act. One time. One woman. I need this."

I believed him. Want shone from his eyes, the way he touched me told me he was a man possessed with desire.

I couldn't deny it excited the hell out of me. Though I had to admit, hell was likely where I'd go for this.

"The Lord sent you to give me strength. This is meant to be, now, us, on this awful violent night. Let us forget about everything but each other and take comfort in that togetherness."

"How can you be so sure?"

"I've been thinking of it for months, if not years. Waiting for the one."

"And you think that's me? I'm the one?"

"Yes." He kissed me again.

Damn the guy could kiss. The pressure was firm and dominant, hungry and urgent.

The fizz of arousal grew between my legs, the need for more, to get down to business, urging me on. I was a horny bugger once I got going.

He tugged at my denim jacket, shoving and pushing until it fell to the stone floor. Our kiss didn't break. His breaths, excited and earnest, blew hard on my cheek and his stubbled chin scratched against my skin.

"You taste like heaven," he said, reaching for the base of my sweater and tugging it up and over my head.

"Do you think you might regret this?" I asked as cool air washed over my hot skin.

"Hell no." He looked at my tatty bra. "This has to go."

I couldn't disagree with that statement.

He unclipped it, with one flick of his fingers, and it fell away.

He cupped my breasts and stroked over my nipples.

"Do they feel how you thought they would?" I asked, searching his eyes.

"Better." He grinned and kissed me again.

For a guy that didn't kiss women he was pretty damn good at it. I guessed it was instinctual in a man that looked like him.

"God, my cock is so hard," he murmured.

"Are you telling me or God?" I stifled a giggle, hearing those words from his divine lips was a mixture of shocking and erotic.

"Both." He released my left breast and cupped his groin.

"Here, let me." I tugged up the cassock until it was bunched around his thighs. Beneath he wore black denims, a bit worn, and hefty boots. There was a definite bulge going on in the groin area. "Are we really going to do this?" I asked.

"Yeah." He nodded. "We are."

We were. I didn't know what kind of penance or Hail Mary's I'd have to do or say, that wasn't my thing. That was up to him. But fuck, I was too far gone on the let's-have-fun-trail to worry.

"In this movie I saw," he said, popping open the top button of his jeans. "This woman, beautiful, a bit like you, she..." He shifted and shoved them to his thighs. His black boxers stayed in place.

"She what?"

"She, you know..."

For a moment I wondered if he were embarrassed, self-consciousness, and the newness of this moment had suddenly gotten to him.

A muffled bang sounded at the back end of the church.

"What was that?" I asked.

"Nothing." He frowned. "Nothing at all." He reached into his boxers and pulled out his cock.

Fuck. He was big, circumcised too, and he'd been dead right when he'd said he was hard.

"Let me," I said, slipping my hand over his and squeezing the shaft.

He groaned. "Yeah ... that feels good."

A sensation of power flooded through me. I was the first woman to touch this guy's cock.

Wasn't I?

"More," he said, "give me more."

I stroked root to tip, several times. "What did the woman in the movie do?" I asked, adoring the way his jaw had slackened and his eyelids were heavy. He was clearly enjoying my touch.

"She sucked his cock." He turned to me. "Like you're going to do now."

"Am I?"

"Yeah. Don't make me beg." He gripped my shoulders and urged me to a kneeling position.

"But I..." Before I knew it, my knees were on a prayer pillow and he was guiding his cock tip into my mouth.

"Take me, Cheryl. Give me the best blowjob you've ever given. Make my first one a moment I'll always remember. One to dream about for the rest of my life. Make it worth the sin."

How can I refuse him that?

Besides, blowjobs were a bit of a specialty of mine.

I sank down, taking him deep. His flavor, musky and spiced, spread over my tongue and his smooth glans slid over my palette.

He clasped his hands on the back of my head, encouraged me to take more even when I'd reached my limit.

I fought my gag reflex and gripped his bare thighs. My eyes started to water.

He'd need to learn a thing or two about receiving. That wasn't polite.

"Fuck yeah, give me it like that. Deep throat."

Deep throat?

He bucked his hips, over and over, holding me firm and fucking my mouth. He gasped and panted. Salty pre-cum slipped over my taste buds.

I tried to push away. It was too much. What was he doing?

"No. More." He gripped my hair, tighter.

Pain shot over my scalp.

Realization dawned. No way was this Father Steve's first time getting a blowjob. I'd read about priest in the news, in the papers, they weren't all they seemed. Sex scandals abounded and it seemed I'd stumbled upon a particularly disreputable one.

I shoved hard, managed to dislodge him from my mouth. I glared up at him.

"Why'd you stop?" he asked with a frown.

A sheen of sweat sat on his brow, and he was breathing hard.

"Have you been honest with me?"

"Of course." He made a cross on his chest with his free hand.

"About everything?"

"Well, mostly." He hooked his hands under my arms, and dragged me upward.

"You've had sex before, haven't you?" I asked, staring into his eyes.

"No, never."

"I don't believe you."

"I don't really care what you believe." He pulled me close, dragging my legs either side of his so I straddled his lap. "All I know is I've got a raging hard-on. I was just about to come and you stopped."

Irritation flashed over his eyes, but it was still laced with desire.

"I stopped because I sensed you'd spun me a yarn."

"Whatever." He yanked at my skirt, tugging it until is sat like a belt at my waist. "And besides, talking is over rated, don't you think?"

"No, actually, I—"

He cut my words off with another one of his lethal, passion-infused kisses. At the same time he tore at my panties, ripping one side of them.

I moaned, the elastic would leave a sore mark. But damn, he was so hot for me and I couldn't deny that was a huge turn on.

He sought out my clit, pressing it with his big fingers.

I bucked forward, needing more. Despite my anger I still wanted him. My body was awash with desire, my pussy damp with arousal.

"Jesus Christ you're a hot little thing," he said against my mouth.

"Jesus Christ is watching you," I said, hoping to induce some kind of shame in him. "From just over my shoulder."

He chuckled. "Yeah, I bet he wishes he was me." He sought my entrance and shoved two fingers in deep. "Poor bugger."

I gasped and rocked backward.

He caught me around the waist with one hand and began to fuck me with his fingers with the other. "Yeah, like that. Good eh? Know what I'm doing, don't I?" There was a certain smugness to his voice. "Instinct, you see."

"Oh God…" The heel of his hand was catching on my clit. He was working me toward orgasm. Virginal priest or not, the bloke knew his way around the female form.

"No, don't pray to God, pray to Father Steve…" He leaned forward and latched his mouth onto my neck, sucking it, creating yet more sensations for my body to get off on.

"Yes, yes…" I cried, my orgasm so close.

He pulled out.

"What?" I opened my eyes and glared at him.

He shrugged. "Now you know how it feels when it stops at the best bit."

"Sex isn't about tit for tat."

"Well, tits maybe." He bent his head and took my left nipple into his mouth. He pulled, sucked, and bit.

I squirmed and wanted to pull back, but I also wanted more.

He lifted up and looked at me.

"I'm going to fuck you now."

"Do you think you should remove this?" I touched his white clerical collar.

"Nah, you like it."

"What?"

"I can tell. Priest fantasy, it's getting you off." He grinned.

Fuck, was it? Maybe.

Except I wasn't even sure if he was a priest anymore. What priest would go at it so rough and ready in front of Jesus and in God's house?

"Sit on me." He held his cock upright. "Now."

"Condom."

"No condom."

"But…"

He maneuvered me forward, aligned his cock, and dragged me down onto it.

He filled me so fast, so thoroughly. Stretching my pussy sideways and lengthways.

I cried out. A long, low, gurgling sound that came from deep in my chest and floated into the high rafters. Pain mixed with pleasure and spread around my body.

A guttural groan of gratification dragged from his throat. "So good."

I panted and tried to adjust to the invasion.

"Now move. Fuck me," he said gruffly.

My clit was buzzing for it and pressed up against his wiry pubic hair. I moved a fraction.

"Much more than that." He gripped my buttocks and urged me into a fast, wild rocking movement. "Please."

I clasped the material covering his shoulders, despite knowing it was holy cloth and shouldn't be victim to my clutches of passion.

But it was too late now.

"Ah, yeah … that's it. Fuck, your cunt is so tight."

"Cunt?"

"Yeah, cunt." He bit my lip and tugged.

The pain intensified as his teeth sank in, then suddenly he let go.

"In for a penny in for a pound," he said. "Reckon I've sinned pretty big time right now, so what's a few more?"

"Have I sinned?" I asked breathlessly. My orgasm was growing again.

"By fucking a priest?"

"Yes."

"I'd say you're going to hell, you dirty bitch."

"What?"

Suddenly I was lying flat on the pew. My left leg draped over the wooden backrest and my right up at his shoulder.

His cock hadn't left my pussy.

"Yeah, dirty bitch, come for me now. I want to see how my big, holy cock makes you come, makes you squirt."

He rammed even higher into me, pulled out, then plunged back in.

I gripped his arms, his biceps were straining beneath the material of his cassock.

"Oh, God…" I was going to come. He was right, his big holy cock was going to create a big holy climax. "Oh, God…"

"He won't help you. God won't help you … just like he won't help me."

"Are you … going to hell?"

"Yes … for this and … many other things…" He shut his eyes and tipped his face to the ceiling. "If you're going to come, do it now…"

I did. I let the pressure release. His body was rubbing my clit violently with each thrust of his hips, and his cock rubbing my G-spot. It was a wild-fire orgasm, it heated my insides, burned over my nerves and red and black dots danced in my vision. My pussy thumped around his cock, spasms ravaging it.

"Yeah, God, yeah…" He gave one last plunge, so deep I thought he'd come out of my throat, then released his load. "So fucking good, bitch."

What is it with the dirty talk?

I ran my hand up to his face and cupped his sharp jawline.

He stared down at me. "That was a good first time."

"That wasn't … your first time."

"Sure it was." He withdrew and dragged up his boxers and jeans. He then made a show of adjusting his black robe and straightening his clerical collar. He shoved a hand through his hair, but if anything it made it messier.

I lay there, on the pew. One leg thrown over the back, the other now with my foot on the floor. My wet, cum-soaked pussy gaped up at him.

"You staying like that," he asked, looking at my cunt.

"What do you suggest I do, *Father*?"

A bang, from the back of the church, like before, caught my attention.

"Is there someone there?" I asked.

"I dunno, but if there is I'm sure he'd like a good go at you too, so why not stay like that." He chuckled and sniffed his fingers. "I'm going to be smelling you all night."

"Don't be filthy."

"What, like you?" He shrugged.

I frowned and sat. I closed my legs and wished he hadn't torn my knickers.

"Who are you?" I asked, "Really."

"I'm the guy that just fulfilled your sick priest fantasy."

"I didn't have a priest fantasy." I reached for my bra, desperate to cover up. Something about his attention now was making shivers tremor up my spine.

"Until you saw me." He stepped from the pew and up to the altar. "Then I gave you that fantasy."

"Cocky bastard, aren't you."

"Is that anyway to speak to a man of God?" He reached for his rucksack and again hugged it to his chest.

"You're not a man of God."

"So how come you've called me God for the last five minutes?" He laughed, the sound a great big boom that echoed around the church.

I clutched my sweater to my chest. He looked crazy now, his hair wild, his cheeks flushed, and his eyes flashing with a devilish look that told me he'd gotten what he'd wanted.

He turned to the effigy of Jesus. "So long, mate. Bet that's the most fun you've seen going on here, ain't it." He made a cross on his chest then once more laughed.

I swallowed. My heart was racing. I could still feel him inside me, on me, his stubble scraping my face. I couldn't deny, it had been one heck of a screw.

"Where are you going?" I asked.

"I'm getting the hell out of here." He strode down the aisle, his heavy boots making sharp banging sounds.

"Is it safe?"

"It is for me."

"Don't go." I didn't want to be here alone.

"I have to."

Quickly I stood. If he was unlocking the door, I was going to lock it up again pretty damn fast.

He did just that. Strode to the door and slipped the bolts.

Holding the large, round handle he turned to me. "Thanks for the fuck, Cheryl, it's definitely one I'll remember." He winked.

Sexy bastard.

Before I could reply he'd slipped out into the darkness.

Rushing forward, I shut the door, and slammed the bolts back into position. In the brief moment I'd seen the street, I was relieved to see it was quiet, it appeared deserted too.

Maybe the worst was over and I'd be okay in here alone until daylight.

I leaned back on the wood and shut my eyes. I had to get dressed, my chest was bare, and I was damp between my thighs.

What the hell has just happened?

Okay so my high libido had gotten me into a few scrapes over the years, I'd had a few unsavory names thrown my way too, and woken up next to a few guys I really should have passed on.

But I'd just fucked a priest in a church.

A new low, or was it a new high?

Sure felt like a high.

Except he wasn't a priest. I'd bet my last pound on it.

Father Steve was an impostor.

It had been good though.

Opening my eyes, I looked at Jesus. "Sorry. But it was seriously good."

As I'd spoken another thought came to me. "So where is the real priest? Whose cassock was Steve wearing?

Again a dull thud came from the back of the church, to the left of the altar. Was it coming from the room there?

I dashed forward, reached for my clothing and quickly made myself decent—apart from the fact I wore no knickers. I then tried the handle, it was stiff but it did release. A shove with my shoulder against the wooden door, and I stumbled into the room.

"What the hell?"

Tied up in the corner was an elderly gentleman. He was gagged with a strip of red material, his eyes were wide and his hands and legs tied with rope and harnessed together. He wore a white shirt that was grubby down the front and black smart trousers that were rucked up to his calves displaying green, rumpled socks. He wore no shoes.

"Bloody hell." I rushed up to him. "Are you okay?" I tugged at the gag.

"Thank goodness." He gasped then licked his lips. "I've been robbed."

"Robbed?"

"Yes, that man, he took everything..." He nodded at a safe in the corner of the room.

The door was wide open, showing off the lack of contents.

"I hope the hounds of hell chase him down." He shook his head, his voice was quivering, as though shock and upset were about to get the better of him.

"Well they just might," I said. "It's wild out there with the riot going on." I set about unpicking the knots at his wrists, being careful not to flash my nakedness. They quickly came free. Steve, if that was even his name, the man I'd just fucked, had done this.

"Thank the Lord you came here, my dear. God must have sent you." He leaned forward and undid his feet, grimacing as he did so.

"Well, I'm not sure about that." If this genuine priest had seen me spread-eagled on his pew having a humdinger of an orgasm five minutes ago that might not have been his opinion.

"Oh my child, He most certainly did." He looked at me, his pale blue, watery eyes studying mine. "God moves in mysterious ways."

Chapter Four

I went to a sink in the corner. There were several mugs and a kettle on the counter, and I filled a cup with water.

"Here." I passed it to the priest.

"Thank you." He took it, drank deeply, and then handed the cup back.

As I too had a drink, he stood. "What's it like out there?"

"Terrible."

He shook his head and frowned. "Mother of Mercy." He crossed his chest. "What has London done to deserve this?"

"I don't know. It's horrible."

"Nothing is sacred. Not even the Lord's house."

"I agree."

He opened the door of a large oak wardrobe and pulled out a cassock. "We should pray," he said, then slipped it over his head.

"Well … I…" Praying wasn't usually my thing.

"We have much to be thankful for, we are alive." He said, setting his steely attention on me. "Plus we must ask the Lord for direction. What to do next. His wisdom will shine the light."

"What to do next? I suggest we stay holed up in here and keep quiet."

"Mmm … we'll see."

"What do you mean?" Panic went through me. Surely Father Duncan couldn't be suggesting going out onto the streets? That was sheer madness.

He straightened the black material that now hung around him, and touched the white collar at his neck. "I'm not sure what I mean yet." He lifted a beaded rosary from the counter and slipped it on. "Come, child. Your soul will be cleansed by His love."

I was about to object, but stopped myself. He was probably right, my soul did need cleansing. Having hot sex with a man who saw no problem impersonating a priest and robbing a church was not exactly wholesome. Though was it really my fault I'd enjoyed it? Or that I thought Steve was one of the most deliciously sinful men I'd ever had an encounter with?

As I followed Father Duncan out into the main body of the church, I wondered where Steve was now. What he was doing? Was he nearly home, and looking forward to lounging in bed with his money all around him? Had he dropped off at a bar to have a pint? Huh, as if bars would be open on a night like this. They'd likely been looted and ransacked, smashed up beyond all recognition.

Father Duncan seemed to glide rather than walk as he approached the altar with his head bent and his hands clasping the rosary. He dropped to his knees before the effigy of Christ and began to mumble.

I stared at his back, wondering what he expected me to do.

A sudden loud bang, from outside, rattled around the pews.

It was quickly followed by another, on the door this time.

I pressed my hand to my chest and turned to stare at the huge oak door.

The church had been noticed by the gangs. Someone had spotted the door that had been previously tucked out of view in the shadows, keeping us safe.

Voices now. Shouting, riled up, looking for a way in.

My heart rate trebled. The big bad wolf was outside and we were in a house made of sticks. No amount of praying would save us.

"Oh shit." I staggered to the left as the tip of an axe shattered through the door. This was it. They were here, the mobs braying for blood. "Father, get up. Please, you can't stay there."

Again the axe crashed through, splintering the wood, the silver tip sending terror through me.

"Now," I said, rushing up and gripping his shoulder. "We have to hide."

He turned to me, his eyes glazed.

"Please." I looked at the door again. The small room I'd found Father Duncan in offered little protection but it was the best I could think of. "Come on."

Finally he stood, though there seemed to be no hurry to his movements.

The door was fractured now. The manic voices and cheers easily pouring through the splits.

The priest looked at it and shook his head. "Five hundred years that door has kept the flock safe, and now look, destroyed in seconds."

"Just like we will be. Is there anywhere else to hide?"

"Yes." He glanced over his shoulder. "This way, child."

"Hey, it's a church. I bet there'll be loads to nick. Gold and shit like that." A deep menacing voice came from the other side of the broken door.

"Hurry," I said, my blood turning cold.

He took my hand, and with a sudden spurt of energy led me past the altar.

A huge tapestry hung to the right. The faded picture embroidered on it depicted the Virgin Mary holding Jesus as a child, and they were surrounded by kneeling women and lambs.

"In here." He pulled the heavy material aside. "Hold this."

I saw another door, small, as if made for people of barely five feet tall. Again it was made of wood with wrought iron furniture.

"Why didn't you hide in here last time?" I asked as he flicked the latch and opened it.

"I didn't have a chance to. That imposter, God have mercy on his soul, surprised me."

"Oh, I see." And yes, Steve did need mercy on his soul. He was a bad man even though he was a damn good fuck. A small tremor went up my spine. When all this was over I'd replay that moment of him taking me to heaven and back. Was it wrong to have enjoyed it so much? Was it wrong to not be utterly mortified now that I knew he was no better than the men breaking into this church at this moment?

I had no time to extend my thoughts. Father Duncan pressed his hand into the small of my back and all but shoved me through the door.

I stooped to prevent banging my head, and then straightened in what appeared to be a small circular room with stone walls. I glanced upward, several ropes hung down and a huge brass bell gaped down at me. We were in a bell tower.

Father Duncan joined me and shut the door.

It didn't have a lock. Just a latch. Not even a bolt.

"Do you think we'll be safe?" I asked, backing up so my shoulders hit the cold wall.

"If they don't tear down the tapestry."

Relying on that fact didn't sit well with me.

A huge splintering crash coming from outside signaled the mob had breached our safe haven.

I pressed my hand over my mouth to hold back a scream. Panic gripped me in its tight fist. It was hard to breathe, hard to focus on the priest who was once more praying with his eyes closed and worrying his rosary.

I looked up again, wondering if there was a way out that way, or maybe another place to hide.

Nothing.

What if they set the church on fire? We'd be trapped.

More crashing. Jeering. Crazy whoops of delight. The church was being trashed. Ancient and sacred artifacts destroyed. The peaceful place where parishioners had come to worship no longer a sanctuary of love. Now it was full of hate, belligerence, and disregard.

I shivered, the tremble going from my toes, up my bare legs, to my naked ass and through my guts.

I wished I had a big tough guy with me rather than Father Duncan. No wonder he'd been tied up and robbed. He was passive, distracted by God, his faith in a higher deity when really he should have been fighting for his life.

I wished Steve hadn't left the church. If he'd stayed and this mob had broken in, at least we'd have had one person with a bit of street sense and muscle.

Steve was definitely the type of bloke who'd be able to stick up for himself. Likely had been all his life. I knew the sort in the East End. Ducking and diving, having to get his fists out to survive. Hell, he'd probably stolen the money to survive too.

Who was I kidding? He was a common thief who'd taken the opportunity for a quick fuck.

What a charmer?

Still, it would be nice to have him in here with us, right now. I'd bet he'd have a plan or at least some kind of idea about what to do.

I wrapped my arms around my body and hugged myself. The shouts and cries were louder now. As though the rioters had reached the altar. I tried to make out how many there were; two, three maybe. Too many for me to take on even if I was a goddamn karate expert—which of course I wasn't.

An ear splitting crash told me the stained glass window had been shattered.

I held in a squeal.

Father Duncan's shoulders twitched but he kept his eyes closed, his lips moving silently. He looked old and frail, as if life had made him jaded and he was ready to say goodbye to the physical world.

"Hey, there's a door here." A rough, sandpapery voice that was also slightly slurred as though the owner had been drinking.

"Oh God..." I stared, wide-eyed, at the latch. I prayed it wouldn't move, that it would stay sat neat and inert.

Of course that didn't happen.

It lifted. The door opened.

A man peered in. His eyes blazed with excitement, his cheeks red, and when he saw me he let out a whistle of delight. "Hey, Robbie, we've got us some fun times in here."

Another man appeared at his shoulder. He had dark skin and wore a red baseball cap. "Oh yeah. Praise the Lord we've got a pretty one to have some fun with."

I gulped. My saliva bitter. Was I going to vomit?

"Father..." I whispered, wondering if the man at my side would save me. "Please..."

He remained stock-still, his thoughts clearly taken up with the words he was saying to God.

"Come to daddy," the first man said, holding out his hand.

"No, fuck off." I pressed harder against the wall. "Now."

"Don't be like that, angel." He ducked and came into the room. He wasn't especially tall, about my height.

I balled my fists. "Get out of here. Leave me alone."

"I don't think so." He sneered at me and took in my outfit. "Not when I'm hard and ready to go."

In a flash he was over me, his hands on the wall either side of my head.

He stank of sweat and beer, the evil in his eyes scared me half to death. He was going to rape me, I knew that. Was murder in his thoughts too?

"Yeah, you do her first, and then I'll have a go." The dark skinned man said, looming at his right and grinning sickeningly.

"You'll burn I hell," I said, my voice shaky.

"Yeah, well, I like the heat," the man trapping me in said. "So I reckon I'm well set up for being mates with the devil."

He pressed his mouth to mine in a disgusting, sloppy kiss.

I cried out, squirmed, and shoved at him.

"Ah you want it really, whore." He dragged my skirt up, exposing my bare pussy.

"And she's ready for it," the other man said. "Why don't we fuck her at the same time. I don't mind taking her ass."

"Nah, I'll have her ass." He spun me around, whacking my cheek against the stone wall.

I kicked backward, and tried to jab my elbow at him, too. But the other man was there now. They were both pinning me down, their hands roaming my body, touching my breasts, and my ass cheeks.

I shut my eyes and screamed. It came right from the very core of my soul. White-hot, electric terror burned through me. It seared my nerves, blazed through my brain. I hated these men. I hadn't known what hate was before this moment, but now I knew it felt like acid in my veins.

A sudden roar filled the small room. It penetrated my eardrums and whirled around my horror-filled brain.

What was it?

Father Duncan? Had he come to his senses and decided to fight for my honor?

One set of hands left me.

A huge crash, the sound of bone hitting the wall.

"Who the fuck are you?" The second set of hands lifted, as did the weight of a chest pinning me in place.

I spun around, opening my eyes as I did so.

A huge man, dressed all in black, slung my short attacker to the right. His body collided with the wall, surprise on his face.

Steve.

He's back.

His face was full of fury, his teeth gritted and his eyes flashing.

I pressed my hands to my mouth. What the hell was he doing here?

Chapter Five

Steve continued to beat on the man he'd just slung against the wall. The long black sleeves of his cassock flapping wildly, and his heavy boots making contact with limbs and torso.

Suddenly the other man sprang back to life. He hurled himself at Steve.

Steve twirled around, aiming a deft right hook with precision.

The man's head snapped backward, a burst of blood sprayed from his lip.

"Raping bastard," Steve shouted. "I'll teach you."

"What the fuck are you? A ninja priest." The black man said, going for a jab at Steve's sternum.

"Yeah, you're going to wish that's all I was."

Steve ducked and evaded a punch going for his temple, then fired off several that rendered his opponent unconscious on the floor.

I was shaking so much my body didn't feel like mine. I looked at the other man, his head had slumped to the side and drool leaked from his lips. His cock lay flaccid from his open zipper.

Steve frowned, his dark eyebrows pulling low, and looked at me. "You okay?"

"Yes ... No."

"Which is it?"

"They were going to..."

"I know." He stepped up to me, reached for my skirt and pulled it downward, covering my nakedness. "I should cut their dicks off."

A sob bubbled up from my chest. Steve was a thief and liar but I'd never been so glad to see an East End rogue in all of my life.

"Hey." He dragged me against him—a rough hug that seemed to absorb me into his body.

I gripped his cassock and leaned onto him. If he hadn't shown up when he had I'd be being raped and buggered right now, likely left for dead so I couldn't identify my attackers.

"Stop that," he said, squeezing me tighter. "They won't hurt you now."

"What … what are you doing here?"

He pulled back and looked down at my face. "I might be a complete bastard," he said, "but the further I got from this church the more I realized that I'd left you to the dogs."

"Why? What's going on out there?"

"Carnage. A woman on her own, as you said earlier, doesn't stand a chance."

I shivered. "So now what?"

"Now I've got to get you out of here."

"Okay." I had no other option. There would be more like the two who had just attacked me. Staying wasn't something I could entertain, neither was leaving without Steve.

I gestured to Father Duncan who still was praying with his eyes shut as if in some kind of celestial trance. "What about him?"

Steve huffed. "He can figure it out on his own."

"But—"

"He was going to stand by and watch those bastards do hideous things to you. A defenseless woman. I think he deserves everything he gets here on Earth and when he gets to the Pearly Gates."

Part of me agreed but still … I didn't like the thought of leaving Father Duncan.

"And when I got here earlier," Steve said, "he was emptying that safe into this bag." He tapped the rucksack on his back that I now noticed was hidden beneath his cassock. "He had a passport in his hand. It was pretty obvious he was doing some looting of his own. I was just redirecting that cash for more worthy causes."

I frowned. "What causes?"

"*My* causes." He grabbed my hand. "Come on."

"Steve."

"What?"

I paused.

"What?" he asked again.

"You're not a priest, are you?"

"You know damn well I'm not." He laughed. "And it took you a while to figure that one out."

I frowned. "Bastard."

"Yeah well." He shrugged. "Right now, I'm all you got, bastard or not."

I nodded. "I know. And … thank you."

"For what?"

"For coming back for me."

"Don't thank me yet. We gotta get about two miles east before we can relax." He bent down and rummaged in the black man's pocket. He pulled something out.

"What's that?"

"We might need it." Whatever it was he'd tucked it under his cassock before I could identify it.

I threw a last glance at Father Duncan, then Steve urged me out of the small bell tower.

The altar looked nothing like it had before, the bible was sprawled on the floor, the tapestry torn and pulled half off its hooks. What appeared to be red wine had been slung at Jesus and dripped from his toes like watery blood.

I shuddered, though as I did so the scent of smoke drifted toward me.

"Quick," Steve said, "Let's go."

The front door of the church was open and I rushed down the aisle, trying to keep up with what was now my only hope. I didn't want to go back out there, into the darkness where danger lurked in every shadow, but I had no option.

We paused at the doorway, it was darker now, the wind having blown out the candles in the church. Outside smoked danced on the breeze. Where the fire was, or rather fires, were I didn't know, but their presence was evident.

Footsteps came from the right. Fast. Running. Slapping on the wet cobbles.

A man, dressed all in black and wearing a balaclava raced past. He paid us no notice.

I wondered what he was running from.

"This way," Steve tugged me to the right.

"That way? Really?"

"Yeah, come on."

I hesitated.

"You're going to have to trust me," Steve said, frowning and tightening his grip on my fingers. "Or I can just leave you here, alone."

"No. No, don't do that." I gripped his biceps. "I'm coming with you."

"Good." He stepped from the archway.

I followed and we stuck to the shadows, hoping not to draw attention to ourselves. But there was no one about, not in the immediate vicinity. Though the riotous crowd was only a street or two away. The cheers and yells, breaking glass, and a helicopter, no doubt police, filled my ears.

We reached the end of the street, where I'd been heading earlier when the first creep I'd encountered took my bag.

Steve paused, looked left and right, then tugged me to the left.

"Hey, hey, what we got here?"

A group of four men were suddenly in front of us. They wore scarves around their faces, pulled over their noses, and hoods pulled up tight.

Menace drifted off them in waves. They were out for blood and a fight. I could tell. Their eyes flashed with excitement and hate.

"A man of the cloth and his pretty woman. Not supposed to be having any of that, are you, Father," the apparent leader of the gang said, then turned to his posse and laughed.

"Well it is a free for all night," one of his mates retorted. "So I reckon he can have a shag, get the dust off his dick."

Steve pushed me behind him, trapping me between his body and the wall. "Fuck off, all of you."

"That's not very fucking Christian of you, is it?" the gang leader said. "We only want a look at the bit of pussy you got there."

"I've got nothing for you. Leave us alone."

I pressed up against the rucksack, knowing it was stuffed full of cash. Why couldn't we just be left to make our way to safety?

"Yeah, he'll have to say a bunch of Hail Mary's for shagging that whore," one of the guys laughed. He had a deep, heavily accented voice, I wasn't sure where he was from but I suspected Spain.

"Get out of my way," Steve said, "now."

"Or else what." The leader stepped closer, with a confident swagger.

"Let us pass," Steve said. "I won't tell you again."

"And I won't tell *you* again, we want a look at your bit of pussy, maybe have a play too." Suddenly he pulled out a knife and held it forward. The steel blade caught the light of a lamppost and it glinted menacingly. "I want her. Now."

Steve tensed and drew in a deep breath. He lifted up his cassock and pulled out a small handgun. "I said, get out of my way, asshole."

"Hey, hey." The gang leader raised his hands above his head. Knife now pointing at the night sky. "Easy man. We didn't mean no harm."

"Sure you didn't." Steve stepped forward.

I followed.

"So just fuck off and go and pray for forgiveness." Steve kept walking.

I stuck to him like glue. I figured the gun had been from the guy back at the bell tower. Thank goodness he'd picked it up.

"Chill out, Father," one of the other guys said.

Steve swung the end of the gun around the group. He held it steady, as if it were familiar in his hand. "You've got five seconds to be out of my sight."

"Or else what?" Despite his words the bravado had left the leader's voice.

"I start shooting. I shot one guy back there which leaves five bullets." He aimed the gun over the gang, fired, and shot a hole through a hanging pub sign. The pub was called The Bull's Head and he fired straight through the eye of the snorting cartoon bull on the sign. "There goes another one." He nodded at the sign, now swinging violently. "And as you can see I'm a fucking good shot."

"Fuck a duck," one of the guys said. "He ain't kidding, bruv."

"Too damn right I'm not." Steve aimed the gun at the leader once more. "Fuck off. I won't say it again."

The leader glared at Steve for a moment then he swung his attention to his mates. "Come on, let's get out of here. Plenty more where she came from."

Their running footsteps clattered around the walls of the high buildings. Within seconds they were eaten by the shadows and it was if they'd never been there.

"Christ Almighty," I muttered, and released the grip I had on Steve's clothing.

"Wankers," he said. "Come on."

He led the way forward, holding my hand and the gun.

I felt safer now I knew he had a weapon. Much as guns abhorred me. I'd never even touched one let alone fired one, knowing he had one and could use it made me think we had a chance of getting out of this hellhole.

We kept on going, took a right onto Ponseable Street, then a left down Newark Avenue. There were people about, drunk youths, a few fires burning in skips, but no one bothered us.

"I can hardly hear it now," I said, breathlessly. "The riot."

"No, we're away from the center of it." He tucked the gun away. "We'll keep walking though. My place is in Newington. We'll crash there."

"That's ages away."

"Yeah, well, nothing we can do about that. No buses running around here tonight."

He was right. This part of London had turned into a ghost town. Despite the riots being some distance away all the houses seemed to be in darkness. Curtains pulled tight, lights off.

****

Eventually we reached Newington Road. Much to my relief Steve stopped at the first block of apartments.

He keyed in a few numbers and the door opened with a buzz.

"In." He set his hand in the small of my back and propelled me into the dimly lit lobby.

As the door shut, blocking me from the outside world, a sense of calm washed through me.

I'd done it.

Made it out of there in one piece.

It had been the worst night of my life. By far. One I never wanted to repeat. But thank goodness I was still breathing and my heart still beating.

"It's a few floors up," he said. "We'll use the stairs, elevator is dodgy."

"Okay." What difference did a bit further make? I'd been marching and running all day.

We came to the fourth floor and he led me out into the open. A long, concrete balcony led to a seemingly endless row of doors.

I glanced at the London skyline. The smoke had hazed the majestic rooftops and landmarks, and helicopters swarmed, their bright lights darting left and right.

I shuddered. I wanted nothing more than a hot shower, a cup of tea and to forget about the nastiness of human nature.

"This one," Steve said, stopping and fishing a small brass Yale key from his pocket. He opened a blue door that was ready for another lick of paint. "After you."

I stepped into the dark hallway.

Steve did the same and shut the door. He slid a chain into place and flicked the lock.

"You'll be fine in here," he said, setting his hands on my shoulders.

"Do you promise?"

"Yes." He paused. "I just got you across London didn't I, the way I said I would?"

"You did, thank you."

"And I haven't made you do anything tonight you didn't want to, have I?"

I turned to him.

He flicked a light switch, and a bare bulb glared from just behind where he stood.

"No. You haven't."

"And you enjoyed it, in the church, when it was just us and you thought you were fucking a priest?"

I studied his eyes. They were full of male cockiness and I had a mind to kick him in the shins. But there was something else. A softness that I suspected didn't surface very often.

I smiled. I couldn't deny I hadn't enjoyed it and he knew that. "So are you going to count your money? From your looting."

"I might, later." He stepped away and shucked off his cassock. He threw it into the corner of the hallway where it lay rumpled. He then let the rucksack fall from his back, catching the strap in his right hand. "But right now I need a fucking drink."

"Me too."

He stepped past me, into a kitchen. "What do you want? Say tea and you can leave right now."

I shut my mouth. The word tea had been about to be uttered.

"I've got whiskey or brandy."

"Brandy, please."

From the cupboard he pulled out a bottle of amber liquid and two mugs. He sloshed brandy into each. "Here."

"Thanks." I took it. "What shall we toast?"

"To getting out of there with assets."

"Assets."

"Yeah, I got cash and a woman. That's a pretty decent night's work."

I raised my eyebrows. "And what did I get?"

"You got me, baby." He knocked back his drink, then smacked his lips together. "Ahh..."

I laughed. It was a strange, almost hysterical sound, not my usual laugh.

"Drink," he ordered, refilling his mug.

I did. The burn of the brandy made me gasp as it scorched down my gullet. Almost instantly it made my knees quiver and sent a tingle over my skin. "Do you mind if I take a shower?"

He tipped his head and studied me. "Go ahead. It's the next door on the right."

"Okay, thanks." I set the mug on the counter and went back into the hallway. The place lacked a woman's touch and needed a good vacuum, not to mention some more modern wallpaper, the flowery stuff that was peeling around the skirting board was nasty.

I found the bathroom. It was painted green and had a bath that needed a good clean and a large shower cubicle that seemed hygienic enough. I flicked on the water and tugged off my boots. I then removed my jacket, sweater and bra, and rolled my skirt down my legs. I needed to get hold of some more knickers soon. Perhaps there were some in the apartment I could have.

The mirror had quickly steamed up, and the air had become damp.

I stepped into the hot water, sighing as it rained down on my tense, aching shoulders. I breathed deep, hoping to cleanse my lungs of the awful smell of smoke and the breath of the man who'd wanted to rape me.

Closing my eyes, I wondered how Father Duncan was getting on. Hopefully the police had found him, if not, he was probably still apologizing to God for his plan to steal all that church money and leave the country.

But Steve had gotten to it first. What was his plan with it? I'd like to think he was going to donate it to good causes but somehow I didn't think so. Shit. Why was the hottest bloke I'd met in a long time a thieving scoundrel? Life played weird games with me sometimes.

"Want some company?"

I spun and opened my eyes.

Steve stood by the shower, gloriously naked and looking like every sin I'd ever wanted to commit wrapped up in one big, muscly package. He had a tattoo on his right pec—a devil's face, complete with horns and manic eyes and holding a pitchfork.

"I guess I could do with help scrubbing my back."

"Oh, baby I'll sort out more than your back."

A shot of arousal went through me as he stepped in. His cock was thick and hard and standing proud. The water hit his body and ran over his flesh in rivers, dipping in and out of the contours of his torso.

What the hell am I doing?

I was going to answer that question tomorrow. Right now, this sexy man who certainly flirted with what was ethically acceptable, was all I wanted. Sure he was an East End thug, no doubt notorious and likely wanted by the police. But my body didn't care about that. I wanted up close and personal with his big, unholy cock and how it could make me feel.

He'd saved me after all, more than once tonight.

I reached for his shoulders and pressed close, enjoying wet skin against wet skin. Instantly my nipples hardened and I pressed my legs together, need growing within me.

He pushed my hair from my cheeks and tipped my head so I faced him.

Water droplets clung to his stubble and his eyelashes were damp. His dark eyes flashed with desire.

"I need to tell you stuff," he said.

"No. Don't tell me anything." I didn't want the moment spoiled with facts. Facts that were likely laced with information that tugged at my moral compass, or possibly threw it completely out of whack and in the totally opposite direction.

His mouth twitched, as though half smiling. "Okay, well, one thing."

"Only one." I ran my palms from his collarbones and set one over his tattoo. "Don't ruin this."

"I'm not who you think I am."

"I know that. And I don't care. Not for tonight. Tonight I just want to feel alive. *Celebrate* feeling alive."

"There's not much of the night left. It will be morning soon."

"So we should make the most of it." I ground against his cock.

He moaned and his eyes fluttered shut. "Fuck."

"Yes. Shall we?"

He opened his eyes and swept his tongue over his bottom lip. "I'm not a hearts and flowers type of bloke. I don't do romance."

"I'd already gathered that."

"But if you decide to stick around, in the morning, beyond…"

I widened my eyes. "What?"

"All I'm saying is I'll show you a good time."

"What with all that cash you nicked?"

"Maybe." He grinned suddenly. "But mainly I'll show you a good time with my dick."

"So start."

His face fell serious. "I'm a one woman man, I might have faults but I don't dip it around. You want to be mine then…"

"Then what?"

"I'll look after you in a way you've never been looked after before."

Jesus. Could I really have some kind of relationship with a tough-as-nails guy like this? A man who had to slip out of view when police cars went past?

I don't know the answer to that.

Suddenly I was hoisted into the air.

"Stop thinking," he said. He twisted so my back was against the cool tiles and his chest pressed into mine.

I wrapped my legs around his waist and clung to his arms.

"Stop thinking and let's start doing," he murmured.

"Okay," I said, happy to let all thoughts of the future leave my mind. This is what I wanted. Now. Here. With Steve. "Condom," I managed as he angled the tip of his erection at my spread pussy. Pregnancy wasn't an issue, but still…

"Why? We've already done it without, in for a penny in for a pound." He tensed. "Are you ready for it?"

"Yes." Oh God, I wanted him. All of him. I wanted him to unleash his passion the way he had in the church. Just fuck. Become raw male need. It was so damn sexy and it turned me on so much.

I could live with that every day.

He pushed into my entrance. Not fast and urgent like before, but slow and deliberate as if feeling every sensation as he buried deep.

"Ah, yeah," he said, his lips moving against mine. "So good, Cheryl."

He kissed me, his tongue probing the way his cock was.

I kissed him back, enjoying the stroke of his lips and him entering me so thoroughly.

When he reached full depth his hard body pressed up against my clit, and he cupped one hand beneath my ass, tipping my pelvis so the connection was even harder.

I trembled. "Yes. That's it."

"You want more?"

"Yes, all of it. All you can give me."

He gripped the back of my head, his fingers slotting into my hair. He held me tight and firm.

I stared at his wet face, the water dripping from his nose and chin, and the way his hair had plastered to his forehead.

"So what other fantasies have you got?" he asked, studying my eyes.

"What do you mean?"

"Well I've fulfilled your priest one?"

I cupped his jawline. "I didn't know I had that one."

"But you admit you did." He pulled out then sank back in.

"Seems that way," I said breathlessly, tightening my internal muscles around him.

He groaned. "Fuck that feels good. *You* feel good."

"Maybe I need to find out your fantasies," I said, gripping his shoulders now. My nails sank into his flesh but he didn't flinch.

"Oh baby, you might find more than you can handle."

"Perhaps you'll have to try me."

He touched the tip of his nose to mine. "Damn, I could get used to having you around. Ticking off all those wicked, filthy fantasies you have but don't even know about." He withdrew, then thrust deep again, faster this time and holding me tight as his balls butted up against my ass.

I pulled him to me, kissed him, wildly, the water slicking between our mouths. Fantasies, yes. I had more. And right now he was the star of all of them.

The tempo picked up. He was running the show, pounding into me, the water cooled but I didn't care. My skin was hot and tingling. An orgasm growing and getting ready to erupt.

"Fucking hell..." he muttered against my lips. "I'm coming."

"Me ... too." A climax ripped through me.

Steve joined me, and my pussy hugged his cock over and over as he released.

"Ahhh, yes. Oh, God," I cried out, my voice swirling with the steam and echoing around the small cubicle.

He grunted and buried his face against my neck.

I felt so small in his embrace and completely possessed by him. This big man who'd tricked me, saved me, and fucked me all in one night had thrown everything I thought I knew about need and want on its head. His variety of sexy, of claiming me, was addictive, I knew that already.

I groaned then sucked in a deep breath. Pleasure was tingling over my skin, my nipples, my toes, and my hairline all fizzing with pleasure.

He nipped my earlobe between his teeth, his breath a storm in my ear. He was shaking, his muscles absorbing erotic bliss the way mine were.

I shut my eyes and let my arms and legs relax.

He held me tight, pressed against the wall, and stilled.

The water rained down as I caught my breath, my chest bashing up against his.

He'd told me one thing about himself, and if there was one thing I knew about myself now it was that I'd be sticking around. I was hooked. Steve, and his promises of fantasies fulfilled, his grotty apartment and his hot as hell body had me hooked. Sinful he might be, but it was the sweetest, sexiest brand of sin I could imagine.

Lord help me.

The End

www.lilyharlem.com

ONE LAST JOB

Alexa Sinclaire

Copyright © 2016

Chapter One

Ivy

Sitting gagged on the floor of the van that Lawson and his men had thrown her into, Ivy had a lot of time to think. And she came to the conclusion that none of this would have happened it hadn't been for her insatiable need to eat a cinnamon roll nearly every day for lunch. Because had she not had that cinnamon roll two weeks ago, she wouldn't have gotten sticky sugar on her fingers and she wouldn't have had to remove her ring in the staff room to wash her hands, and Lawson would have never seen her tattoo, and he never would have touched her hand and stared at her with those ridiculous deep brown eyes that were as enticing as the damn sugar on her cinnamon roll. And then he wouldn't have asked her for dinner and they wouldn't have had the most amazing sex she'd ever had, staring into those damn beautiful eyes again.

Had none of that happened, when the group of masked men that came into the jewelers this morning and started robbing the place, Ivy wouldn't have whispered Lawson's name when she saw those same eyes staring at her through a mask. And like the idiot she was, Ivy actually said his name loud enough for one of the others guys to hear her and decide that the fact that she knew who one of them was meant she was a liability.

Now she was kidnapped and listening to a bunch of criminals argue about whether she was going to be killed or used as blackmail. It wouldn't take long for them to figure out that there was no one in her life worth blackmailing and eventually they'd decide to kill her. All she could do was hope that she'd find an opportunity to escape before that.

Ivy glanced up at Lawson. Until now he hadn't said anything, hadn't given his opinion of what her fate should be. He'd sat mute, staring at her. After they'd driven for what felt like an hour, he finally leaned over and yanked off her gag.

"You weren't supposed to work today. Why were you there?" He sounded furious, as if the current situation was her fault.

"Marcie texted me last night. Her little girl was sick. She knew I had the day off and I didn't mind taking her shift."

He sat back, seemingly satisfied with her answer but the look of resentment remained firmly on his face. Ivy was beginning to realize that any sort of connection she'd felt between them had been clearly one-sided and she couldn't rely on him to help her out of her current predicament.

Four months ago Lawson Trent started working as a security guard in the jewelry shop. He was one of those silent and brooding types, with rugged features to make the image complete. Emphasis on rugged. She could see why he'd been hired to work security with his massive build but he looked like he belonged in an underground cage-fighting circuit, not a mid-range jewelry shop where most of the clients were safe and boring middle-class members of society.

But there he was nonetheless, with his broad shoulders and tree-trunk thighs, sinfully filling out his uniform and driving her to distraction. And his rough stubble that he seemed to maintain effortlessly that she imagined rubbing against the sensitive skin on her inner thighs. *And* the scar he had on his right eyebrow that she desperately resisted running her fingers over on almost a daily basis. It was all that and more that made her want to get to know him. That and the fact that she saw something underneath all that, something she thought was worth working for.

On his first day of work, they ended up in the staff room having lunch at the same time. Ivy cut her cinnamon roll in half, after heating it in the microwave, and slid it across the table until it sat next to his sandwich. He stared at for a few moments before looking up at her. She'd already eaten her tofu and lentil salad and was picking off warm chunks of sugar-coated dough and moaning softly as she savored each morsel.

"Didn't I just see you eating tofu?"

Ivy gave him a big smile after licking the sugar off the tip of a finger. "Yup. And lentils. I'm a big believer in the power of legumes."

"What the hell is a legume?" This was by far one of the least sexy conversations she'd ever had, but it was better than nothing. As far as she knew, he'd been monosyllabically polite with the rest of the staff.

"It's a class of vegetables. Lentils, peas, and beans. That kind of thing. Legumes are some of the healthiest foods you can eat."

He gestured to her half of the roll. "Do you realize the kind of crap they put in these cinnamon rolls to make them taste and smell like that? It's probably been sitting on a shelf for two years. How else do you think they make it taste so damn good that you're sitting over there moaning over it like you're trying out for a porno?"

The fact that hearing her moan made him think of sex was only a good thing, as far as Ivy was concerned. "Well yeah. Why else do you think I eat the legumes?" She gave him another big grin and took bite of her roll, resisting moaning again.

He snorted in response. "You're a bit of a contradiction, you know that?"

She dropped her smile. Ivy hated when people pointed that out about her, especially since she already knew it was her biggest personality flaw. Being a contradiction wasn't a good thing. It was a polite way to call someone unpredictable and while being unpredictable was occasionally fun because it meant she could be spontaneous, but really it meant unstable. And her life had been the definition of unstable.

Shunted around from foster home to foster home, Ivy had grown up with the ground constantly shifting beneath her feet. To say she had a slight impulse control problem was an understatement. But she figured out early on that acting out didn't do any good and managed to control her erratic behavior as best as she could.

She realized quickly that grown-ups didn't like kids who acted out. Grown-ups also didn't like quiet kids who seemed so damaged they were gone beyond repair. So instead Ivy tried to be the happy, upbeat, yet slightly manic kid who did well in school, despite everything, and got along with everyone.

Of course she couldn't keep that up consistently. Her school record was smattered with months of perfect grades, then expulsions or suspension for acting out: breaking a cheerleader's nose, knocking her desk over, and swearing at a teacher. She would go weeks getting along with a foster family until she snapped and ran away. She had endless examples of her inconsistent moods and her behavior drove her social workers crazy.

As an adult, she was still trying to figure out how to be the mistress of her own destiny. And of course, how to not be an excessive people pleaser just to keep life simple because that one always came to bite her on the ass.

To protect herself, she kept a firm emotional distance with the rest of the world. Friendships took a lot of work and could turn bad fast, so she minimized them. That's not to say that she wasn't pleasant and warm. Any of the girls at work would describe her as reliable and considerate. She'd just baked cupcakes for Elaine's birthday last week, because she was that kind of friend. But none of them knew where she lived, or what her background was like. Only a few of them had her phone number and she rarely saw them outside of work.

She knew she was full of contradictions, and she hated hearing it from a guy she was crushing on pretty hard. The fact was Lawson was one of the first guys she'd let herself even *think* about in a non-platonic way for a very long time. And describing it as a crush was putting it lightly. She was having a hard time not constantly fantasizing about ripping her clothes off and impaling herself on the ridiculously large cock he could barely contain in his uniform khakis.

When it came to men, Ivy learned that she tended to give in pretty quickly, and as such she stayed away from them. She knew she was attractive. Her delicate features, long blonde hair, and curves most women worked hard to get because they probably hadn't discovered the secret of the dual power action brought on by cinnamon roll consumption and legumes, ensured that she got plenty of attention from the opposite sex. But like everything, it usually came at a price. There was always a balancing act to figure out and she wasn't all that good at getting it right.

That's not to say that she didn't like men and sex. Ivy liked sex, although she hadn't had a lot of good sex. Just a lot of mediocre sex and a healthy commitment to her vibrator. Both of which always left her wanting *more*. She didn't really know what that was. Just *more*.

She wanted them to hold her tighter and longer.

She wanted the sex to be rougher and harder.

She wanted his hands around her throat while he pounded into her, making her feel like he would never let her go.

That's why she had to keep to herself. There was no way she could turn over that kind of power to a man. At least none of the men she'd met. The few times she'd come close to even experiencing that with a guy, it always turned sour quickly since he thought she wanted to be controlled.

Again—another one of her contradictions.

It wasn't about a guy taking control, it was about finding that space where she could let go and lose herself. The distinction was vague and she wasn't even sure there was one, but she just knew when it felt right, which it never had. That kind of indistinctness led to chaos and Ivy was trying her hardest to avoid chaos. And basically any situation that smacked of ambiguity.

Until Lawson.

She could tell he obviously lived a hard life and as such he looked older than thirty. She knew how old he was because Elaine, who worked in the office with their sleazy boss, had seen his file. He didn't look like he drank or smoked too much. Just that he'd seen his fair share of hardship.

Just like Ivy.

But he was still always polite. It went against the brooding, silent thing he had going on. And that's why she was drawn to him. *He* was a contradiction. And that's why she was confident that he'd accept her cinnamon roll because despite keeping to himself and maintaining a certain distance, he was polite.

Just like Ivy.

But then after that moment together at lunch, probably sensing that she was interested in him, he worked hard at keeping a distance between them.

However, like a moth to the mother of all erotic flames, Ivy was drawn him to him. And she was getting close to admitting the attraction was probably one-sided, despite catching him looking at her on almost a daily basis, and despite the comment about listening to her moan, until he saw her ring tattoo.

The tattoo had been one of her more spontaneous decisions, naively made when she was younger and didn't realize how hard it was to get a job with a visible tattoo. Thankfully, it was easily hidden with a real ring and no one at work even knew she had it. Until Lawson walked in and saw her washing sticky sugar off her fingers. She'd removed the cheap silver-plated ring she wore to hide it and he took her hand from under the running water and touched it, almost like he couldn't control himself. Grabbing a paper towel, he dried it off and just stared at it.

"Does it mean something?"

Her stomach flip-flopped as his coarse fingers caressed her hand and she tried to keep her voice calm. "Of course. Don't all tattoos?" It wasn't really an answer and they both knew it. His eyes swept up to meet hers and she swallowed audibly. He didn't look happy. "It's a reminder. Just a little reminder."

"Of what?"

There was no way she could explain all it reminded her off, not sitting in the staff room where it still smelled like reheated macaroni and cheese and stale coffee.

"Everything," she whispered.

The next day Lawson sat down while she was having lunch and asked her to dinner at his place. Just like that. And being a lust-struck young woman, she enthusiastically accepted.

Ivy showed up at his apartment, which was in a neighborhood just as bad as hers, something that didn't really surprise her. Most men, at least on a first date, would hide living in such a dump. But Lawson wasn't the kind of man to hide who he really was, Ivy told herself.

He fed her gorgeous heavy calorie-laden lasagna and poured cheap red wine but she didn't care because the whole thing was perfect and amazing and she knew that Lawson was dark and beautiful and by far the most exciting man she'd ever met.

After dinner, they stood side by side doing the dishes. And she did that thing that all women do at some point when they're connecting with a man: she pretended they were a real couple and she pretended that after cleaning their tiny kitchen, he would sweep her up in his arms, walk into their bedroom, and take her hard and rough, and she pretended he would tell her how much he adored her before they fell asleep with their arms around each other.

And it actually happened. Sort of.

Having finished drying the last plate, Ivy turned to him and was about to tell him how lovely the dinner was when his mouth descended on hers and he kissed her.

He really kissed her.

Lawson pushed his tongue into her mouth, giving her no option but to open up to him. He tasted like red wine and dark spices and she moaned against his tongue. God, he even tasted rugged. She threw her arms around his neck, needing to hold onto something since her legs were about to give out but also because she was afraid he'd pull away and she needed him to keep kissing her until she died, it was that good.

In the back of her mind, Ivy heard a tiny alarm bell ringing, warning her that if the man kissed this well, she was going to have trouble resisting anything and everything he tried to take from her further down the line. But she didn't care.

Lawson's arms wrapped around her waist and he effortlessly lifted her up. Ivy didn't even need to think twice before she wrapped her legs around his hips. He moved his hands to hold her under her dress and it was his turn to moan as he discovered the bare skin of her ass, thanks to her choice of thong over panties.

He walked them the short distance to the couch, still dominating her mouth, still making sure she knew who was in charge, and Ivy loved every second.

Sitting down, with Ivy straddling him, he finally broke the kiss. His hands ran up and down her thighs, sweeping ever closer to her pulsing core. She leaned her forehead against his and swiveled her hips. There was no way she could ignore the stiffness wedged between her open legs. She wanted to see it, to taste it, to lick it and worship it, and then she wanted it in her.

"Jesus, Ivy, you're so fucking sexy. Do you know how hard it's been to sit and eat dinner with you? When all I wanted to do was…" he stopped talking and pressed his face into her neck, licking and nibbling at her soft skin.

"Was what? Please." She wanted to hear it. She needed to know that it was just her who had been fantasizing about what sex between them would be like.

He growled into her skin, making her shiver and grind her hips even harder.

"Fuck. If I told you, I'd probably scare you."

Ivy shook her head back and forth. God, if he only knew the things she fantasized about him doing to her, he'd probably think she was some sort of pervert. "No, please, I promise, it won't scare me."

He lifted his face from her neck and stared into her eyes. "I wanted to bend you over my kitchen table, flip up that pretty dress you wore for me, and pound into you. Every time you took a sip of red wine and I had to watch that little tongue of yours slip out to wipe your lips, all I could think about was getting you on your knees and face-fucking you until I came down your gorgeous throat." Ivy closed her eyes and groaned. "Open your eyes, Ivy." His hips were thrusting up to meet hers as they worked themselves into a frenzy through their clothes. "I'm not even done telling you all the dirty things I want to do to you."

"Yes, more, tell me more," she managed to breathe out. She opened her eyes and kept contact as he started talking:

"I want to get you on my bed, use my belt to tie your hands behind your back, while I take you from behind. And there's nothing you can do but take it." His voice was getting deeper and deeper, a gravely tone that in itself was enough to turn her on. He could have been reciting recipes and it would have gotten her hot.

God, the belt scene—how could he have known that being bound with a belt was one of her deepest fantasies?

"Yes, Lawson, I'll take it, I will, like a good girl," she whispered back.

He chuckled as his hands came up, leaving her thighs feeling cool and she wanted him to put them back.

That is until he roughly yanked down the sleeves of her dress, pulling her bra straps off her shoulders at the same time and ripping open the front opening of her bra, breaking the small snap. Her breasts spilled out but he kept eye contact with her as he started palming them, pinching and twisting the nipples, hard and then soft, driving her wild with each twist and turn of his thick fingers.

"Do you know how many times I thought about seeing these naked? You wear that plain white blouse every day to work and all I can think about is ripping it down the middle, jacking up that tight skirt of yours and pushing you down face first over that damn display counter. I know you'll take it. You'll let me fill you up and then I'll flip you over and wrap my hands around that pretty neck of yours." His large hands came up and circled her throat. It wasn't tight, it wasn't meant to hurt her, Ivy knew that much. "I'll hold on to you and watch your face as I push into your ass. And again—you'll take me. For as long and as hard as I want."

That was it. The mention of her ass. She'd never done anal sex because that was something that even though she wanted to try it, *badly*, she knew it had to be with someone she trusted, and she never let a man get close enough for that. But the thought of Lawson doing that to her was too much. She needed him. The ache between her legs was now bordering on painful.

Ivy's hands moved to hold his face as she kissed him passionately, putting all her wants and desires into that kiss, hoping that she could convey the arousal she had no way of expressing without looking like a maniac.

"Please, please, do it, do everything to me, but now. I'm going crazy here, Lawson. I need you." She was begging, she knew she was but it was the first time she'd ever let go and she loved the way it felt. She loved that she needed him. And from the way he was acting, he seemed to need her as badly.

"I know, baby, I know what you need."

Flipping them so she lay on her back on the couch, Lawson crouched over her, undoing his jeans and pushing them down just enough to release his cock. Ivy barely got a look at before it before Lawson slipped on a condom and moved to guide it in her. For a second, a split nanosecond, she thought they should slow down, but then he pulled her thong to the side and started to slide in.

"I'm not going to be able to let you go, Ivy." He paused a few inches in and glanced up at her, his voice barely audible. Despite the fact that she was mostly naked under him and all he'd done was unzip his jeans to take himself out, she didn't feel vulnerable or exposed. He felt it, she knew he felt it, whatever this was between them.

She lifted her knees up, opening herself up further. "Then don't."

As soon as she lifted her knees, pressing them high against the side of his chest, he wrapped his arms around her, holding her tight to him as he pushed in with one thrust.

"Fucking hell." He stilled. "You're so tight."

And he was so big but the fullness wasn't overwhelming. It was perfect.

"It's been a while," she gasped before moaning as he pulled out and pushed in again. He wasn't soft. He didn't treat her like a doll that would break under his meaty hands.

Instead, he took what he wanted, giving her everything in return.

They started to move, their bodies jolting together, desperately trying to consume each other, barely staying balanced on the couch, now seemingly small compared to their fused rutting bodies.

Ivy's arms wrapped around his neck and she held on as she started to peak. She clenched around him and his movements sped up, either in an attempt to come with her or because he couldn't help himself. Either way, Ivy cried out his name as she came and a few thrusts later, he was panting over her, his eyes glazed, his cock swelling even more before releasing into her with a growl.

Far too quickly, he slipped out of her, causing her to whimper. She wanted him to stay in her, on top of her. And now it was the beginning of the end, or so she thought.

Instead, Lawson whipped off the condom and unceremoniously dropped it on the floor, before pulling her up to standing. Silently, he tugged her dress off that had bunched up around her waist. He then slipped her thong down her legs, and dropped them on the floor too, before picking her up and carrying her to his bedroom.

For the rest of the night he proceeded to take more and more of her, giving her as much as she could take and then some. And it was all that she'd imagined, standing in the kitchen that evening, pretending that life could be as simple as a man and woman losing themselves in each other.

Until the next morning when she'd woken up to a different, withdrawn Lawson.

Ivy could hear him on the phone when she slipped out of bed and put on one of his t-shirts. It was huge on her, hanging off one shoulder, looking like just one wrong move and it would slip off and give him a good shot of what he'd had last night.

She'd slept over and not in a clingy way but in a Lawson-fell-asleep-spooning-her-naked-with-his-arms-wrapped-around-her-so-tightly-she-though-he-wanted-her-to-stay kind of way. But standing in the doorframe of his bedroom, watching him talk on the phone in a hushed voice, she knew something was wrong. His naked back muscles were bunched up and his shoulders were tense as he spoke into the phone.

"Yeah, I got it. I know what the plan is. I'm not a fucking idiot, Ray. I'll see you later." He hung up, slamming his phone so hard on the kitchen counter top, she was sure it was broken.

Ivy cleared her throat; suddenly wishing she'd slipped out and gone home, instead of trying for more. Lawson whipped around. The anger in his body didn't dissipate as she'd hoped it would when he saw her. It was just that now she could see his face and he wasn't angry. He was furious.

"You're up. Finally." He barked out the statement as if she'd slept all morning. It was only eight o'clock and as far as she knew, both of them had the day off work. Making a conscious decision to try and figure this situation out with as much pride as possible, despite where this train-wreck of a-morning-after was clearly going, Ivy gave him one of her big smiles.

"Yup, I'm up!" she gave him to the count of five to answer her and give her a clue as to how he wanted to play this. After all, he was angry before he saw her, she reminded herself. But when he said nothing, she took that for what it clearly meant and gingerly stepped forward to pick up her dress, broken bra, and panties from the couch, where he'd neatly piled them up at some point. Bending down as gracefully as possible, without giving Lawson a money-shot, Ivy grabbed her shoes that were lined up at the end of the coffee table, noting that again, neatly aligning her shoes was an oddly considerate thing to do, especially since he was clearly waiting for her to leave.

Ivy gave him a glance over her shoulder as she made her retreat back to the bedroom. Despite everything they'd done last night, the thought of getting dressed in front of him now was too much to take.

Not giving herself a chance to even begin to think about how stupid and naïve she was, Ivy quickly dressed. She wasn't going to worry about the fact that she had to work with Lawson almost every day. They didn't need to interact that much at work and it would be easy enough to stay out of the staff room when he was there.

To say she'd misjudged Lawson's expectations was putting it mildly. This was a one-night stand, nothing else. Whatever connection she thought they had, whatever she'd seen when she looked into his eyes, it was gone now. Or maybe it was never even there. Maybe she was so desperate to feel something with someone else that she'd read too much into Lawson's action.

Running her hands through her hair, she grabbed her broken bra, took a deep breath, and stepped out of the bedroom, making a beeline for her bag that was, unfortunately, on the floor near the kitchen counter where Lawson was still standing. Slipping the strap over her shoulder, she shoved the bra in the bag, before she met his gaze. It was still as dark as it had been five minutes ago.

"Well, thanks for a lovely dinner." He nodded in acknowledgement but kept his mouth shut. "Okay, I'll see you on Monday then."

Giving him a little wave, because as awkward as that was, she didn't know what else to do. Shake his hand? High-five him? Less than seven hours ago, he'd had his cock in her and was telling her he wouldn't be able to let her go. Now he couldn't even bring himself to verbally good-bye.

As she opened the front door, barely able to keep the tears at bay, she heard him approach her from behind.

"Are you going to be all right getting home?" he roughly asked.

Ivy turned to face him, because that was the polite thing to do. And she was polite. Slightly heartbroken and embarrassed but polite nonetheless.

She patted her bag. "Yup, I've got my trusty bus pass, so I'm good."

"The bus?" he echoed with disdain. Shaking his head, he yanked his wallet out of his jeans and pulled out a few bills. "Get a cab home," he held the money out in front of him.

She stared at him, her jaw dropping open. What the hell was this? Was he worried about her waiting for the bus in his sketchy neighborhood? Or was this payment for services rendered? Either way, she wasn't prepared to take the money and make him feel better about his behavior.

"You know what? I'm good with my bus pass so you can just keep *that*," she pointed at the cash.

"Ivy, come on, do me a favor and just take a cab home." He waved the cash in front of her again.

"Do *you* a favor? No thanks. Like I said, I'm good." She made to leave when Lawson lunged forward. Whatever irritation he felt about her being here this morning was now spilling out of him.

"Jesus Christ, just take the goddamn money!" He grabbed her bag and yanked it open, before shoving the cash into it and aggressively pushing the strap back onto her shoulder. The second he'd moved toward her, she'd stood still and even now as he stepped back and ran his hands over his face, she remained motionless. "I just need you to take the money." He voice was shaky and he took a few steps back, like he couldn't even stand to be near her. Knowing better than to wave a red cape in front of a bull, Ivy acquiesced.

"Sure thing, Lawson," she quietly said, keeping her voice neutral. She felt him watching her as she turned slowly and opened the apartment door. Closing it carefully behind her, she didn't exhale until she was in the stairwell.

Her hands were shaking and she took a few deep breaths, drawing the air far into her lungs and tried to calm down. It's not that she thought Lawson was going to hurt her, but whatever was going on with him was more than morning-after guilt and for some reason, she'd been the recipient of it.

As she walked through the dingy lobby of his apartment building, she spied the row of mailboxes. Finding Lawson's, Ivy quickly folded the money up and slid it into the box. To make it worse, she saw that he'd given her $200. This wasn't cab money. This definitely fell into payment for services rendered. If she hadn't felt cheap enough upstairs, braless, holding a wad of cash, after being made to feel less than welcome, she certainly did now.

Chapter Two

Lawson

From his window, he watched her walk down the sidewalk, annoyed as hell that she was making no effort to hail a cab. He hated the thought of her waiting for the bus, especially in that goddamn dress that did nothing to hide her luscious body, and especially with no goddamn bra on. And despite acting like a fucking lunatic and shoving the money in her bag, Lawson knew she wasn't going to use it. In fact, wouldn't be surprised if she returned it to him on Monday morning.

It was meant to be a job. It was meant to be the *last* job. Looking back over the past fifteen years of his life, Lawson had nothing to show for it. They say crime doesn't pay and they were right. Despite all the robberies he'd done, he had nothing real, nothing substantial in his life. Once the stash was split and the celebrations were over, there was never much left. At least not enough to warrant the risk he took each time.

Lawson had managed to save some cash in the past few years, just enough to start over. It had almost been a subconscious decision, probably knowing that he was getting sick of this shit: always looking his shoulder, never trusting the guys he worked with. The messed up part was that these were guys he'd known since he was a kid. But they weren't friends. They weren't a band of brothers. They were criminals. And they looked out for themselves, not each other.

But walking away from them wasn't going to be so easy. Lawson knew too much, he'd seen too much. That only gave him one option: run. Normally, he wasn't the kind of man who ran but he knew that it was either run or end up behind bars. And that was an easy choice. But he was stuck with this one last job. Thankfully it was simple, clean. Nothing he couldn't handle easily.

Until he saw Ivy.

Until she gave him her big smile on his first day as the security guard for the jewelry joint that was the target. Her blonde hair was pulled up into a neat bun on the top of her head, a few strands had fallen out and they framed her face perfectly. Her big brown eyes brightened as she smiled and he held his breath as she told him her name with a soft voice that matched her delicate features. Except for that mouth. That mouth was meant for sin and he couldn't stop staring it at it. Pink lush lips that seemed to be almost artificially plump.

And he knew he was screwed.

Lawson had to make her his.

It was that small tattoo that did it. Up until then he'd kept an acceptable distance. She flirted with him, nothing too tacky or aggressive, but he knew she wanted him. After she shared her cinnamon roll with her and he had to suffer through watching her eat it and resist blowing a nut in his boxers, he knew he needed to stay away from her. Then he saw her washing her hands and that was it.

The tattoo was nothing more than a simple thin black band that wrapped around the ring finger of her left hand. Watching her graceful hands move under the water, the tattoo caught his eye and something came over him. He touched her, for the first time. And like a fucking idiot, he went home and stalked her online to see what else he could find out and then invited her to dinner the next day.

It drove him crazy that the tattoo didn't match the rest of her. She showed up to work in her uniform: a fitted white blouse and tight black pencil skirt, plain but sexy heels that made her ass look fantastically squeezable. Her makeup was simple and nothing about her screamed rebel.

In fact she was almost wholesome, with her damn hippy homemade lunches and inspirational quotes about love and happiness that she was always telling customers when she closed a sale. Whether it was an engagement ring or a graduation bracelet, she always had something to say to make the moment special. Coming from anyone else it would have sounded cheesy but she was so damn sincere, it just sounded right. So fucking wholesome.

Except she wasn't. At all. And it wasn't just those lips that belonged on a porn star and that tattoo. There was the other side to her—a dark side, something evasive and odd about her.

He'd done a background check on her, found out about her growing up in foster care. Ever since she turned eighteen, she'd moved around a lot and didn't seem to have any connection to any place or person. She was friendly with the other sales girls but Lawson could see she kept a wall up.

He tried to ignore it. He told himself that he didn't need to know, that she didn't need saving, especially not by someone as messed up as him. The tattoo, her flirting and yet guarded behavior. It was too compelling. She didn't stand a chance with him.

But then reality came crashing down the morning after he slept with her. He'd completely lost it, ripped her bra off like some caveman and told her all his dirty dreams about her. Lawson liked his sex a bit rough but it was always just sex—a means to an end. He had no problems using women to get what he needed. Until her.

Lawson had wrapped himself around her, not even giving her the option to think about getting up and leaving his bed. He'd watched her sleep, like some stalker, pushing her hair away from her face so he could memorize her features.

Ivy was the first and only woman who'd ever made him see red at the thought of another guy touching her. Just the thought of some other man seeing her braless tits, swaying through her thin dress, drove him crazy.

There was something about her though, that made him want to take and take and take from her until there was nothing left. He wanted her to give him every last piece of herself. He wanted to make her weak with lust and then fuck her until she begged him to stop. He wanted to see her body dripping with his sweat and cum, knowing that she'd craved, begged, and yearned to end up like that.

And for that one night, he ignored the reality that he would have to cut her loose despite their night together. Despite the fact that she'd let him take her, let him break her open and he couldn't get enough. He'd never get enough.

His phone woke him and it was Ray, wanting to talk about meeting up. They only had two weeks left and still so much shit to go over. Especially on Lawson's end. After all, he was planning on making a break after this, not that Ray knew that, but instead of focusing on the job, he was standing in his kitchen, still smelling her scent on him, listening to fucking Ray jabber on in his ear about the heist. And Lawson knew he couldn't keep her.

So he was a prick and made it clear he wanted her gone, watched her clench her hands in his t-shirt she'd pulled on, waiting for him to say something, anything to wipe the look of disappointment and shame off her face as he made no effort to reassure her that he hadn't just been stringing her alone, that he hadn't just been using her. He watched her try and keep it together as he shoved that money at her. She tried so hard to not cry and he couldn't blame her.

He'd claimed her last night, there was no question about that. And now he was acting like he couldn't even stand the sight of her. It took everything in him not to reach out to her, to tell her everything and beg for forgiveness.

The next two weeks were hell. Lawson ignored her the best he could. And in the end he tried to keep her safe. He made sure she wasn't working that day in case something went wrong. But there she was standing behind the display case. Ivy whispered his name, recognizing him despite the mask and Ray panicked and dragged her into the back of the van.

Now Lawson was staring down at the woman he'd do pretty much anything for, listening to the guys talk about how they wanted to have a taste of her before getting rid of her. Lawson wouldn't last much longer before he flipped.

The best thing about being a moody prick is that people think you're unpredictable. Despite always being in control, Lawson gave the impression of being a crazy asshole and it scared the guys he worked with. Not much scared them, but he did. And that was the only thing he had going for him now.

As he felt the van pull up to the run-down motel where he'd arranged to be dropped, Lawson crouched down and undid Ivy's hands and took off the gag. She didn't move, except to rub her wrists a bit.

"What the hell are you doing? I don't want to have to deal with the bitch untied, man!" Lawson ignored Ray and stayed focused on Ivy, keeping his voice low.

"I'm going to get out and lift you out of the van. You're going to walk with me into the motel room and not make a fucking sound. You scream, try to get attention, try to run? I'll throw you right back in here and let them have you. Got it?" Her eyes widened but then she quickly nodded and rose up on to her knees, adjusting her clothes.

"What the hell? You can't fucking take her!" Lawson spun around and faced Ray, he was the only he'd have to deal with, the rest of the men were too gutless to try and face Lawson down.

"Can't I? It's *me* she recognized. You think I'm going to put my future in your hands? You think for a second I'd trust *you* to deal with this?" Ray opened his mouth to speak but Lawson didn't give him the chance to respond. This wasn't a negotiation. He didn't need to hear what Ray had to say. "No, this is a minor glitch. One that I'm going to deal with since I'm the one she'll name if she gets away. Now sit the fuck down and shut up."

Lawson stared at him and for once, Ray acted smart and obeyed. But of course, Ray wasn't smart or else he would have realized that it didn't make any difference that Ivy had recognized Lawson.

He hadn't used his last name or a real social security number so even if she had told the cops she knew him, it wouldn't have gone anywhere. They would have eventually figured out that Lawson was involved in the heist anyway. The only real thing she had on his was his address, but Ray didn't know that. And even that was a dead end. Lawson could have easily let her go and she wouldn't do any real harm. But he wasn't about to tell that to Ray. Or Ivy.

Slinging his bag over his shoulder, Lawson opened the back of the van and jumped out. He helped Ivy get down and kept a firm grip around her waist as they walked toward the door of the motel room. He already had the key and by the time he opened the door, the van was driving away. If everything went to plan, that was the last time he'd ever see Ray and the guys.

Ivy wrenched herself away from him as soon as the door was shut, and sat on the bed. He could feel her eyes on him as he checked out the room. So far he had no idea what he was going to do with her. Ever since Ray had picked her up and thrown her in the van, Lawson had been acting on instinct. Which would only get him so far. He needed a plan, a new plan. All he knew for sure was that that plan wouldn't include letting her go.

"You weren't supposed to be there."

"Yeah, I figured that." She sounded tired and he knew she was going to crash soon from the adrenaline rush. "What are you going to do with me, Lawson?"

He ignored her and checked his bag. He knew exactly where everything was but he needed to keep his hands busy, keep his eyes off of her.

"Are you going to kill me?"

"Fuck no! Jesus, Ivy." Lawson shook his head, glaring at her. What kind of man did she think he was? "I'm a thief. You think that makes me a killer too?"

"But in the van, those other guys—they were talking about killing me, like it was something they'd done before—something you'd done before." She phrased it as a statement but he knew what she was asking and he couldn't answer her. He'd be lying if he said he was different to those guys. He'd killed people before, but never like this, never someone innocent like Ivy. And he sure as hell had never taken a woman by force.

"Forget about them. I'm not going to kill you."

"Are you going to hurt me?" There was no way he'd ever hurt her. He was still angry that the binds Ray had put on her wrists had left marks. But Lawson wasn't going to tell her that. Now that she knew he wasn't going to kill her, he needed something to make sure she was afraid.

"That depends."

"On what? I won't tell anyone. I swear. I doubt I even know your real name and I didn't hear anything that can be used against you. I mean, you could just tie me up and leave me and you'd be miles away before anyone found me and by then I'm sure you'd be safe." She shifted on the bed to face him, sitting on her knees in supplication.

"It's not the simple, Ivy. Besides the risk of you leading the cops to me, have you thought about what would happen to you?" She frowned, obviously confused. He moved to sit next to her on the bed, close enough so his leg brushed against her bare knees. He wanted to push her back on the bed, run his hands up between her creamy, soft thighs and delve into her.

Lawson softened his voice and explained.

"You had a prior relationship with one of the robbers, and you've got no ties to anyone else, it would only take a few questions to the rest of the staff for the cops to realize that you kept to yourself. I bet you've got just enough money put away to pay for next month's rent and that's it. You look like someone who's ready to run. Someone who'd be open and willing to use her inside knowledge for a nice lump of cash."

"No, but that guy—he *grabbed* me, he pulled me out of the shop. That'll be on the cameras! And I don't have any inside knowledge, I don't know anything!" Her hands were balled up on her lap as she protested her innocence. Slowly, he took hold of one and uncurled her tense fingers, methodically running rubbing the palm of her hand.

"We took the cameras out. Also it would make sense if you were putting on act for the rest of the staff.

And it seems pretty convenient that you just happen to be sleeping with one of the guards involved."

"Once! It happened once. We didn't have, I mean, we don't have, a relationship." His hand tightened around hers as she tried to pull it away.

"Not because I didn't want one." He leaned in closer, breathing her scent in, the ephemeral hint of coconut oil in her hair driving him crazy. "I did it to keep you safe."

"That doesn't even make any sense. You slept with me to keep me safe? Look how that ended up."

"No, baby, I slept with you *once* to keep you safe. I knew I couldn't keep you, I couldn't risk making you part of this. But I needed one taste, one taste and I thought I'd be able to walk away from you." He reached up and released her hair from its clip. It fell down her back in messy waves and he wrapped it around his fist.

"But I'm here anyway, Lawson." Her breathing was becoming shallow and he didn't know if it was from fear or arousal. Probably both. Lawson breached the distance between them and ran his nose along her jaw, chuckling at how right she was.

"I know, trust me, I know." Reaching her neck, he softly kissed her skin, waiting for her to push him off, to struggle, to scream and fight and tell him to get away from her. He'd kidnapped her and locked her in a motel room with him. She had every right to be scared and hysterical. But she was letting him touch her and until she said no, he wasn't going to stop.

Ivy's hands reached up and rested on his shoulders as he continued to lose himself in the velvet skin of her neck, the feel of her pulse against his tongue as he tasted her causing him to tighten his grasp on her hair.

"Oh my God, Lawson, what are we doing? What I am doing? I don't understand any of this…" Ivy moaned and tilted her head to the side, giving him more access and he knew he had her.

Rising up, Lawson wrapped his arms around her and lowered her down until she lay on her back, staring up at him. Her mouth was open slightly as she panted under his touch. Cradling her with one arm under her neck, he kept eye contact as his hand slid down her body, brushing over a stiff nipple. Her breath hitched but he kept on going until he reached the hem of her skirt. His hand slipped under and he glided up those creamy thighs he had fantasized about just minutes ago.

Ivy slightly opened her legs, easing his access. Her eyelids partially shut as he drew a finger up her core, over her damp panties. Slipping a finger under the edge of her panties, he nudged at her wet folds. Adding another finger, he slipped both inside her and felt her clench around him.

"You're soaked for me, Ivy."

She shook her head back and forth, protesting. "I can't do this, I don't know…" she couldn't finish her sentence. He knew it was a lot to take but if he got her off, it would help her settle and stop focusing on what was happening. All she would be able to feel, to think about, was him touching her.

"Yes you can," he ordered. Just like their first night together, Lawson felt her shiver when he told her what to do. To confirm his theory, he started to tug at her blouse. "Take this off, baby, I want to see all of you." She scrambled to unbutton her top as Lawson found the zip on her skirt and yanked it off her. He had to pull his fingers out of her and she whimpered and rubbed her thighs together.

"Bra too, Ivy, I want all of you," he bent down and kissed her pubic bone, slipping off her moist peach-colored lace panties. "You're such a naughty girl, baby, wearing these little panties under your skirt at work. Were you thinking of me when you slipped them on?" He knew it wasn't fair to ask, especially since he'd effectively ignored her for the past two weeks, after sending her packing like a cheap one-night stand.

Lawson glanced up at her face, bringing the lace up to his nose and inhaling. "Tell me you were wearing them and thinking about me." Irritation flashed through her eyes and she shook her head, once again trying to hold back on him.

Crawling up her body, he licked her now bare breasts before kissing her hard and fast as he shoved two fingers into her. She gasped and pulled away from his mouth, sucking in air as she tried to catch her breath. His thumb worked her clit as he thrust his fingers in and out. She was so goddamn beautiful, the way her body moved against his, her hips trying to find the rhythm of his fingers while at the same she was trying to get away, trying to fight her need for him.

"Tell me what I want to hear, Ivy, tell me you wore them and thought of me, tell me you made them all wet thinking about the way I fucked you." His lips found her pulse on her neck and he held her naked body close to his as he worked her hard with his fingers.

"Yes." It was barely a whisper.

"Yes what, baby? Come on, don't be shy." He ground his thumb hard into her clit and she yelped in surprise.

"Yes, I wore them and thought of you, I thought of you every time I touched myself, I thought about how good you felt inside me. And every day since then my panties have been soaked thinking about that night."

It was so much more than he expected. He was going to burst through his jeans he was so hard. He wanted to give her what she needed, even if she hated him for it. The noises coming out of her were driving him insane as she writhed against him, her face tucked into his neck.

"Touch me. Take me out and touch me."

Without hesitating, she reached down and fumbled frantically with his zipper. He was more than ready, his cock honing in on her warm, wet center as soon as she pulled him out, but he forced himself to stop when the throbbing head made contact with her hot folds.

Lawson didn't have a condom and despite the danger of their situation, he wasn't so stupid or reckless to do something they might regret later. Instead, he rolled them so they lay side by side and hoisted her thigh onto his hip. His fingers were still deep inside her and he wedged his cock against her clit, leaving little room for anything else beyond friction and sweat to get the job done.

"Lawson, please, please, put it in me," she begged into his neck, wrapping her slender arms around his shoulders. "I can't take it." God, hearing her beg was music to his ears but he wouldn't be pushed.

"No, baby, like this. Just to take the edge off," he started pumping his hips. She was soaking wet by now and her juices began to cover his length with every stroke. He wasn't going to need long before he burst and he wanted her there with him.

"You're going to ride my fingers, Ivy, just like this and I'm going to feel you come."

She groaned in frustration but she didn't stop grinding her hips against his cock. "No, I need more."

"Shhh, don't worry, I know exactly what you need. Because this is mine," he pushed two fingers in hard before slipping a finger out of her. He shifted his hand until he could reach back and feel her puckered entrance. He knew she'd never done anal and that was part of the appeal. He needed to push her over the edge, show her that even if part of her wanted to hold back, her body was already his. "And this is mine too."

He rubbed a wet fingertip over her back entrance and felt her stiffen up. "No, Ivy, I told you I know what you need and you have to trust me." Without giving her time to respond, he pushed his finger in up to the first knuckle.

Ivy squealed and bucked her hips forward, trying to get away but she only ended up thrusting against his engorged cock even harder and he felt some pre-cum leak out. "No, baby, it's all right, I promise you'll like it."

Lawson adjusted his hold on her and began to move his fingers in and out, slowly at first, sliding into her wet pussy and tight ass at the same time.

He pushed further and further in with each pulse until he was buried inside her, each finger lodged firmly up to the last knuckle. She squirmed at first, her body protesting at the foreign invasion but eventually, as he pulled his fingers out to push back in, she began to push back.

Her breathing hitched and when a gush of arousal moistened his cock even further, he knew she was close. Ivy clung to his neck, her hands clenched in his short hair and she stiffened in his arms, whispering his name as the orgasm hit her. Feeling her clench around his fingers, Lawson held her tightly as his hips jerked and he came against her stomach.

Assuming she would pull back, Lawson tightened his grip on her, after gently pulling his fingers out of her. Ivy hoisted her leg higher up his waist. Her hands released from his hair but only to slide down and rest on his chest. She was so soft against him, and he let himself breathe her in as he stroked her bare thigh, his fingers trailing patters along her exposed ass cheeks.

What the hell was he going to do with her now?

Chapter Three

Ivy

Ivy didn't know how, but she'd slept like a baby. After coming on her stomach and fingering her ass, Lawson cleaned her up with a washcloth and then slipped his shirt over her head. She remembered rolling back into his chest, his large arms surrounding her, keeping her close, keeping her safe, keeping her from running.

But now Lawson was waking her up and she didn't like the look in his eyes. He looked guilty as hell. He stood over her, fully dressed, and extended his hand. Silently, he led her to the bathroom where he proceeded to tie her hands behind her back before making her sit on the floor, wedging her between the toilet and sink and tied her already bound hands to the pipes.

The tears started flowing then. She couldn't help it. She hadn't cried when that guy had dumped her on the floor of that van and then talked about killing and raping her, or when Lawson had threatened to leave her with them. But now she was losing it. She couldn't help it. After what they'd just done, it seemed too harsh.

"Don't do this, please, don't tie me up. I promise I won't leave. Or you can take me with you. Please, Lawson!" He wouldn't look at her as he wrapped a gag around her head. She ducked her head and clenched her jaw shut but he was too strong and Ivy was too distraught to put up much of a fight.

"Be good." He shut the bathroom door and she heard him leave the motel room. He must have had a car ready for him because from what she'd seen when they got out of the van, they really were in the middle of nowhere.

She wiggled her hands, trying to see if there was anyway she could escape but the knots were too tight. Frustrated, she rested her head against the toilet and tried to calm down. She couldn't stop imagining Lawson driving off and never coming back, or Lawson calling those other guys and letting them deal with her.

Ivy needed to trust him with so much to keep from really losing it. And like a moron, she'd assumed that by trusting him, he would start to trust her. But he didn't or else she wouldn't be tied up, sitting on a disgusting bathroom floor, with no panties on, hoping that he hadn't left her to rot.

The sun had started to set and the minimal light that came through the small bathroom window was fading fast. She didn't know how long he'd been gone but it felt like hours. She needed to pee, badly, her wrists were a mess, her legs and back had started to cramp up from sitting in one position for so long, and her anger had faded to despondency. When she heard him open the bathroom door, Ivy didn't even bother looking up. He was going to do whatever he wanted to anyway.

Without a word Lawson bent down and untied her. By now she was getting used to the silent treatment. She staggered as she stood up and he caught her, murmuring soft words of reassurance. It wasn't an apology but at least he sounded concerned.

But she didn't want his concern. Not now. It was childish and stubborn but she was done with the emotional tug-of-war he kept playing. Stepping out of his arms, she cleared her throat.

"I need to pee." When he made no move to leave she looked up. His arms were crossed and he looked perturbed, as if he'd been expecting her to act differently. "I'm kind of desperate. Can I please have some privacy?" He scowled before turning to walk out.

"You've got two minutes. We've got stuff to do before we leave. Don't lock the door."

What did he think she was going to do? Try and crawl out the tiny window that was barely big enough to fit her head through, let alone her body? She quickly used the toilet and was washing her hands when he came in without knocking and placed a box of hair dye on the counter next to her.

"I'll cut it then you dye it. I've got you some new clothes you can change into after."

Ivy eyed the box of dye. At least the color wasn't that extreme. He'd chosen a chestnut brown with a subtle tint of deep red. Anything darker would have looked ridiculous with her complexion.

"How much are you going to cut off?"

"Does it matter?" Lawson raised his eyebrows and stared at her in the mirror as he held up the scissors.

She shrugged. He had a point. As much as she loved her hair, it was the least of her problems. "Go nuts."

He stepped behind her and she tried to ignore her body's reaction to his proximity. She was still only wearing his shirt and the heat of his body, so close against her back, seeped through and warmed her skin.

This morning she'd welcomed his touch. She'd needed it to take her mind off of what was happening and to convince herself that Lawson wasn't a bad guy, that he wouldn't really hurt her. But after sitting on the bathroom floor for so long, drooling from the gag, she'd changed her mind about him.

Apparently her libido didn't get the message.

Lawson gently pulled her hair back and started snipping away. Ten minutes later he was done after taking off at least half her hair. It now hung just above her shoulders in a basic blunt cut that looked remarkably trendy.

"It suits you." Lawson smiled at her in the mirror, obviously proud of himself for not completely messing it up. He blew off some stray hairs against her neck and Ivy rolled her lips together to stop from moaning. "Now it's your turn. Get the dye on." Slapping her ass hard enough she felt a sting, he walked out, leaving her tingling and furious.

By the time she came out of the bathroom, now a brunette, Lawson had undergone his own transformation. He sat on the bed, leaning against the headboard with his legs stretched out and crossed at the ankles. Gone were the dark jeans and Henley shirt: bad-ass criminal Lawson was gone. He now wore a dark grey polo shirt, relaxed khakis, and leather sandals, looking practically respectable.

Laid out on the bed was her own new outfit: a dark blue maxi dress, gold flip-flops and a floral bag. She could see pack of plain underwear, deodorant, and other sundries he obviously thought she might need.

"We're taking a little road trip, a romantic weekend away with my girl. Got to look the part. You're hair looks great. Now get dressed."

Tightening the towel that was wrapped around her after her quick shower, she started to gather up her outfit to take to the bathroom.

"No. Get dressed in here." His pose was casual but his words were far from relaxed.

"Why?" Ivy knew it was an order and she was at the whim of this man, but despite all that she couldn't help but challenge him, even if it was over something insignificant.

"Because I said so. And you're mine. Or did you forget everything from this morning? Maybe you need a quick reminder."

This morning, despite how unbelievably erotic it had been to have his fingers in her like that, had been a mistake and he knew it. Keeping eye contact with him, Ivy dropped the towel and ripped open the pack of simple cotton thongs. Slipping a pair over her ankles, she shimmied them slowly over her hips and smoothed her hands over the front, biting her lip to stop from smiling as she heard Lawson groan. There was no bra in sight and from what she could see he'd gotten rid of the clothes she was wearing this morning.

"No bra, huh?" Ivy casually asked as she lifted the dress over her head slowly. She gave an extra wiggle as she started to drop it over her head, knowing full well his eyes were trained on her swaying breasts.

"Nope. You don't need to wear one with me around. And I like the idea of having easy access. Just one little tug, and they're all mine." An image flashed through her head of Lawson yanking down her dress and feasting on an exposed nipple. She shouldn't have wanted that. Not now. Not after he'd made it abundantly clear how that he intended to treat her like a prisoner.

She finished pulling the dress down and looked up. Despite herself, a soft flush had spread through her cheeks. Seeing Lawson's face mirroring her own ache made her squeeze her thighs together. His eyes lingered on her now covered breasts before sweeping up to meet her own lustful gaze.

"Come here, Ivy."

"I thought we were in a rush. You said we had to go." Ivy stalled, not wanting to be near him again. If she went near him, she'd have to exercise self-control, something she was clearly lacking when it came to Lawson.

He crooked his finger at her, his face hardening and she knew hesitating any further was a bad idea. Weren't her raw wrists and sore jaw lesson enough?

Ivy walked around the bed. By the time she reached him, he'd swung his legs off and he pulled her in between his spread knees. Silently, Lawson reached up and pulled down one of the straps of the dress, revealing her left breast.

"Lawson, wait—" she managed to get out but whatever protest she was trying to make turned into a low moan as he leaned forward and enveloped her hard nipple in his hot mouth. Instinctually her hands gripped his hair, holding him closer to her as he sucked hard, hard enough so that she winced. After a few seconds, he pulled back, her nipple popping out of his mouth crudely. He pulled the strap of the dress back on her shoulder and stood up, gently running his hand over her now over-sensitive nipple through the material.

"Easy access," he murmured and leaned down, brushing his lips softly against her still open mouth.

Picking up the bag near the side of the bed, he took her hand and led her out to a car parked in front of the room. Guiding her into the passenger seat, he handed her the floral bag that he bought to go with the rest of her outfit. It was only then that she noticed there was stuff inside. A quick look and the mystery of Lawson only grew bigger. He'd bought her lip gloss, sunglasses, a hair brush and a few bands, mascara. And condoms. A pack of condoms. Ivy blushed and shut the bag. Glancing over at Lawson she saw he was smiling at her.

"Don't worry, there's more in my bag." Ivy turned and looked out the window instead of responding. He chuckled as they pulled out of the motel parking lot.

They drove for hours. Deep into the night, Lawson kept going. Despite the ridiculous nap she'd taken earlier, Ivy felt herself falling asleep. She tried to stay awake, hoping that she could take advantage at some point of Lawson's inevitable fatigue. But she couldn't keep her eyes open and the next thing she knew, Lawson was stroking her cheek, trying to rouse her.

"Ivy, baby, come on, we need to go inside."

She blinked and tried to get her bearings. They were at another remote motel, practically identical in its state of abandon as the first place they stayed. A beat-up truck sat in the lot but other than that, the place looked empty. Lawson came around to help her out of the car and she leaned on him as they made their way to the door. Still half asleep, his warm arms around her in the cool air were too comforting to turn away.

Once they were inside, Lawson started getting set up to sleep. Ivy watched hazily as he locked the room door and then put his gun, car key, and phone in the safe that sat next to a TV. He locked it before proceeding to pull a coil of rope out of his bag and place it on the bedside table.

Crossing his arms, Lawson towered over her. He looked worn out and she wanted to run her hands over his creased brow to help smooth away his worries.

"I need to rest. I'm giving you two choices. I can tie you to the bed, which will make for a shitty night's sleep but at least I won't need to worry about you trying to sneak out. Or I can trust you to stay put. Bearing in mind we are once again in the middle of fucking nowhere. Even if you do manage to get out of the room without me noticing, you won't have keys to the car, so you'll have to take your chances with the pervert at the front desk, who looks like something the guy from the hotel in Psycho and we all know how that ended up. What's it going to be?"

"I'll be good," she immediately blurted out, "I promise. I'm tired too. I just want to rest and my wrists really can't take any more rope burn." They weren't that bad but she couldn't handle the thought of being tied up again. He stared at her for a few more seconds.

"All right, get undressed and get into bed." Her eyes grew wide at his order. Capitulating, she stood up and kicked her flip-fops off before sliding her dress over her head and draping it over a chair, deciding that being topless and braless in front of Lawson was only as uncomfortable as she made it. Keeping her eyes down, she crawled onto the bed and slipped under the covers.

"Good girl," he murmured before stripping down to his tight boxers and turning out the light before getting under the covers. Ivy gasped as he pulled her back against his chest and shoved a leg between her thighs. Her head rested on his arm and his free hand lay high on her stomach, just barely brushing the skin under her breast.

Ivy stiffened, unsure of what she was supposed to do. She wriggled her hips but then stilled as she felt him push his erection against her ass. The small thong she was wearing left her mostly exposed and she shivered as her sensitive bare skin rubbed against his covered groin. How the hell was she supposed to fall asleep when she was this aroused?

"Jesus Christ, Ivy, if you don't stop wiggling I'm going to roll you over, pull that damn thong off and fuck you until you pass out," he growled into her neck, his arm tightening under her ribs.

"Oh my God," she whispered, and involuntarily her hips thrust back as she tried to squeeze her thighs together.

"Now you're being a naughty girl. Trying to keep me awake when you know how tired I am, rubbing your sweet ass against me." Lawson moved his hand up and cupped her breast, rolling her nipple between his fingers. "You want me to break out those condoms, don't you Ivy?" She nodded her head, blushing at his dirty words, and pushing her breast further into his hand. She felt like her skin was on fire and she started to pant at the thought of Lawson doing exactly as he'd threatened.

He began to move his broad thigh against her core, rubbing the soft material of her thong against his hairy leg. She moaned his name when he squeezed her breast hard, eliciting him to shove his hips against her.

Suddenly he released her and pushed her into her stomach. She looked over her shoulder to see him yanking his boxers off and donning a condom he pulled from under a pillow. God, she'd played right into his hands. But at that moment, she didn't care.

Not even bothering to fully remove her thong, Lawson yanked it down her hips until it was just above her knees, stretching into her flesh. His own boxers sat just under his ass and he leaned forward, kissing the middle of her back before thrusting in with a groan.

Unable to control the noises coming out of her mouth, Ivy shoved her face into the pillow in front of her, her hand grasping at the cheap sheets while Lawson moved above her. She tilted her hips up further.

"Fuck, yes, just like that. You've been driving me crazy all night in that damn dress and no bra." He lay down on top of her, barely keeping his weight off her as he slipped a hand under her body to squeeze at her breasts.

Feeling his hot breath on her neck, Ivy turned to kiss him, shoving her tongue in his mouth. She felt him bump against her cervix with every thrust as he rutted into her. A haze come over her and her thighs quivered as she came.

Pushing his face into her neck, Lawson powered through her orgasm, his hold on her shoulder and breast tightened as she felt her muscles clench around him.

"Yes, baby, that's right, give it to me, give me everything, Ivy." He stiffened and his deep groan spread across her neck. His cock pulsed inside her and she closed her eyes, reveling in the sensation of his body in hers, losing control, just as she had.

Lawson pulled out of her and she mourned the loss of his heavy heat against her back but she was too tired to move. After a minute, he returned to her side and gently pulled her thong back on into place, his fingers traced over her back, his lips trailing up and down her spine with tender kisses. The last thing she felt before she let herself slip away was the Lawson's voice as he kissed the back of her neck.

"I'm not letting you go, Ivy. Never letting you go."

Chapter Four

Lawson

He watched her sleep, resisting waking her up despite the fact that they should have been on the road hours ago. She had bags under her eyes and her wrists were still a bit sore. He needed today to be different. Despite everything he'd done to her, he needed Ivy's cooperation from here on in. Finally he roused her, quietly telling her to get showered and dressed.

A half hour later, as they finished gathering their bags, she finally asked "What happens now, Lawson?"

He watched her wring her hands together, her slim fingers subconsciously flitting over the marks on her wrists. "We leave. That's the plan. I've got enough money to keep us going until we figure out where we want to get set up. It's not a lot but it will cover the basics—new ID, tickets, the works. I'm not talking caviar and champagne but I'll take care of you. That's all you need to know."

"We? What if I don't want to leave?"

Lawson stared at her. God, he loved seeing her trying to act so tough with him. She wasn't asking to be let go but she wanted options, options he wasn't happy to offer her. After everything they'd been through, she was still holding back, still pretending that this wasn't something worth fighting for and it was beginning to piss him off.

"Why would you want to stay? What do you have here that isn't easy to walk away from?"

"My job! My friends! My life!" She threw up her hands in exasperation.

"Right. You mean your wonderful friends who know so much about you? Oh and your great job with the awesome salary, that gives amazing medical coverage and time off? Or maybe it's your beautiful pent house apartment that you're going to miss so much? I get it now." He snapped his fingers. "It's your close-knit family who you go to church with on Sundays and spend every holiday with." She turned away from him, her shoulders hunched over. "Oh wait a second! You don't have any of those things, do you, baby? No real friends, who actually know anything about you, a shit job, shit apartment, and no family. Nobody to turn to, nobody to call. Worst case scenario you're looking at jail time for being an accomplice and best case scenario you go back to your lonely life, where the most exciting thing that happens to you is a buy-one-get-one-free deal on fucking cinnamon rolls. So tell me, Ivy, because I really want to know, what's this great life I'm taking you away from? Because it's not like you've been fighting me to get back to it, this wonderful life of yours."

Her shoulders shook and Lawson knew she was done. All he wanted to do was wrap his arms around, tell her that everything was going to be all right, but he held back. She needed to think that there was nothing left for her. He knew it was twisted and wrong but the more hopeless she felt, the more she was likely to come with him on her own.

He grabbed the door key, needing to get away from her at least until he'd calmed down.

"I'm checking the car. I'll be right outside so don't try anything stupid," he growled.

"You're an asshole, Lawson," she said, her voice shaking with emotion.

"Yeah, I've heard that before," he barked out before slamming the door.

Twenty minutes later, Lawson was calm, or at least as calm as he was going to get until he was sure she wasn't going to leave him. Twenty minutes though was all Ivy needed to move from hurt to livid.

A flip-flop hit him in the face as he walked in the room. He stalked toward her, knocking away the deodorant she hurled at him.

"People have told you you're an asshole before? Well, maybe you need to hear it a bit more!" Her hair was a mess, like she'd been running her fingers through it, and her red-rimmed eyes now flared with rage instead of pain. "You lying scumbag. How dare you judge me? You're a goddamn thief! What the hell do you have to show for your life?" She screamed and batted her hands at him as he reached her. "Don't fucking touch me! Don't you dare touch me!"

Lawson wrapped his arms around her as she struggled to escape him. Her bare feet kicked against his shins. She was too small to do any real damage and he easily pinned her to the bed, while she bellowed a stream of insults.

"You done?"

"Let me go, Lawson!" She wriggled furiously and he grew hard as her soft curves pushed against him.

"Why? So you can find more stuff to throw at me?" He knew the second she felt his erection pushing into her stomach. She stilled and her eyes met his. She might pretend to hate him, but she couldn't hide her reaction from her body. He shifted between her legs, making sure he was nestled against that sweet spot, holding back a smile as her breath hitched under his movements.

"Yeah, I think you're done." He made to kiss her but she turned her face to the side.

Ignoring her little act of rebellion, Lawson softly kissed her cheek instead and moved his mouth to her ear, whispering.

"Everything I said before was true, and you know it. You can't be angry with me for telling the truth. Yeah, I didn't have to be such a prick about it but it's still true. I wasn't judging you. It's just the truth. And as for my life? You're right. I've got nothing real to show for it. Nothing to be proud of, nothing I can't easily walk away from. Except you. I can't walk away from you. The only time I ever lied to you was when I threatened to leave you in the van. I never would have done that. You can call me a lot of things, but don't call me a liar." He could feel her heart beating in her chest.

Her voice was still shaking from emotion when she finally spoke. "You are a liar though. You lied when you made me believe that we were the same, that there was that thing in both of us, that darkness. And I let myself believe that I could let you in and it would be all right. I let myself forget—"

Lawson remembered her tattoo and he sought out her hand that was still caught between them. Rubbing his finger over the ring, he threaded their fingers together.

"Forget what?"

She closed her eyes but he wasn't going to let her block him out again. "Ivy, forget what? What happened to you that you always need to remember?"

She sighed and opened her eyes. "Nothing happened. I mean, lots of things happened, but that's not what I'm talking about. I got it to remind myself that no matter what, no matter how safe I feel, no matter how much I think I can trust someone, I'm on my own. It reminds me that I don't *need* anyone and no one needs me. And that's a fact. It's not bad. It's just the way life is."

Lawson wanted to tell her that was a messed up way to look at the world but he couldn't because it was the same attitude he'd taken to keep himself safe. Until her.

"That darkness, baby, I know it feels bad but it's something beautiful. I made you feel that the first time we were together. That darkness is cloudy but when I let you in, and I did, it cleared, and became something else." He released her hands, shifting slightly off her to let her know he'd let her up if she wanted. "All you have to do is stop fighting it."

"Lawson," she breathed out as her eyes become heavy. Her hands slid up his arms and around his neck as she yanked back down to meet her lips. Their mouths clashed together and the pain, anger, and frustration they were both feeling, erupted through their bodies.

Ivy fisted his hair and nipped at his lip, almost drawing blood. He pulled back and yanked her dress off her in one swoop, pawing at her breasts as soon as they were free. Her hands moved down and fumbled with his jeans and he helped her undo them and pull him out. A few moments later he slipped a condom on, running on muscle memory more than anything and shoved home. She arched her back and released his mouth, moaning as he pushed into her again and again.

Despite what they'd just shared, it wasn't soft or gentle. They didn't make love and stare into each other's eyes, he didn't whisper into her mouth. He fucked her.

Hard.

But she gave as good as she got.

Her nails scored his lower back as she held him close. The sweat rolled down her neck and he licked it off her skin, wanting to taste her, consume her, take all of her, as much as he could get.

He wrapped a hand around her neck, to feel her pulse, her need pumping through her veins. Her eyes flared and when she reached up and wrapped her hand around his wrist, it was to keep him there, not push him away. That small action hit him hard in the gut seeing her reach out to him, trying to trust him.

"I need you, Ivy. I need you," he whispered. His lips descended softly on to hers, a fierce juxtaposition to his almost violent thrusting. She opened her mouth, gently sweeping her tongue against his, tenderly letting him know she'd heard him.

Lawson's control was slipping and he reached down and pinched her clit hard. She winced but then stiffened as her muscles tensed and then he watched her find her exquisite release. Her hot, wet muscles clenched around him and he was gone.

Trying to catch his breath, he looked down at her. She was still holding onto his wrist and he loosened his grip around her neck. It hadn't been tight enough to hurt her, just keep her in place. He slid his hand down a few inches until it rested flat on her chest, between her breasts.

"It got clear," she said. He closed his eyes for a moment, feeling the beat of her heart resonate through him. He felt that darkness that scared her, that darkness she didn't know what to do with, so full of need and a desperation to be owned, to be protected, to belong. It pulsed through him just as strongly and then when they came together it crystalized into perfection.

Ivy stayed silent as they got packed up and into the car. There was no point pushing her anymore. Either she got there or she didn't and he could only hope now. She didn't ask him where they were going, just sat quietly and looked out the window.

It was late afternoon when Lawson finally pulled over for gas. He filled up and instead of making her come with him like he had the other times they'd stopped, he opened the car door and stuck his head in.

"I'll be right back. Sit tight."

He knew she was surprised he wasn't making her get out. But it wasn't that big a risk. They were in the middle of nowhere and they'd only passed two cars in the last hour. She needed time to think and he had to give her that, even if it was just a few minutes on her own in the car.

Lawson grabbed some bottled water, a bag of cookies, and then backtracked to pick up a pack of cinnamon rolls. They looked stale and he didn't get why she ate that shit but at least she'd know he was thinking about her. That's what normal couples did and fuck, they had to start somewhere.

Trying to balance all the junk he'd bought, he didn't see the police cruiser until it was already parked up. Lawson had no idea how long it had been sitting there, he just knew it hadn't been there when he drove in.

Ivy was leaning against the car, her arms at her side, staring at the cops. Her sunglasses were on but it was clear where she was looking. The door behind Lawson jiggled as it shut and she glanced over at him, finally.

There was no way he could get to her in time. And even if he did manage to get his hands on her, what then? They would see she was struggling and come after him.

Ivy pushed her sunglasses onto her head and pushed off the car. Walking toward him, he swore she put an extra swing into those sexy hips. She stopped when they were practically toe-to-toe.

"Crappy, stale gas-station cinnamon rolls? You must really love me." She beamed up at him and stood on her tiptoes, her lips brushing against his.

"You know I do." Stepping back, she took the bottles out of his arms and slipped her hand into mine.

"Then let's go."

Chapter Five

Ivy

Sitting in bed, watching Lawson dry off from his shower, something Ivy would never get bored of, she had some time to think. And she came to the conclusion that none of this would have happened it hadn't been for those gas station cinnamon rolls.

Six months ago, she'd watched that police cruiser pull in and she knew she had a real chance to escape. All she had to do was get out of the car and walk toward the officers and she'd be free. Free to go back to her crap job, her distant friends, and most importantly, free from Lawson. He'd go to jail and she'd never see him again.

And the thought made her sick.

Ivy stepped out of the car and waited for him. She leaned against the car and watched Lawson through the window as he paid for the gas. Even as he walked out, she was still pretending that she hadn't made up her mind about what she was going to do. But then she saw the cinnamon rolls. Despite everything that was going on, despite the craziness of all that was happening, he'd got her those stupid rolls. Suddenly it was crystal clear.

And she stopped lying to herself.

Lawson sat on the edge of bed, having pulled on some boxers, to Ivy's disappointment.

"What are you thinking about, baby?" He leaned over and stroked her hair, which was finally back to blonde. She grabbed his hand and rubbed the tattoo on his finger that matched hers.

"I was remembering those cinnamon rolls. And how I knew then that I loved you." Lawson smirked at her as he pulled his hand away and yanked down the sheet that covered her naked breasts.

"Cinnamon rolls? You know what I remember about those cinnamon rolls?" he whispered, as he pushed her onto her back. "I remember sitting across from you that first day of work. I thought you were so fucking cute and then you tortured me by licking your fingers. I almost came in my damn uniform."

Ivy smacked him on the shoulder. "I'm telling you how I fell in love with you and you're talking about sex."

"You want me to spout some romantic shit to you? Is that what you want?" he asked as he kissed her collarbone and slowly licked his way down to her nipple.

"Yes," she breathed out. Her eyes fell closed as he enveloped her breast in his mouth.

"Yes what, Ivy?" He let go of it with a wet pop.

"What?" she couldn't remember what the question was now. She felt him laugh against her skin.

"I don't think you want me to tell you anything. You want me to show you, don't you? I'll show you how much I love you." Lawson moved lower, shouldering her legs apart, smattering kisses as he worked past her stomach, then her hipbones, before finally reaching his goal.

Ivy ran her fingers through his hair, holding him close to her, even though she knew he wouldn't leave until he'd accomplished his goal. Her back arched as he sucked her clit hard and pushed two fingers into her. A few strokes of his hand, she was close and she ground her hips up into his face. After six months, she'd stopped being embarrassed about how wild she got under his tongue, his hands his cock. And she knew he loved seeing her respond to him. He growled against her and she involuntarily squeezed her thighs against his head as she came, crying out his name over and over as the wave crested over and through her soul. Without missing a beat, Lawson was up on his knees, his boxers shoved down, pushing into her as he held her hips.

She stared up at her beautiful man as he moved above her. It was these moments together, when she was coming out of the erotic fog that descended whenever he touched her, that she lived for. These moments, born out of darkness, that ended up illuminating how strong the connection was between them. She sat up on her elbows as he moved inside her. Reaching up, she placed a hand on his chest, feeling his heart pound. He released a hand from her hip, the one with the tattoo, and placed it over hers.

"Baby," he grunted as he came, squeezing her hip and hand at the same time as he pulsed out his orgasm. This was what he'd given her. No caviar, no champagne, but in their small one-bedroom apartment in once again a rough neighborhood, he'd given her that crystalized perfection, that helped her see through the darkness.

The End

www.alexasinclaireauthor.com

CAPTIVE ARTIST

N.J. Young

Copyright© 2016

Chapter One

Jax

Ellis Jackson slowly pushed his broom along the wall where the abstract watercolor hung prominently in the main room of Wentworth Art Gallery. Jax appreciated fine art, but for the life of him, he'd never understood abstracts. Standing up straight, he rolled his shoulders as he evaluated the painting more closely. Circles, lines, and triangles. Hadn't he seen a similar painting on his sister's refrigerator? A grin played at his lips as he thought about replacing some of these *masterpieces* with the work of his five-year-old niece. Would anyone even notice?

"You like the Berkeley painting too, huh?" said a voice from behind him. "It's one of my favorites."

Jax stiffened for a moment, annoyed that he'd let someone sneak up on him. Then he turned to see Carrie Wentworth staring up at the painting with a look of wonder on her beautiful face, and everything inside him softened. One side of her blonde, wavy bob was tucked behind her ear, revealing a graceful neck. He swallowed and tried not to think about running his tongue along that little spot just below her ear.

Gripping his broom tighter, Jax turned without a word to finish sweeping the marble floor and shuffled past Carrie.

If she thinks the colorful scrawl in front of her is wonderful, what would she think if she knew what's really underneath it?

With one more glance over his shoulder at the gorgeous blonde, Jax turned the corner. As soon as he was out of her sight, he snatched up his broom and started down the long hallway of the art gallery. He'd nearly made it to the supply closet, where he had his tools ready to go, when his cell phone buzzed from the pocket of his jumpsuit.

Clicking the mute button quickly, he stepped into the supply room, shutting the door behind him before he hit Answer. "I told you not to fucking call me while I'm working," he barked as a greeting.

Ben's exasperated sigh on the other end of the line told Jax that his partner didn't really care about his rules.

"Fuck you, Jax," Ben snapped at him. "You don't make the rules. Just tell me you have the fucking painting, and I can stop checking in on you."

Jax's teeth gritted as his fingers clamped tighter around the phone he held to his ear. "I will get it. Just give me time. I've done this before."

"She's still there, isn't she? The blonde?"

He firmed his lips at his partner's question.

"Well, I'll just take your silence as a yes. Jesus Christ, Jax. Just kill her. Then you can get the painting, and we can get our fucking money."

Jax's temper was quickly unraveling when it came to Ben. Maybe his partner had important contacts in the art world, but Jax had other … talents.

He deepened his voice to convey exactly who was in charge of this operation. "Last time I checked, Ben, you don't give me orders. You also don't tell me who to kill … I can decide that all on my own."

Silence filled the line as Jax's veiled threat hung in the air.

"Just call me when it's done," Ben snapped.

The phone clicked in Jax's ear, and he blew out a breath as he looked at the time on his phone before slipping it back into his pocket. Seven o'clock. *Shit.* Carrie was usually gone by six. *I could kill her. It's not like I've never killed anyone before.*

But most of the men he'd killed in the past had deserved it. He really had a problem killing an innocent woman. And the thought of watching the life fade from Carrie's bright blue eyes made his stomach turn over.

Great, a thief with a conscience. He'd be so damn lucky once he was done with this job. The money from the stolen painting would be enough for him to retire a few lifetimes over.

A soft knock sounded on the door of the supply room, and he stiffened. "Jax, are you in there?"

He yanked the door open with more force than necessary, causing Carrie to jump back in surprise. His fingers tightened on the doorknob as he looked down at her curvy little figure. Saying nothing, he just arched a brow in question. *Please leave. I don't want to have to hurt you.*

"I … uh…" Carrie began in a shaky voice. She wore a blue peacoat over her prim black skirt and matching blazer, and her fingers played nervously with a dangle on the black clutch she held in front of her. She cleared her throat. "I … uh … I'm heading out."

Thank God. Blowing out a breath, Jax stepped into the hall and into Carrie's personal space, letting the door to the supply room close behind him.

Carrie backed up nervously. "I, uh, I just wanted to say goodnight."

Jax nodded slowly, his eyes sweeping her form. "Miss Wentworth."

A shy smile played at her lips as color rose in her cheeks. "Well, um, I'll see you tomorrow. Uh, have a good night." She looked up at him expectantly.

"'Night, Miss Wentworth." His eyes followed her as she nodded and turned to walk back up the hall to the front door of the art gallery. "Drive safe," he called at the last minute before she reached the door.

Carrie turned back and offered him a wide smile before she punched the buttons for the security system. She walked out of the building, clicking the door shut behind her.

As much as he enjoyed the view when she walked away from him, he didn't enjoy the fact that that was the last time he would ever see Carrie Wentworth.

"Get a hold of yourself," he mumbled as he opened the supply room door once again to get the tools he'd hidden under a tarp. It was time for him to get to work.

Chapter Two

Carrie

As soon as she was in her car, Carrie rested her forehead against the cool steering wheel, hoping she hadn't come across quite as pathetic to Jax as she'd seemed in her own head. *At least he can't hear my internal thoughts. Then he really would have run screaming.*

Leaning back in her seat, Carrie pushed the button to start her Lexus then pressed the palms of her hands against her tired blue eyes. She wasn't smooth with men, and she blamed her parents for that. After Carrie's cousin had become pregnant at age sixteen, her own parents had completely flipped. Wentworth women were expected to be pristine, go to the right schools, marry the right men, and have perfect children.

That kind of life sounded so boring she'd wanted to slit her wrists, but her parents hadn't seemed to care what she'd wanted. Their solution had been to keep her away from any scent of testosterone. She'd gone to an all-girl boarding school, and then studied art history at Wellesley. Not a lot of dating experience in there. Oh, she'd gone out with a few white-collar prep boys whom her parents had found acceptable, but they'd had personalities as exciting as a piece of cardboard. And none of them were anywhere near as mouthwatering as Jax.

Carrie sighed as she put her car in drive and turned out of the parking lot. Her days had been perfectly pleasant before Jax had walked into her art gallery. She vividly remembered the day her brother Tate had hired the new janitorial staff. Jax had walked in—all tall, dark, and bulging muscles—and she'd had to pick her jaw up off the floor.

Three months later, she didn't feel anymore comfortable around him than she had that very first time. Her lame attempts at conversation with him had fallen flat. The few times she'd tried to crack a joke, he'd just stared right through her with those black-as-night eyes. His eyes were what she couldn't stop thinking about. She'd caught him staring at her many times, and those eyes held such heat that she would swear he could melt her insides if he tried hard enough.

The ringing of her phone pulled Carrie out of her reverie. She hit the button on the dash that synced her Bluetooth to the overhead speakers, and her brother's voice filled the car.

"Hey Carrie, have you left yet?" Tate asked.

"Yep. Almost home." She turned down her street, feeling more relaxed as she got closer to her elegant stone cottage, and very grateful that she only lived a few minutes from the gallery.

Tate's sigh told her that this might not be the relaxing evening she'd hoped.

"What? Do I even want to ask?" She was pretty sure she didn't.

"I really need the Martin file," her brother said. "Any chance you brought your laptop home with you?"

Crap. "No. You know I always leave it in the dock on my desk to charge overnight. And why do you need the Martin file now?"

"He's claiming that the Seville he purchased is supposed to be delivered next week."

"Wait. What?" She felt her ire rise. "That man has been nothing but trouble. I know it says in his contract that the painting will be delivered to him after the exhibit on the fifteenth. I drew the contract up myself."

"That's what I told him, but he says different. I need to look over the contract first just to make absolutely certain." Tate waited a beat before continuing. "Any way you could head back to the gallery and email me a copy of it?" he asked hopefully.

Carrie had the urge to whine and stomp her foot as she pulled into her driveway. "Can't you just tell him you'll get back to him in the morning?"

"He's really insistent about getting this settled tonight. Come on, Carrie. Please?"

With an exaggerated sigh, she put her car in reverse and backed out of the driveway. "Fine. But you totally owe me."

"I do. Absolutely. I'll bring you Starbucks first thing in the morning—triple venti white mocha with extra whip."

"All right," she grumbled. "I'll email it as soon as I get back to my office."

"You're the best, sis."

The phone clicked as her brother disconnected, and Carrie tried to look at the bright side. At least she'd get to admire Jax one more time. Even the shapeless janitorial jumpsuit he wore couldn't hide those sculpted muscles. Maybe she'd get lucky, and he'd be bending over to empty the trash or something, and she could admire his backside. She grinned as she pressed down on the gas.

****

The bolt on the door slid free after Carrie punched in the seven-digit security code. When she entered, the first thing she noticed was the quiet. She wasn't sure what she'd expected. Jax singing at the top of his lungs while whizzing by on a floor waxer? Just the thought made her smile.

She walked down the dimly lit hall. Paintings lined the walls, leading a path toward the main exhibition gallery in the center of the building. The large room displayed their featured artists. While there was added security around the paintings themselves, she hadn't acquired any artwork yet that would necessitate the security methods found in larger galleries.

As she approached the exhibition area, she noticed that the overhead lights were still on. She could have sworn she'd turned them off when she left. *Jax must be cleaning in there.*

What she saw when she turned the corner took her breath away. The large frame that had hung in the center of the main wall had been removed. The frame was propped against the wall, and the Berkeley painting that it had encased lay on the floor next to it. A large cardboard-looking tube stood upright with the lid off.

Carrie inched closer, not believing what she was seeing. It looked as though the Berkeley was lying atop another painting. She could see what immediately looked like an older piece sticking out from beneath the newer abstract on the floor. She started to bend down to move the Berkeley aside so she could see the painting it covered when she heard a distinct click behind her.

She froze. Maybe it was from binge-watching all those crime shows, but she knew exactly what that click was … the cocking of a gun.

"Turn around," said the familiar deep voice behind her. "Slowly."

No, please don't let that be who I think it is. With a shaky breath, Carrie turned slowly and found herself face-to-face with Jax. Only it wasn't the Jax she was used to seeing. He wasn't wearing his usual dark green jumpsuit. She'd guessed that he had muscles—had fantasized about his muscles—but her imagination paled in comparison to the reality. His biceps bulged against the black t-shirt he wore, and faded jeans hugged his hips in a way that nicely displayed the large bulge of his crotch. As she stared, she could have sworn she saw it twitch.

Pay attention, Carrie. The man has a gun on you.

She forced her gaze up to his hard black eyes, but she was unable to focus on anything except the barrel of the gun he had directly pointed at her forehead.

"Jax." Her voice trembled. "I-I don't know what you're doing, but y-you don't have to. The painting … it's not worth a lot. You wouldn't get—"

"Shut up, Carrie." He cut her off.

Her mouth snapped shut, and she backed up instinctually.

"I told you not to move," he said, stepping closer. "I don't want to hurt you." His grip tightened on the gun with one hand. His other hand ran through his short-cropped black hair in a frustrated motion as he muttered a curse under his breath. "Fuck, Carrie, please don't make me hurt you. Just do what I say, all right?"

She opened her mouth to speak, but then thought better of it and nodded instead.

"Good. I'm glad we understand each other." His eyes flicked to some sort of a tool box on the floor and then back to her. "Lie down on the floor."

Up until then, she'd felt an odd sense of calm, but at those words, fear sliced through her. "Jax, no. Please, you don't—"

"I'm not going to rape you, Carrie." His mouth twisted in disgust. "Just lie down on your stomach, and put your hands behind your back.

Her face flamed. She knew she was overweight, but the repugnant look on his face made her want to curl into a ball. *I'm upset because he doesn't find me attractive enough to sexually assault? What's wrong with me?*

She did as he said, lying on her stomach, and pressing her cheek against the cold marble floor. She heard shuffling of tools and then a ripping sound, as though Jax were tearing duct tape off a role. In moments, he had wound that tape around her wrists so her arms were secured together behind her back, and then he wrapped another long piece tightly around her ankles.

Yanking her to a sitting position, Jax propped her against the nearest wall. "Keep your back against the wall. Don't move. And don't speak, or I'll have to gag you. Do you understand, Carrie?"

She nodded. Speak? She could scream. She hadn't even thought to scream. But it's not like anyone was around to hear her. Even if her voice could be heard outside the building, it was located on a hill on the edge of town with no other buildings around it. No one would be able to hear her. No, she needed to use her energy to figure out the best way to get away from Jax.

Chapter Three

Jax

Fuck, fuck, fuck. Jax threw the tape back into his toolbox as Carrie watched him with wide blue eyes. What the fuck was he supposed to do with her now? If Ben had been here, he would have suggested killing her. Again. But Jax couldn't do it. He couldn't fucking do it. This was a really bad time for him to have a sudden attack of morality.

He snatched the Berkeley painting up and began putting it back in the frame when Carrie's startled gasp stopped him.

He looked up to see her staring at the painting on the floor, the one that was underneath the Berkeley, with her mouth open in shock. *Fuck.*

"Is that what I think it is?" She almost whispered the question.

Of course she would know what the painting was. She'd studied art history, for crissake. He sighed. "What do you think it is?"

"The Concert." Her eyes flicked to him and then back to the painting laying on the floor. "The Concert by Johannes Vermeer, painted in 1664. It was stolen from the Isabella Stewart Gardner Museum in Boston in 1990."

She looked him in the eye. "It's thought to be the most valuable unrecovered painting in existence. It's estimated to be worth over"— she swallowed—"over two hundred million dollars. My God, Jax, where did you get this? We have to call the police. We have to—"

"No." Jax ran a hand over his face. "I'm not a Boy Scout, Carrie. Do you think I just ran across this painting by accident?"

"But, where did you…?" She looked at him and then looked again at The Concert, then at the Berkeley he was quickly putting back into its original frame. As he snapped the last piece of the frame back in place, he watched as Carrie's eyes flicked faster and faster between the two paintings. He was sure she was assessing the situation and putting two and two together.

"We just got the Berkeley in yesterday," she finally said. "Was it … was The Concert…"

"Behind the Berkeley painting," he finished. "Yes." He hung the Berkeley back in its original spot. "Give the lady a prize."

"You're smuggling stolen artwork through my gallery?"

He didn't answer her, but began deftly rolling up The Concert and putting it in the tube. Out of the corner of his eye, he could see her face go through a wide range of emotions, but she seemed to settle on anger. "You are smuggling stolen artwork through my gallery!" It wasn't a question this time. "You son of a bitch!"

When he didn't respond, she continued. "So, you're going to what? Just leave me here then disappear into the night with a two-hundred-million-dollar painting? Are you going to sell it and buy an island somewhere to live out the rest of your days, you bastard?"

"Language, love." He walked out of the room and dumped his tools back in the supply closet before coming back and assessing Carrie who had come out of her shock enough to begin struggling at the tape that bound her hands. "And you almost have my plan figured out except for one thing."

Her eyes shot fire as she looked up at him. "Oh yeah? What's that?"

"I'm not leaving you here." He reached down to yank her up. Her face registered fear for one quick moment before Jax swung her over his shoulder as if she were a sack of potatoes. "You're coming with me."

****

The crunch of gravel as Jax turned off the main road signaled that they were getting closer to his house. Carrie seemed to sense it too as he heard the "Mmmmm!" sounds she was making get louder. He hadn't had a choice but to tape her mouth before putting her in the back of his SUV.

But now that they were drawing closer to home, he had to figure out what the hell to do with her. He was no closer to figuring out that problem than he'd been when he left the gallery.

He drove down his long, winding driveway, and thanked his lucky stars that he'd decided to pay and have the drive heated. With his house halfway up the damn mountain, he got a ton of snowfall, and he really hated shoveling. When he neared the end of the drive, the trees opened up, and the three-story brick mansion loomed in front of him. His housekeeper had left it lit up, just as he preferred. He'd spent so much of his life in the dark, on the streets, that now he wanted everything bright.

"Mmmmm!" Unfortunately, the person whose light shone the brightest was screaming in his backseat.

As he pulled into the south garage that was connected to the house, his phone buzzed.

"What!" He answered.

"Do you fucking have it or not?" Ben barked back at him.

"Yes, I have it, so stop bothering me. I'll get it prepared for the client tonight, and we'll drop it off tomorrow. Then we'll both have our money, and you can disappear."

"I'm hurt, Jax. You don't want me to stick around?"

"Fuck you, Ben. It's bad enough that we had to pull a job in my own backyard."

"What are you complaining about? You get twenty million out of this." Ben's voice got serious. "So what about the girl?"

"What *about* the girl?" Jax replied.

"Did you have to take care of her, or did she go home?"

Jax looked in the back seat, where Carrie was struggling. "She left." It wasn't really a lie. She had left. She'd just come back.

"Good. Look, I'll be over later. We can prep and finalize everything."

"No! Ben, you don't—"

But he'd already hung up.

Fuck, fuck, fuck. What the hell was he supposed to do with Carrie?

Chapter Four

Carrie

"Help!" Carrie screamed as Jax gently peeled the tape from her mouth. She kicked out as hard as she could with her bound ankles and caught him square in the knee.

"Fuck, Carrie." He backed up rubbing his sore knee as she continued to scream.

Jax had carried her into a room that looked like a library. Two of the walls were lined with bookshelves, and a large oak desk stood in the center of the room. A cushiony, overstuffed red couch sat against one wall, and that was where Jax had deposited her.

Under different circumstances, she would have admired the room. But right now, she was intent on screaming her head off. Maybe she could alert the owner of this mansion, and someone would come and help her.

Unfortunately, Jax didn't seem very concerned.

Carrie screamed and screamed and screamed. "Help! I've been kidnapped! I'm being held hostage! Call 911! Help me! Call the police!"

Jax leaned against the wall near the large oak desk and crossed his arms over his broad chest.

After becoming convinced that no one was rushing to her rescue, Carrie began struggling to get the tape off of her wrists. She vaguely remembered a story on Dateline that talked about how to get away if you were ever duct taped. What the hell had they said?

A good five minutes passed before she finally ran out of energy. Panting heavily, she eventually stopped struggling, trying to wipe her forehead with a shoulder because she could feel a bead of sweat trickling down her face.

She looked up at Jax, still leaning against the wall, and damned if the bastard didn't look amused. His eyes sparkled with mirth, and the corner of his mouth tipped up in the closest thing she'd ever seen to a smile from him. One dark eyebrow slowly arched. "Done?" he asked.

She took a few more deep breaths. "Fuck you."

This time, he didn't try to hide a grin, but his face broke into a wide smile, revealing perfect white teeth and a dimple—a fucking dimple—in his left cheek. Dammit if her heart didn't skip a beat.

Pushing off the wall, he walked toward where she sat on the couch. When he reached her, he bent down as if he were going to tie his shoe. Instead, he lifted the pant leg of his jeans, and Carrie looked down to see a holster of sorts at his ankle.

With a *schwing*, Jax pulled out a knife. It wasn't a huge knife, but it looked very sharp and very pointy.

Carrie felt that prickle of fear again at the back of her neck. "What are you going to do with that?"

Jax rested the point of the knife against the hollow spot at the base of her throat and bent his head until his face was mere centimeters from her own. Carrie drew her tongue across her lips, and she could have sworn Jax's eyes darkened as he let out a little groan.

He trailed the point of the knife lightly along the side of her neck and down her throat, lower between her breasts. She knew she should be afraid, and deep down, there was a part of her that was, but anxiety seemed to dissipate into an emanating heat at the center of her very being, as something told her he wouldn't hurt her. She didn't know why, didn't know what it was, but she knew he wouldn't hurt her.

She focused on his full lips, loving how they parted slightly. The heat from his body seared her, and he wasn't even touching her. And his scent … warm, musky, and deliciously male. Searching his face, she locked eyes with him and held his gaze for what seemed like an eternity, but was probably only mere seconds.

"Hold still, love," he finally said. Trailing the knife down her legs, he kept his eyes on hers. She shivered at the sensation of the cool metal … or was she shivering because of his nearness? When he reached her ankles, he sliced through the tape in one quick jerk of the knife.

He ripped the remnants of tape off, and Carrie breathed a sigh of relief since she was able to separate her ankles. With the tape off, she could keep her balance so much easier. When Jax stood up, she asked, "Aren't you going to do my wrists?"

With a quick headshake, Jax slid the knife back into his ankle holster and stood up. "Not quite yet. We need to talk first."

He looked so somber, but then again, this was a serious situation. Carrie watched him stalk over to one of the two leather chairs across from the oak desk. Even though they looked heavy, Jax lifted one as if it were light as a feather and flipped it around to face her. He sat in it and crossed one ankle over his knee.

"Okay." She took a shaky breath. "Talk. Tell me what's going on. How did you end up with a two-hundred-million-dollar painting? What was it doing in my gallery? Whose house is this? And what … what are you going to do with me? Are you going to uh…" she gave a tug at the tape on her wrists. "Are you going to kill me?"

"Carrie." Jax said her name softly as he ran a hand over his dark stubble. Even though he came to work each day cleanly shaven, it seemed as though he usually had a five o'clock shadow by about two each afternoon.

"First things first," he finally said. "This is my house."

"Your house?" She looked around at the elaborate furnishings. "How could you afford this on a janitor's sal—oh, right." If she'd had a free hand, she would have smacked herself in the forehead. "Your parents must be so proud," she said sarcastically.

The laugh that Jax gave held no humor. "Yeah, well, if I had any parents, maybe I wouldn't have become a thief."

She stared at him for a long moment. "You don't have any parents?"

"Not everyone grows up as lucky as you, princess. With money and cars and clothes. Private schools, universities." He jerked his eyes away as if he couldn't stand to look at her anymore.

She felt her anger rise. He'd stolen, he'd abducted her, and now he was trying to make her feel guilty? "You don't know anything about me."

When Jax turned back to look at her, his eyes were cold. "I know enough. I've had to work for everything I have, Carrie. Can you say the same?"

"Work? Work!" She looked at him in disbelief. "Being a thief is not work, Jax. And for your information, life hasn't been as easy for me as you might think."

He shook his head and rose from the chair. "I highly doubt that."

"Don't be so sure. Maybe you didn't have parents, but that can't be any worse than having parents who didn't even want you."

He looked at her long and hard. "What are you talking about?"

She straightened her spine. "You think I went to all those fancy boarding schools because my parents loved me? Hardly. My dad wanted a son—an heir. He didn't have much use for a girl, at least not until I was old enough for him to marry me off." She looked away. "He groomed Tate, and he shipped me off somewhere, to a girls school, where I wouldn't be tainted."

"Tainted?"

She looked back at him, ignoring the question. "Thank God for Tate. He could have turned out like my dad, but he was the only one who showed me any compassion."

"What about your mom?"

"My mom? If my mom was awake, she was drunk. I used to hate her for it, but now?" She shook her head. "Honestly, I can't say I blame her. She coped the only way she knew how. They think the car accident was her fault. Their car drove over a cliff, you know."

"So I read. That was your mom's fault?"

"Well, the car exploded on impact, so they can't really prove anything, but they do know my mom was in the driver's seat. Drunk driving was the only thing that made sense." She looked up to see sympathy on Jax's face. "Forget it. I don't know why I just spilled all that to you. Maybe I just wanted you to see that we're not so different."

"In some ways, I suppose." He walked over to sit next to her on the couch. "We're both survivors. We both make the best of a situation even if we're dealt a shitty hand. But I'm guessing that's where it ends, doesn't it, Carrie?"

"The disparity is that I know the difference between right and wrong." And it didn't matter how sexy or enticing he was, he was wrong, this whole situation was wrong. "Tate's going to find out what you did. He's going to come after you. You can't get away with this." She jerked again on the tape.

Jax sighed. "We're wasting time. I have enough to worry about without throwing your pansy-ass brother into the mix." He rose from the couch and began to pace. "Listen to me. We're going to have company soon. His name's Ben. Just follow my lead when he gets here. Can you do that?"

Carrie jutted her chin out. "I'm not doing a damn thing until you answer me. Why would someone put such an expensive painting under the one coming to my gallery? It doesn't make sense."

He sighed. "There's big business in art smuggling, Carrie. Ever since World War II when Germany stole so many paintings. You'd be amazed at the paintings and sculptures being bought and sold on the Black Market."

"So you're smuggling paintings? For who?" She furrowed her brow. "I don't understand."

He circled the chair again and sat down. "Look, a buyer makes it known that he's looking for a certain piece of art. People like me go in search of that piece. When we find it, we broker a deal between the buyer and the seller. Expensive paintings are easily transferred underneath lesser-known paintings. We make the transaction, and we get a cut of the profit."

"So you're like the middle man?"

He shrugged a muscular shoulder. "For lack of a better term."

"You haven't answered my big question, Jax. What about me? I'm guessing it's not a good thing for you that I know about this." She looked up at him, searching his handsome face for answers. "Are you going to kill me?"

Chapter Five

Jax

She was so fucking beautiful. He knew he couldn't hurt her, but he needed her to be afraid of him, at least until he got Ben in and out of there.

"I'm not going to answer that, love. Because it depends."

"Depends? On what?"

He really loved the way she jerked on that tape every so often. The thought of sinking his cock into her soft little body when she was tightly bound made his spine tingle. What would she do if he took her down the hall to his dungeon?

Focus, Jackson.

"Carrie, someone's going to be here soon. We have to—"

The slamming of a door down the hall stopped him. "Fuck," he muttered.

"Hey, man! Where the fuck are you? Let's see this thing!" Ben's footsteps sounded down the hall.

Jax should have done a better job explaining the situation to Carrie instead of flirting with her. But all he could do was pray that she went along with him on this. Flipping the chair back around, he grabbed the length of rope that he kept in the desk for the times when he liked to tie up a submissive in this room. Walking toward Carrie, he noticed her face flinch as she saw the rope in his hand.

"Please, Jax, don't. I'll—"

"Shh, baby." He quickly yanked her up. "I'm not going to hurt you." He kept one arm around her waist as he walked her to the corner and reached up for the retractable hook he'd had installed in the eight-foot ceiling. "I don't have time to explain. Just, please. Please follow my lead."

Reaching down, he yanked the knife from his ankle holster once more and reached around to slice the tape from Carrie's wrists. He wished he had a moment to let her stretch her sore shoulders, but there was no time.

"Jax, what the fuck?" Doors slammed down the hall. "I know you're here. I saw your car!" Ben was getting closer to them.

Jax looped the rope around Carrie's wrists and tied it in a simple square knot before pulling her wrists up. She cried out a little bit, most likely because her shoulders were so stiff.

"I'm sorry, baby." He looped the rope over the hook in the ceiling just as the door to the office swung open.

"Are you in here, man? What the fu—" Ben stopped as he spotted Jax in the corner of the room with his arms circling Carrie. "Jesus Christ." Ben's face was red as he approached them.

Jax immediately stepped in front of Carrie to shield her, and he could feel her body shaking behind him. He didn't think Ben would hurt her, but if his partner thought Carrie was his submissive, then that was a guarantee he would back off. "Jesus Christ, man, don't you ring the fucking doorbell? How did you even get in?"

Ben craned his neck to look at Carrie, and Jax could only imagine how terrified she must look. Ben was a big guy. Even when he smiled, he looked menacing. When he was pissed, he looked down right deadly. And at that moment, he certainly wasn't happy.

"You have got to be fucking kidding me." Ben's eyes flicked back and forth from Carrie to Jax.

Jax forced himself to stay calm. "I told you this wasn't a good time. Or I tried to anyway, before you hung up."

"Yeah, you also told me the bitch left, not that you had her tied up in your fucking house."

Jax took a step toward his partner and couldn't stop the savage growl that escaped his throat. Ben swallowed and backed up.

"What I do with a submissive in my own house is none of your damned business," Jax spat out. "And you'll refer to her with respect."

Ben's eyes widened incredulously. "Submissive? You haven't kept a submissive in ages."

Shrugging casually, Jax turned to Carrie, reaching to brush a few stray blond hairs from her face. He hated the fact that she looked so frightened.

He directed his words to Ben, but his eyes stayed on Carrie. "So? Maybe I haven't found a sub worth keeping until now."

"Really?" Ben ran a hand through his shaggy brown hair in disbelief. "And you find one who happens to be running the gallery where we have a job? What about that? What if she goes to the police?"

"Why would I do that?" Carrie asked. Jax could hear the fear in her voice even though she tried to keep it from wavering. "Jax is giving me a cut of the money. It's not like I'd do anything to ruin that." Her eyes flicked to him. "Right … Sir?"

Raising both of his eyebrows in surprise, Jax was rendered speechless for a moment. But his cock responded to the word "sir" in an instant, hardening in anticipation. "Uh, exactly."

"A cut of the money?" Ben's mouth hung open. "Have you lost your fucking mind, Jax?"

He rolled his eyes. "Sweet Jesus, don't be so dramatic. What I do with my cut of the money is none of your concern." He took another step toward Ben, slowly backing him out of the door. "Now, if you don't mind, I'd appreciate it if you got the hell out of here. I'd like to fuck my submissive."

Ben stared at him for a beat and then sighed. "Fine. But what about the painting? And what makes you so sure she's not going to leave here and go straight to the police?" Ben shot a glare at Carrie. "No matter what she says."

Jax didn't like the way his partner was looking at Carrie. "I'll prep the painting, so don't worry about that." He glanced at Carrie. "And she's not going anywhere tonight. By the time she leaves tomorrow, the painting will be safely in the hands of the client. Even if she were to go to the police—which she won't—there won't be any proof of anything. So you contact the client, tell him everything is on schedule, and don't bother me again until morning."

Ben's face turned red. He was frustrated. About that, Jax had no doubt. But he'd addressed all his partner's concerns, and took satisfaction in the fact that Ben had seemed to run out of arguments.

Finally his partner huffed out a breath. "Fine." He turned and walked out the door of the library, slamming it behind him.

Chapter Six

Carrie

For a moment, Carrie wondered where the heavy breathing was coming from, and then she realized it was her own. There had to be something wrong with her. That was the only excuse. She'd been scared, downright terrified, when that Ben person had walked in, all big and growly. But the second Jax had said he wanted to fuck his submissive, she had been laser-focused on him and on what that would actually feel like.

She didn't want to be tied up. She *didn't*. She also didn't enjoy being kidnapped. But if that were really true, and she really didn't enjoy those things, then why did Jax's smoky dark eyes make parts inside of her clench that she hadn't even known existed before tonight?

Carrie took another deep breath, trying to force herself to remain calm. But after Ben had left the room, Jax turned to stare at her with a look in his eyes that she couldn't quite place. His eyes had darkened, and the way he circled toward her like a wolf stalking his prey made liquid heat pool at her center. She hadn't had much sexual experience, but she knew for certain she'd never been so turned on in her life. "Are you going to let me down now?"

He walked back over toward her, and the slight quirk of his lips lightened his otherwise menacing features. "You still think you're in charge, love?"

She would have shrugged a shoulder, but it was a bit difficult with her arms secured over her head. "I did as you asked. I kept my mouth shut."

She looked up at him when he reached her. When he lifted a hand, she thought he was going to unhook her, but instead, he ran the backs of his knuckles softly down her cheek making a *"tsk tsk"* sound.

A little whimper escaped the back of Carrie's throat as she leaned into him. Was it wrong that being bound this way turned her on? She didn't even care anymore. She lifted her face to his. "Jax." She meant to shove him away somehow, demand to be untied, to be let go ... but she wanted him to kiss her. She'd never wanted anything so badly in her entire life.

He must have sensed it. His hand turned to cup her cheek, his fingers pressing in lightly as he lowered his head and finally claimed her mouth. Her moan was covered by his mouth as he pulled her to him, his meaty arms holding her close. She felt the hard line of his erection against her, and every nerve in her body seemed to light up. When his tongue met hers, she thought she'd died right there. She'd never felt anything like this. Her blood shot like electricity through her veins. *This must be heaven. It must.*

She wanted to reach for him, to touch him, but her arms were bound.

Turning her head to the side, she broke the kiss. "Please," she panted. "Please untie me."

His mouth trailed down her neck, his tongue tracing little circles. "It doesn't work that way, love." He turned her face back to his until their eyes met. She saw a wanting there, a desire she'd never thought possible in a man's gaze. He wanted her. This big beautiful man wanted her.

"You may be used to being in charge, to giving orders, but that stops with me." His voice seemed deeper now. "When you're with me, you do what I say, what I command. You give in." His hands played up and down the sides of her body as he held her gaze. "Let your mind and your body submit to me, Carrie, and I can give you more pleasure than you ever dreamed."

His words left her breathless. Right now she didn't care about anything else. She didn't care that he'd lied to her. She didn't care that he'd stolen. She didn't even care that he'd threatened her. All she cared about was that she wanted him, and he wanted her. She tried all the time to be so strong, to be firm and commanding. Just once, she wanted to let go, to trust someone other than herself. She was so tired of being so tough all the time. She wanted to lean on someone, to lean on Jax.

She didn't know what this connection was between her and Jax, didn't know what it meant, only that it was deep. It was primal.

And she knew at that moment, she should tell him. She should tell him she was a virgin.

She opened her mouth to speak, to say just that. Then his teeth found a corner of her neck, and he bit lightly, nibbling until electricity shot through every pore of her body. And all she knew was that she didn't want him to stop.

Finally he raised his head, dropping a kiss on her mouth. "You looked like you wanted to say something." He reached up to cup her face, his thumbs making little circles on her cheeks. "Is there something you want to say?"

She took a deep breath. She needed to tell him. "I'm ... I'm..."

His touch was so distracting. So much. She wanted him so much.

"You're what, little one?"

"I'm ... I'm sure I don't want you to stop. Please don't stop."

She was going to tell him. But if she did, she was pretty damn sure he would stop. And that couldn't happen.

As he kissed her again, she breathed him in, and thought to herself that maybe, just maybe, he wouldn't notice.

Chapter Seven

Jax

Never in his life had he met a woman with so much passion, such fire. He'd expected her to turn away. To scream and tell him to fuck off. As much of a bastard as he was, he wouldn't take her if she said no. He didn't need to rape a woman to get her into bed. But she didn't turn him away. She'd trusted him. Even though he hadn't given her a reason in the world to trust him, she had.

He'd planned to untie her until he'd realized just how much she liked being tied up like this. Oh, she might claim that she didn't, but he knew the truth. He could see the heat flair in her eyes. Every time he kissed her, he could hear the little moan that escaped the back of her throat and feel the way she tensed, her breathing speeding up as she instinctively yanked on her bonds. She was a sweet little submissive, and she didn't even know it.

There was so much he wanted to show her. He wanted her to see how good he could make her feel by tying her to a St. Andrew's cross and flogging her sweet, heart-shaped ass. He wanted her aroused after he'd pinkened her ass with his firm hand. But right now, more than that, he just wanted her. He wanted to sink his cock into her sweet little pussy.

Reaching down, he unsheathed the knife from his ankle holster once again.

"What are you doing with that?" She asked in alarm.

"Shhh," he soothed. "Do you trust me?" When she didn't answer, he asked again, "Carrie, do you trust me?"

Finally, she gave him what he wanted—her submission. She nodded. "I do. I don't know why ... but I do."

He didn't know why Carrie did it for him, but she did. She was sweet, and smart, and funny, and stubborn, and sexy as hell. He'd walked around the last few months with a continuous erection, hoping she wouldn't notice. He didn't know how he'd ever thought he could hurt her.

He slid her skirt and panties slowly down her legs, watching her face the whole time, waiting for her to protest, but all she did was wiggle her hips to help him slide her skirt off more easily. When it reached her ankles, she kicked it off, and stood in front of him naked from the waist down.

Gazing down at her pussy for the first time, he licked his lips in urgency. The smattering of dark blonde hair on her delicious mound made his mouth water. He wanted to shave her. He wanted to tie her legs down and shave her nice and smooth. She would feel the sting of a crop so much better on a clean-shaven pussy.

He'd nearly forgotten he was holding the knife, he was so used to the weight of it in his hand, but he caught site of Carrie's eyes, which were following each movement of the blade as he twirled it back and forth in his fingers.

For a second, he studied the pretty pink blouse she wore. He could unbutton it and set her breasts free without even untying her if he wanted to. But then, what fun would that be?

With a grin, he lifted the knife up and slid it between the gap in her shirt. The rise and fall of her chest betrayed her calm exterior. She couldn't hide the quickening of her breath. Jax focused his eyes on the porcelain skin of her face, and felt his cock twitch at the sight of her teeth sinking into her lower lip. He was pretty damn sure she was going to kill him. She was the sexiest woman he'd ever seen in his life.

With a quick jerk of his wrist, the knife sliced through the thread holding on a button, and it flew off with a little *ping*. Instinctively, Carrie stepped back, but he circled her waist with a commanding arm. "Stay still, love." Sliding the knife lower, he sliced off the next button. *Ping*. And the next. *Ping*. Until the tattered silk of her shirt hung open.

He tossed the knife on the end table next to the couch and reached for her, pulling her to him. He kept one arm securely fastened around her waist, as the fingers of his right hand trailed up the sensitive skin of her belly. He loved the way she quivered beneath his touch. Reaching her bra, he deftly unfastened the front clasp, and moved the cups aside so her breasts spilled free.

Her large, full breasts stood at attention. Cupping each one, Jax savored the full weight of them in his hands. Damn, he loved large breasts on a woman. And Carrie's were truly the most perfect breasts he'd ever seen. He pressed a kiss to the areola on each one just above the nipple, and grinned at how she sucked in a breath. She was so soft, so smooth. And she tasted sweet, like strawberries. He'd never think of strawberries the same way again. On a groan, he gently squeezed one full breast, his thumb sliding a circle around the pebbled nipple.

He looked at her face, eager to see her reaction. Her eyes were closed, her head back, exposing the line of her throat.

"Look at me, Carrie. Open your eyes and look at me."

When she didn't immediately comply, he increased the pressure on her nipple with his thumb and forefinger, and her eyes popped open as a little squeak sounded in her throat.

"Good," he said. "Keep your eyes on me."

She locked eyes with him as he slowly lowered his head and took her other nipple in his mouth. His fingers continued to toy with the first one, and every time she would groan in pleasure and close her eyes as he lavished one nipple with his lips and tongue, he would twist the other one firmly until her eyes opened again. When he noticed how her hips wiggled and gently thrust forward each time he gave her a little tweak of pain, he began giving her nipples and her breasts little bites until her pelvis was involuntarily thrusting toward him as she yanked at the rope around her wrists.

"Jax." She said his name almost on a whine. "Please."

Everything about her did it for him. Her smell, her taste, and her voice. "That's right, little one. Beg me. I want you to beg me."

She yanked at her hands again at the same time she thrust her lower half toward. "Please, Jax … I … please."

"Tell me what you want." He fisted a hand in her hair as he captured her mouth, plunging his tongue deep, signaling what he wanted to do with his cock. He held her head still as he took her mouth over and over again. When he raised his head, he looked into her big blue eyes, and one more time, she said, "Please."

"Carrie, I can't wait anymore. I need you. Now."

Chapter Eight

Carrie

She kept her eyes on him, every cell of her body lit up, on fire for him. Somewhere in the back of her mind, there was a voice saying that this was a mistake, but the rest of her mind was quickly beating that voice into submission. She wanted him, and nothing could keep her from having him.

She watched as he stepped away from her and reached for the hem of his black t-shirt. He whipped it over his head and tossed it to the side. She couldn't help her mouth from dropping open. His caramel-colored skin was smooth, and the bulging muscles weren't just on his arms. She wanted to feel the sinewy muscles of his chest pressed up against her breasts. And his abs… "That is not fair," she said.

He stopped as he was unzipping his jeans and peeked up at her face. "What's not fair?"

"That whole chiseled ab thing you have going. No matter how much time I spend at the gym, my body would never look like that, not in a million years."

His dark eyes swept over her, making her shiver. "Baby, your body is perfect. It's the most perfect body I've ever seen, and I don't want you changing anything, do you understand me?"

"Yes, sir," she said without thinking.

At her words, she saw his hands noticeably clench the waistband of his jeans. "Jesus, Carrie, what are you doing to me?" He muttered the question almost to himself. And he worked quicker now, his movements more determined.

He didn't slide his jeans off as she'd thought he would. Instead, he opened the zipper and reached in to pull himself free, as if he couldn't wait to be inside of her.

"Oh, holy God." She could feel her eyes go wide, and hoped they weren't bugging out of her head. He was enormous. She couldn't take her eyes off his cock as he slowly stroked the long, thick shaft with his hand, stopping only to run his thumb over the mushroom-shaped head.

"Wow." How the hell was that ever going to fit?

As he reached into his pocket, he tilted his head at her. "What's wrong, love? Bigger than you're used to?"

"I, uh…" *Tell him! Good lord, he's going to rip you apart. Tell him!* "It, um, yes … much bigger than I'm used to."

He ripped open the foil packet he'd taken out of his pocket and sheathed himself quickly before stepping closer to her.

Wrapping his arm around her waist, Jax pressed their lower halves together, and she felt his thick erection against her skin, hot and hard.

Leaning the top half of his body away from her, Jax looked down in between him where his cock rested against her belly.

Yeah, that thing is never going to fit.

"Don't worry. I'll fit," he said as if reading her mind.

Her eyes jerked up to his face. His beautiful, chiseled face. He even had pronounced muscles in his face. So not fair.

His hooded eyes glittered as he looked at her. "You need to know, Carrie, I'm not a gentle lover. I don't go slow. I want to fuck you. I want you, hard and savage, and now."

She would have melted at his words into a puddle at his feet if her hands hadn't been tied above her head. Words like that shouldn't turn her on so much, should they? They shouldn't make her pussy throb in response. Her pussy ... she'd never thought in those terms before. But even though she didn't know what she was missing, she suddenly felt empty without him.

Jax reached down to grasp her hips. "Wrap your legs around me," he said against her mouth. His hands cupped the round globes of her ass, supporting her as she did what he instructed. She wrapped her legs around his waist, feeling his large erection pressed against that sensitive spot on her pussy.

She moaned out his name, and he captured her mouth again, his tongue rubbing against hers in a sensual dance as he lined himself up. He rubbed the engorged head over her swollen sex, getting himself slick with her wetness. Then, she felt the head of his cock against her opening. She felt him nudge the head gently inside of her, but before she could get used to the feel of him, he thrust himself forward hard as he yanked her hips against him.

She wrenched her head to the side as something tore deep inside of her, and a white hot pain shot through her. Her hands clutched at air as she cried out, her eyes squeezing shut.

Then, stillness.

Panting hard, she opened her eyes to look at Jax's face and watched a range of emotion play over his beautiful features—shock, confusion, concern, and finally anger.

He started to pull back. He was going to leave her. She tightened her legs around him, crossing her ankles at the base of his back.

"Dammit, Carrie." He practically growled her name.

"I don't want you to stop." It hurt, it still hurt, but the pain was dissipating.

He looked at her for a long moment. "I'm not stopping, but why didn't you fucking tell me?"

"I just … it didn't come up," she said lamely.

"It didn't come up?" He looked at her with his jaw clenched so tightly that a muscle stood out in the side of his neck. "I am so going to punish you for this."

"Punish me? But, I—ahh" Her words ended on a cry as he pulled out and thrust back in.

"We're not talking now, so shut up." He leaned his head down, taking her mouth almost savagely this time. He stayed still inside of her until his kisses had her so hot that her lower body was trying to thrust against him.

Only then did he move. He pulled out again, slower this time, and slid back in. He slid in easier now, the pain turning to something … good, his cock dragging across nerves that she'd never known existed.

"Jax." His name came out on a whimper as he set a rhythm for her. He would pull nearly all the way out then thrust back in, grinding his pelvis against hers, sending sparks shooting from her clit to the rest of her body.

As his thrusts quickened, she felt something inside of her begin to build. His fingers sank into her hips in a bruising embrace. He held her tightly the whole time, so there wasn't an uncomfortable weight on her arms and shoulders.

His lips tore away from her mouth, and his face buried in her neck, and Carrie sensed his control slipping away. "Carrie, please, please come," he begged.

She wanted to come, needed to. Even though she'd never felt this, she knew that whatever was building inside of her was about to overflow. Almost like a balloon that couldn't hold any more air, but was blown up so tightly that if one more breath was added, it would be too much.

One last hard thrust of Jax's cock was the one last push she needed, and the balloon inside of her burst. "Oh God, Jax." She cried out his name, every muscle in her body spasming. His name became unintelligible on her lips as he continued thrusting, fucking her through her orgasm. She twitched from head to toe, shudders rolling through her body. She'd never felt anything so powerful. It was so intense that she wanted it to stop, but she also wanted it to never stop. Nothing made sense. There was no logic, no thought, there was only him.

Every muscle in Jax's body was rigid. She opened her eyes to look at him, and when she locked eyes with him, he let go. "Fuck, Carrie." He thrust deeply one last time and held himself still as his body jerked. She felt his cock bulging and releasing inside of her as he emptied himself.

Chapter Nine

Jax

Jax's arms encircled Carrie's waist as he squeezed her tightly to him, not ready to let her go. Her legs were still wrapped tightly around him, and as he drifted back to earth, the emotions came back. She'd been a virgin, and she hadn't told him. He should feel horrible for putting her in a situation where she'd felt forced to open herself to him. But he didn't feel horrible. He'd offered her the chance to say no, and she hadn't taken it. Instead, she'd given herself to him. She'd offered herself up and hadn't hesitated.

Would he have taken her if he'd known? He certainly wouldn't have been as rough, he knew that. He pulled back to look at her, and she tried to adjust her shoulder with a little grimace. Shit, her arms. He looked up to see her hands a bit pale but still pink.

Carrie winced and gave a little cry as he pulled out, letting her feet slide to the ground. She didn't say anything, but hung almost limply in her bonds at that point. Satisfied and glowing. She had a little smile on her face that had Jax's cock twitching again. He disposed of the condom and tucked himself into his jeans, then buttoned them up as he took in her body. As much as he wanted to do nothing more than carry her upstairs and take her again, he had business to take care of. *They* had business to take care of.

As her weight rested on her wrists, her hands quickly began taking on a purplish hue, and he snatched up the knife where he had deposited it on the table. Supporting Carrie with one arm, he raised the knife and deftly sliced through the ropes, freeing her.

"Ow." She grimaced as her arms fell, and he knew it would be uncomfortable as the blood rushed back into her limbs.

"It's okay, love. Come here." He carried her to the couch where she'd sat earlier, then covered her up with a blanket, massaging her shoulders.

With her nakedness hidden, she looked up at him a bit sheepishly. "Are you mad at me?"

"Mad?" She was worried that he was mad at her? This beautiful, sweet woman. All she'd wanted was to trust someone. No matter what she said, she wanted … needed someone to take care of her, to love her.

Love her. That's not you, Jax. You're not capable of that.

"Carrie, I'm not mad at you. I just wish you'd told me. Why didn't you?"

She shrugged one sexy shoulder. "You would have stopped," she said simply. "I didn't want you to stop."

Her whole life she'd waited to give herself to someone, and she ended up choosing him at that moment. He didn't understand. He needed to put a stop to this now. He wasn't the man she thought he was, and he needed her to understand that.

"Carrie, I don't know what you think this was, but we can't—"

"Hey, Jax! I forgot to…" Ben burst into the room at that moment.

Fuck. Fuck. Fuck.

"Well," his friend took in Jax's shirtless form and leered in Carrie's direction, "you two certainly didn't waste any time, did you?"

Carrie tucked the blanket tighter underneath her chin, and Jax turned to shield her from Ben's prying eyes.

"What the fuck are you doing back here, Ben? I told you to contact the client, and we would talk in the morning."

"I did talk to the client. He's, uh…" Ben looked at Carrie. "He's not happy."

Fuck! Just from the look in Carrie's direction, Jax knew his partner had told the client about her even though he'd told him to keep his damn mouth shut.

"Goddammit, Ben, I told you—"

"Look, you can yell at me all you want to later, but you need to hear this. Put some fucking clothes on, and meet me in the living room." Ben slammed the door, setting Jax's teeth on edge. He didn't take well to being ordered around in his own home.

"Fuck." He got up and reached for the t-shirt he'd discarded earlier. "Get dressed, Carrie."

The blonde had the blanket wrapped around her like it was a shield, trying to cover as much skin as she possibly could, as if he hadn't just been inside her and had her nipples in his mouth.

"I can't," she said.

"You can't? Can't get dressed? Why not?"

She gave a little huff and rolled her eyes. "You sliced the buttons off my blouse, remember?"

He couldn't help but grin. "Right." He tossed her his t-shirt. "Here. Put this on. I'll get another one." His grin faded as his eyes trailed to the door. "I have to go deal with Ben. I'll be back shortly."

"Jax," she started.

He had a hand on the doorknob and turned to look at her, arching a brow in question. There was so much he wanted to say.

Carrie blew out a breath. "Nothing," she finally said.

He gave her a long look then finally turned and walked out of the room.

Chapter Ten

Carrie

Holding the t-shirt to her face, she took a long sniff. My God, the man smelled so good. His scent had to be some sort of drug. Tossing the blanket aside, Carrie quickly pulled the shirt on then went in search of her skirt. Once she was dressed, she rubbed her sore wrists. At least she wasn't tied up anymore. Not that it had been all bad.

Part of her thought she would wake up and find out this was all a dream. Things had changed so drastically in the last few hours, she still couldn't quite wrap her mind around it. A priceless painting was smuggled through her gallery, she'd been held at gunpoint, kidnapped, and then she'd lost her virginity to her kidnapper. She hadn't even decided if she fully trusted Jax yet.

Loud male voices pulled her out of her reverie. She inched closer to the door. She couldn't hear what they were saying, but they didn't sound happy. Opening the door, she could hear little snippets of the argument coming from somewhere down the hall to her left.

"Why the fuck would you tell him about her in the first place?" Jax was saying.

"It doesn't matter. You're missing the point, man. You can't let her go. He wants her dead." Ben's words sent an icy fear shooting down her back. She strained to hear more, but the voices became muffled again.

Why would someone want her dead? She thought they'd had a good cover story. Apparently, it wasn't that believable. She noticed how severely her hands shook as she closed the door to the library. Would Jax kill her? He'd just made love to her.

Don't be an idiot, Carrie. It wasn't making love. It was fucking. Even though he'd been her first, she damn sure hadn't been his. She was being delusional if she thought she held a special place in his heart. Even if she did, was that enough for him to put his life on the line? Or enough for him to give up twenty million dollars? She highly doubted it. Even if he couldn't bring himself to kill her, he'd probably just have Ben do it.

The burning anxiety in her chest spurred her into action. She had to get out of there before they came to the realization that they had no choice but to kill her. What was she going to do if she left? She couldn't walk down the mountain. Searching the room frantically for some sort of inspiration, her eyes landed on the set of keys on Jax's desk. Of course! When he'd brought her into the room, he'd deposited her on the couch and tossed his keys on the desk.

Rushing to pick up the keys, Carrie tried to remember the layout of the house in her head. The garage was down the hall to her right, past the kitchen. The men's voices were coming from somewhere down the hall to the left. She actually might have a chance to get out of there. With the garage at the opposite end of the house, she could start the car and leave without the men hearing it.

Carrie quickly slipped her shoes on then inched to the door. Opening it a fraction, she listened closely and still heard muffled voices from down the hall. Now was her chance. She would have to be fast ... and quiet. On second thought, she slipped her shoes back off. Clutching her heels in one hand and Jax's keys in the other, she slid out the door and tiptoed down the hall in the opposite direction of the voices. When she reached the kitchen, she sped up, all but running to the garage door.

When it creaked open, she went completely still, barely breathing, listening as hard as she could for any sounds. When she heard nothing, she opened it just enough to slide through the doorway, then shut it quietly behind her. Once in the garage, she exhaled. Then she looked up and nearly did a fist-pump when she saw that Jax had left the garage door open.

Once in his SUV, which resembled a small bus, she locked the door. She was a bit scared to start it for fear the engine would alert the men inside the house, but she knew she was running out of time. As soon as the engine turned over, Carrie threw the car into reverse and backed out of the garage. She sped down the driveway without looking back.

It wasn't until she reached the end of the drive, that she realized she wasn't quite sure where she was. *Shit!* She'd always been directionally challenged, and since she'd been lying down in the backseat when they'd driven out to the house, she had no idea which way they'd been going.

Looking around the car wildly, her eyes landed on the screen on the dash. A GPS. Of course! It was just like the one in her Lexus. She just rarely used it since she was familiar with her small community. As she punched in her address, she could have sworn she heard an engine starting up somewhere behind her.

Oh no! Hurry, hurry! She breathed a sigh of relief when the directions to her brother's house popped up on the display. She'd go directly to Tate's. He would know what to do. She turned out onto the road and sped down the mountain toward town.

Chapter Eleven

Jax

"What is so fucking important that this could not wait until morning?" Jax slammed into his home office at the front of the house, yanking on a t-shirt he'd grabbed from the dungeon. Ben trailed right behind him. Not only was he annoyed Ben had interrupted his moment with Carrie, but he was still trying to wrap his brain around the fact that he'd just taken her virginity. Christ, he hadn't fucked a virgin since he was sixteen years old. Carrie hadn't deserved to be taken like that. She should have had candlelight and music and wine, and hell, a fucking bed. He had to make this right with her. The sooner he could get rid of Ben, the sooner he could be with Carrie.

"Jax, listen to me, the client is really upset."

"The client," he said almost mockingly. "I am sick of this fucking client." He needed to take his confusion and anger out on someone, and Ben had the unfortunate position of being directly in his path. "I don't even know who this fucking client is, and at this point, I honestly don't care. Tell him he will get his fucking painting tomorrow."

He started to shove past Ben when his partner grabbed his arm. Jax was about to shake him off when Ben said the words that stopped him dead in his tracks. "It's Tate Wentworth."

Turning slowly, Jax clamped a hand to his mouth as if holding in a curse. He stared at Ben, his mind running wildly for a few moments before he finally trusted himself to speak. "Tate Wentworth? Is your client? Carrie's brother?"

Ben must have sensed that Jax's temper was simmering slowly beneath the surface because he didn't respond with a flippant comment. "*Our* client. And yes, but unfortunately, that's not the worst of it."

Narrowing his eyes at his partner, Jax waited for the other shoe to drop. He watched as Ben swallowed deeply.

"He wants her dead," Ben finally said.

Fuck, fuck, fuck. Carrie had no idea. He remembered the words she'd uttered earlier this evening. *Thank God for Tate.* On a sigh, he ran a hand over his face. What the fuck was he going to do? How was he ever going to tell her?

As if echoing his thoughts, Ben asked, "What are you going to do?"

"Well, do you have any suggestions?" He gave Ben a grim look and jabbed a finger in his direction. "And don't you dare fucking say kill her, or you'll be the one in the body bag." His partner's reputation of a tough guy who killed first and asked questions later was well-known. So why did Ben look scared shitless right now?

"I'm not going to say kill her."

"Really? Because you've said it plenty of times already tonight."

"Fuck," his partner whispered. "Because Tate was adamant she was out of the way."

Wearily, Ben took a seat in the chair near the window and looked out into the night. "It wasn't just the painting that was Tate's priority. The gallery is the perfect vehicle for him to smuggle paintings in and out. The problem is Carrie's the one running the place. She's the one with all the knowledge of art." Ben blew out a breath. "Apparently, she's also the one with the conscience. With her in the way, it's going to make … acquiring and moving art much more difficult for Tate."

"So he wants her dead?" Jax stared in disbelief. "He's already worth a fortune. How much money does he need? And he wants to kill his sister for it?"

When Ben rose from his seat, Jax positioned himself between his partner and the door. "You're not going near her."

Ben rolled his eyes. "I'm not planning to kill her, but you're missing the point. Tate sent his sister back to the gallery tonight knowing you would be in the middle of removing The Concert from behind the other painting. He wanted her to walk in on you. He thought you would kill her."

Fisting his hands, Jax had to stifle the urge to plant one through his partner's face. "Why the fuck would you tell him about her in the first place? That she was here?"

"Well, don't you think he was going to wonder where she was when her body wasn't found at the gallery?" Ben waved his hands in frustration. "It doesn't matter. You're missing the point, man. You can't let her go. He wants her dead."

"Why use us? Why didn't he just kill her himself if he wanted her dead?"

"And get blood on his hands? That's not how the rich operate. But I have no doubt he'll kill her if he has to."

Jax leaned against the wall. He felt exhausted. He never should have agreed to this job. He had enough money. But the dollar signs from this job were so big, he'd gotten greedy. It was time for him to quit putting money first.

For the last three months, he'd watched Carrie, studied her, fantasized about her, and now he felt like he owned part of her. He wasn't about to let her die. But how the fuck was he going to tell her about Tate?

"Uh, Jax?" Ben was staring out the front window. "We have a problem."

"No shit. We have a lot of fucking problems."

Pointing out the window, Ben said, "Uh, you might want to take a look at this one. I'm pretty sure that's your car pulling out of the garage."

"What!" He rushed to the window and looked out in time to see his car speeding out of sight down the drive.

"Fuck!" He'd left her alone, he'd untied her. But he hadn't thought she would run. Turning, he shoved Ben out of the way and ran toward the door. He had a feeling that she wasn't going home, and she most likely wasn't going directly to the police. She would go to Tate first, ask him for help. And if she got to him before they got to her, she was dead.

Chapter Twelve

Carrie

Pulling into Tate's driveway, Carrie had barely thrown the gearshift into park before she pulled open the door and rushed out of the car. She banged and banged on Tate's front door.

When he yanked it open, he had a menacing look on his handsome face. But it quickly changed to surprise.

"Tate! Oh, thank God!" She barely registered the look of astonishment on his face and the fact that he had his phone pressed to his ear before she wrapped her arms around him in a relieved hug.

He clicked his phone off immediately and shoved it in his pocket. "Carrie! Are you okay? What happened?"

Relief filled her as he pulled her inside and shut the door. He led her into the family room where a fire was roaring in the fireplace.

"Let me get you a drink," Tate said, helping her sit down on the big leather couch.

Carrie shook her head, her eyes on her fingers as they clenched and twisted around each other. "Tate, I need you to call the police." Her eyes filled with tears.

"The police?" Tate moved over to the bar that held several glass bottles full of amber-colored liquid. "Carrie, what are you talking about?" He calmly filled two glasses with some sort of alcohol and carried them over, shoving one in her face. "I think you need to calm down. Whatever happened, I'm sure you're overreacting."

"Tate! Listen to me!" She shoved his hand away. "I'm serious. It's Jax. He—he—" After uttering his name, she didn't know if she could continue. "I'm so confused." Her words came out on a sob.

"It's okay, Carrie. I won't let him hurt you." As Tate spoke, he walked over to the safe she knew was hidden behind a sliding bookcase.

Shaking her head, she got up and went to Tate's desk, where there was a landline.

"What are you doing?" Worry filled Tate's voice as he made shuffling movements behind her.

"We have to call the police. The painting." She took a deep breath. "Tate, he's working for someone—I don't know who—but they're smuggling art through our gallery." With shaking hands, she began to dial 9-1-1. "We have to contact the police."

Before she could dial the last number, Tate's hand slammed down on the receiver, making her jump. "I can't let you do that, Carrie."

She felt her brow furrow as she looked up at her brother. His blue eyes were filled with an icy cold rage that made her back up in fear. That's when she noticed he held a small pistol, and it was pointed directly at her.

"Tate, what are you..." Her voice trailed off. It suddenly made sense now. All the "borrowed" paintings that seemed to travel in and out of the gallery so quickly. The employee turnover, the odd delivery times, the weird men in business suits that would show up, and all of Tate's money. She knew they'd both inherited well, but she'd thought Tate had just really known how to invest.

"You ... you're smuggling art?" Her entire body trembled. "Tate, why? Is it the money?"

Tate shrugged, but his gun never moved. "The money, sure. But Carrie, it's more than that—it's the power." His eyes glittered in a way she'd never seen, and for the first time, Carrie wondered if her brother was truly insane.

"Carrie," he continued, "I'm one of the most powerful players in the international art community. You have no idea what that's like."

"Tate, it doesn't matter," she said in a hiss-whisper. "This is wrong. Those paintings. They belong in a museum. They're not your personal playthings."

Tate let out a humorless laugh. "God, now you sound like Dad."

"Dad?" Carrie heard the wobbling in her own voice. "Dad knew?"

Tate made a *tsk tsk* sound. "He didn't get it either. He didn't see the big picture. I didn't want to get rid of Mom and Dad, Carrie, but Dad just didn't leave me a choice."

"Get rid of … you killed Mom and Dad?" The tears spilled over. "Tate," she sobbed. "How … how could you?"

"Like I said, I didn't have a choice." He raised the gun and leveled it at her head. "And you don't leave me a choice either, Carrie. I didn't want to do this myself. Jax was supposed to—well, it doesn't matter now. I'm sorry, Carrie. I really am."

He cocked the gun, and she flinched, squeezing her eyes shut.

"Carrie!" A slamming noise followed Jax's voice, and for a second, it sounded like the big bad wolf trying to blow the house down. Then she heard splintering and realized Jax had broken down the door.

"What the fuck?" Tate turned as Jax entered the room. "You're a little too late. I've got this taken care of." Tate leveled his gaze at Jax and sniffed as though he was too good to breathe the same air as him. "And you're paying for my door."

Jax's black eyes found hers, and she thought he sighed in what looked like relief. But she didn't know what to think anymore. Was he here to help Tate? To kill her?

Everything seemed to still for a heartbeat, then Jax made the first to move. Carrie watched as he pulled a gun from his waistband and stepped toward her. A cold sense of dread spread through her. But then, he moved so he stood between her and her brother, and he turned, aiming the gun at Tate.

Both men stood facing each other, pointing their guns directly at the other's chest. Jax backed up and used his free arm to shove Carrie behind his big body.

"What the fuck are you doing?" Tate asked, stunned.

"You're not hurting her." Jax's voice was deadly calm. "You'll have to go through me."

"That's fine with me." Tate leveled his gun.

Carrie squeezed her eyes shut and gripped Jax's waist. She wanted to shove him out of the way, but he was too big, too strong.

A shot rang out, and she flinched back.

She cried out and waited for Jax to fall.

But when she opened her eyes, Jax was turning and gathering her close. Her eyes flew to Tate who lay on the floor, a red stain blooming on his chest.

"Oh God. Oh God." She buried her face in Jax's chest.

"Shhh, it's okay, love. It's okay. No one's going to hurt you now. Everything's going to be okay."

But how? How was anything ever going to be okay again?

Chapter Thirteen

Jax
A few weeks later…

The coffee machine bubbled and gurgled to life as Jax stood in his kitchen and watched it. For the first time in his life, he hadn't run. Instead, after the night that had turned his entire world upside down, he'd waited. Once they were sure Tate was dead, Carrie had forced him to leave before the police had arrived.

After a quick goodbye to his partner, Ben had left town in a rush. His partner had tried to persuade Jax to leave town with him, but he hadn't. The only place he wanted to be was here, near Carrie. In some ways, he felt responsible for her, and he probably always would.

Carrying two cups of coffee down the hall, he turned and walked into the dungeon.

"It's about time. My God, you're slow to make coffee." Carrie was turning into quite the little brat.

He sat both cups of coffee down on the smooth black table and picked his favorite flogger off the wall, admiring the way his girl looked. She stood against a St. Andrew's cross, black straps binding her naked form. "Is that how you talk to me, sub?"

He loved the way those blue eyes widened as he walked over to her and brushed the flogger gently over her body.

"I'm sorry, Sir." She shivered lightly, but he was learning her body quite well, and he knew it wasn't because she was cold. No, when her little pussy got wet, shivers of excitement ran through her luscious curves. "You have to admit this is a little strange, though. You tie me to a St. Andrew's cross, turn the TV on to CNN, and then leave the room?" She shook her head in confusion. "I know I have a lot to learn, but I'm pretty sure that's not some weird sex thing … at least, I don't think it is."

"Stop talking, love, or I'll gag you."

"Gag me, but I—" Carrie gasped as Jax pulled her close and rubbed his erection against her. He only wore a pair of sweats, and his cock was trying as hard as it could to break through that barrier and get to her.

Before she could say another word, he grasped her face in both hands and crushed his mouth to hers. His tongue forced its way through her lips, taking what he wanted. Oh, she was his, all right. He just needed to make sure she knew it.

When he heard the voice on the TV, he broke the kiss, leaving her breathless, and turned, grabbing the remote and turning up the volume.

"Jax, what—"

"Shh, I have a surprise for you."

As the news reporter began to talk about The Concert, Carrie focused on the TV with rapt attention.

"... and the art world is shrouded in mystery today as a stolen painting—Johannes Vermeer's The Concert—was returned earlier this morning to the Isabella Stewart Gardner Museum, the same place where it was stolen from in 1990. When the museum's director came into work this morning, he found the painting prominently displayed on a wall in the museum, near where it once hung. There is no word on who returned the painting, or how the benefactor even got into the museum. Authorities are investigating."

Carrie's eyes shot to him. "Jax … you … but…"

He reached up to trace a finger over her lips, and gave her a little smile. "You're not speechless very often, love."

"But, why? I thought, I thought—"

He stopped her with a quick headshake. "It was the right thing to do. Being around you … well, let's just say that you make me want to do the right thing."

Carrie's eyes shone with tears as she regarded him.

Pulling her close, Jax buried his face in her hair. The scent of strawberries must be what heaven smelled like. As long as he lived, he'd never get tired of her sweet, delicious scent.

His plan had been to untie her and make her breakfast, but he needed an appetizer first. He raised his head to look down at her, and then dropped a quick kiss on her mouth before kneeling in front of her.

Her little gasp made him smile. "I thought we were going to have coffee."

He raised his eyes to hers, giving her a wicked grin. Then his tongue snaked out, tracing a circle just above her smooth mound. "I have other ideas."

"But—but, the coffee will get cold," Carrie said breathlessly.

"Don't worry, baby." He gripped her buttocks, dragging her lower body forward to meet his mouth. "I have other ways to heat you up."

Her cries were music to his ears as he licked and sucked her pussy until her sweet nectar flooded his mouth. She was his. He could keep her tied up right there, and make her come all day long.

And that was just the beginning.

The End

www.njyoungauthor.wordpress.com

THE SHADOW

Elena Kincaid

Copyright© 2016

Chapter One

He came out of nowhere, like a shadow hiding in pitch darkness.

"Help! No!" Emily continued to scream and kick, but the sound was muffled underneath the Shadow's powerful gloved hand, her feet dangling as he lifted her against him.

"Shut the fuck up or this won't end well for you," he spoke quietly, voice deadly, in her ear.

How had he managed to make such an ominous threat sound almost seductive though? Maybe she was losing it. Who in their right mind in any case could find their captors voice enticing? The adrenaline, the fear, was making her thoughts irrational.

Only moments ago, while she rode the subway home after work, she felt eyes watching her. Invisible eyes on a crowded New York City train, no one actually making contact, but she *felt* them peering into her. She still saw no one watching her when the crowd began and continued to thin out as the train neared the end of the line. And when she stepped out of the train, the sole passenger to get off, she waited for the eerie sounds of footsteps behind her, but they never came.

Paranoia, she had tried to convince herself. It had been two years after all, since the restraining order. Why would Louis have waited this long to grab her if that was his purpose all along? No, he was a man filled with pride, a pride he cherished more than his enormous power. He had wanted her to come back to him willingly.

She rushed down the steps of the elevated train station and only when her foot hit the very last step did she realize that her paranoia had not been paranoia at all. Ice cold fear traveled through her veins as her Shadow lifted her and held her tightly against his solid, muscular frame, one iron-like vise around her waist, and a black-gloved hand covering her mouth. Her muffled curses and yells did nothing but piss off her antagonist. And as if she weighed nothing, he carried her toward a black SUV parked close to the stairway. Emily spied a few people across the street, just coming off the train on the other side, but they all went about their evening completely oblivious to what was happening just several feet away from them.

Meanwhile various thoughts raced through her mind. The most prominent of which, she had to keep fighting no matter how much angrier *he* became, because she was pretty certain that if he got her into that car, it would be the end of her. And once again, Louis popped into her mind. Could he be behind her abduction despite the fact that this was so not his style? If he had really wanted to take her, she pictured him pulling up in a dark limo, two goon-sized guards grabbing one of each of her arms and walking her toward said limo, and the car door opening to reveal Louis sitting casually inside with an arrogant smile on his face. Perhaps then this was just a case of being in the wrong place at the wrong time. If only she hadn't stayed two hours late after work today, it would have been someone else playing the role of a helpless victim. She then immediately felt bad about wishing her fate, whatever *it* may end up being, on someone else.

Helpless victim. Emily thought about those words and decided that, yes, she most certainly is a victim, but helpless … no. She was angry. She would not go down without a fight. Be more trouble than you're worth, she thought. Isn't that what all the self-defense classes and police officers who lecture safety at schools teach you?

The Shadow's hand reached for the handle to the backseat of the SUV and in her last ditch effort to free herself from his clutches, she head butted him with the back of her skull. She thought she heard a crunch underneath and she definitely felt something hot and wet on her neck.

"Mother-fucking fucker!" He shoved her hard against the car. "You bitch," he said in her ear, sounding like it was through gritted teeth.

She had hurt him. It seemed that not only had he pinned her against the car, but that he was leaning on her for support. Still, her plan amounted to completely nothing except for the satisfaction of causing him pain. His hold on her never even wavered slightly, which scared her even more. Emily wondered if he was some kind of pro at kidnapping. *Oh god*! *What if this is some kind of sex slave thing?*

"I'm not even that pretty," she cried out. She had been so busy with work lately that she'd been skipping her yoga classes. Sure she had a decent body and considered herself attractive with her mid-shoulder length curly blonde locks and sea-foam green eyes, but her thighs were meaty, her stomach soft and round, and she could definitely use a haircut, and further grooming everywhere else. There was nothing about her that should have stood out, not even to a man like Louis.

"What?" He sounded surprised before his ire returned in full force. "Do that again, princess and the next time I hit back. Consider yourself lucky it's not broken."

His threat made her body tremble. She could only imagine what a hit from him would feel like. If his iron hold on her was any indication of his strength, not to mention the fact that he barely flinched when she head butted him despite how badly it must have hurt, she knew his punches would definitely not feel like love taps.

"I'm s—sorry. Please, just let me go." Fighting didn't work. Maybe begging would.

"No. And I said shut up!" He pulled her against him, opened the backseat door, and shoved her inside, face down on the back seat. "You need to start following instructions, princess, or things will go far worse for you." The car door slammed before he finished his sentence.

"She got you good, didn't she?" another man's voice came from the front seat with a chuckle. "Try not to get any on my leather."

Fuck, there were two of them!

"Drive," ordered her Shadow. His tone was completely cool despite the fact that she still felt his blood trickling against her as he tied her hands firmly behind her back. He must have been a Boy Scout, too, she pondered, with how expertly he tied her hands in some sort of intricate knot. The rope he used felt thin and surprisingly pleasant as if made from some soft fabric. She managed to turn her head to the side, but had no time to take in her surroundings when he blindfolded her. Her legs were pushed further into herself to make room for him in the back seat.

This was it, she thought. She wasn't the praying type, but if begging didn't work on her emotionless abductor, perhaps a higher power might hear her and intervene. She couldn't help the whimper that escaped her. "Please," she whispered.

"Hmmm." Shadow seemed to be pondering something. "I didn't think I'd enjoy you tied up and begging, but surprisingly I do."

Another chuckle from the peanut gallery had Shadow's slightly softened tone hardening again. "You just can't follow simple instructions, can you, Cal?"

No, no, no, no, no. She hadn't seen their faces yet, knew nothing about these two men. There may be some small chance of survival if she couldn't identify them. But Shadow carelessly using the driver's name meant only one thing—they were going to kill her. Surely, he would have been more discreet if he had planned on letting her go.

"I said drive!"

Chapter Two

The car pulled to a stop. Emily had no idea how long it took for them to arrive at their destination. She remained terrified of what actually waited for her there and was too consumed with horrific scenarios to take note of time. In any case, fear tends to often make time seem prolonged.

The engine cut off, two car doors opened, and Shadow pulled her to him. Within seconds she found herself being thrown over his shoulder in a fireman's hold, her hands still tied behind her back. She heard gravel crunching beneath his feet before he must have stepped on a smoother surface. She heard the driver, Cal, go ahead of them and open a door and then Shadow carried her straight inside, the winter chill turning into warmth. Another door opened and down the stairs Shadow carried her.

Emily's heart thumped loudly in her chest as he set her down on a bed. He undid her coat, took off her hat and gloves, and redid the ties on her hands, binding them in more intricate knots to the bed. She was lost in the darkness, pondering just how hazardous her Shadow would turn out to be. He kidnapped another human being and yet remained steady and cool like he did this every day. *Which he probably did.* He breathed heavy as he tied more intricate knots, this time binding her ankles together. Yet again, the ropes felt surprisingly pleasant. Maybe now was not the time though to discover that she had a fetish for being tied up, but it seemed that her Shadow was definitely getting off on it too.

"You're enjoying this?" Emily couldn't help but ask.

A slight pause on his part, one she may have missed had she not been so attuned to him at the moment. "Yes."

At least he didn't tell her to shut up this time, she thought. Maybe she could get some answers and decided to tread carefully. "Do you tie women up a lot?" Emily's voice quavered as she spoke.

"I do. To the women who beg me to," he replied matter-of-factly but Emily didn't miss the slight tremble in Shadow's voice either.

"But *I* didn't beg you to."

Another quick pause in his ministrations. He remained quiet while he finished binding her legs. After he finished with the ropes, the bed dipped as he sat beside her. She felt his breath near her face when he next spoke. "I am making an exception." His voice altered from speaking softly to her, sounding slightly aroused, to deadly steel in seconds when he added, "The fact that I like seeing you tied up like this changes nothing."

"Please, just let me go," she pleaded. The ice in his voice terrified her.

His response was an emotionless "no."

Somehow she knew that pleading would amount to nothing, his coldness indicative of that. And his anger at being turned on by her was completely baffling. After all, wasn't that the point of kidnapping her? What could he possibly want from her if not to rape or to sell her to someone who would? She certainly didn't come from money. The living she made as an accountant, though quite decent, did not make her a Rockefeller. She came from an average middle-class family with parents who had kids later in life and were both living in a retirement community now.

"I won't tell anyone." She had to keep trying, at the very least to find out why he kidnapped her. Being prepared was at least better than not, she supposed. "I didn't see your face, I can't ident—"

And then he pulled off her blindfold.

Her eyes widened. She felt like Psyche for a moment, forbidden to see the face of Cupid and yet she would have wanted nothing more, even though in this case it most likely had led to her death. To say this man was as beautiful as he was frightening was an understatement. Cupid may have even been envious of the Shadow with his mess of rich brown curls hanging down to his collar bone, striking gunmetal eyes, a perfect aquiline nose, a strong square jawline, and full lips with a natural pout. She figured he must have wiped the blood off his face in the car since she saw no visible traces of it. The chest he had held her against looked as firm as she imagined with visibly defined muscles bulging through his scoop-necked black ribbed sweater.

His chuckle startled her out of her ogling state and his face remained beautiful even when his lips curved into a cruel smile. "I know I'm pretty to look at, but I imagine you'll soon hate the sight of me."

"Why?" She whispered. "Why me?"

"Payback!"

With that, he got up and left the room, a room that looked like it was part of a finished basement. She had no time to really take in her surroundings since he turned off the lights on his way up the stairs, plunging her back into complete darkness.

Chapter Three

"Fuck," Brody Beckett mumbled as he entered the kitchen.

"You're letting that bitch get to you?" Cal snapped. "Don't get all soft on me, Brody. We've been planning this shit for too long."

Brody walked toward Cal slowly, like a predator stalking his prey. "Soft?" he roared into the significantly shorter man's face. "Soft, motherfucker? You had one job and you pussied out. I had to step in and do it for you."

"She changed her s-schedule," Cal stuttered, backing away from Brody. "What was I supposed to do?"

"Exactly what we've been planning for the last four fucking months," Brody roared again. "You adapt, asshole."

Brody pinched the bridge of his nose to calm himself down. It wasn't like him to lose his cool in front of anyone. He'd always been good at keeping his emotions in check. And Cal was right. This girl had gotten under his skin. His emotions were warring inside of him with exactly how much damage to do to her ever since Cal started gathering intel and bringing him photos of Emily Renard. One particular image haunted him ever since he blew it up to enlarge her face. Haunting green eyes had stared back at him for months, as if even then they had been pleading with him not to hurt her. The way her wide eyes had looked at him downstairs had his dick hardening even more than when he was tying her up, something else that shocked the hell out of him. She of all people should not be having that effect on him, especially from what he saw of her in the video. Payback *is* going to be a bitch, he thought, haunting eyes be damned.

"Go get everything ready," Brody ordered Cal in a more even tone. "Can you handle that at least, you chicken shit?"

Cal nodded and left the room. Calvin Dunne had just as much reason for doing this as he did, but he should have known better than to trust that unskilled weasel with any of the actual heavy lifting. And Brody suspected that Cal started using again after the death of his brother. A strung out junkie hell bent on revenge could easily make things go south for the both of them. Brody may have been just as hell bent on revenge, but at least he wasn't a drug addict. He relied on his control too much for that.

His cell phone rang. "Is it done, Beckett?" Stephen Nowicki, a man Brody loved and trusted like a brother, asked. Other than Stephen, there were only four others that Brody trusted in this world, and he had no doubt that his former Navy Seal brothers were on standby, waiting for all the shit to go down.

"I went and got her myself," Brody replied.

"I knew that little prick had no balls!"

"Make the call, Nowicki."

"Done. ETA for first video?"

Brody thought for a moment. "Give me an hour," he said before disconnecting the call. A short little video every hour should do the trick, he thought.

Brody imagined how the conversation between Stephen and the scum drug lord Carter would go as he went over to the sink to try and get the blood out of his black leather jacket.

She's going to pay for that one, too.

Right about now, Nowicki was informing him that they had the girl and for every hour that Carter did not deliver his right-hand man, Zeke Fallow, to face justice—to be delivered by Brody and Cal, of course—Emily would be the one to suffer for it.

She deserves it as much as Fallow, he tried to convince himself.

"Shit!" he muttered, breathing heavily. He nearly scrubbed a hole in his black leather jacket trying to get all the blood out.

After blotting the jacket nearly dry, he walked over to the small kitchen table and draped it over one chair while taking a seat in another. He rested his elbows on the table and placed his head in his hands, fisting his unruly curly locks. His phone buzzed again. A text this time.

Stephen Nowicki: **Not the reaction I expected. When I told him we had his girl, he seemed almost unconcerned. He said he'd think about it.**

Brody Beckett: **Wtf! He'll change his tune after the first video.**

Brody angrily shoved the phone back into his pocket and slammed his fist down hard on the table. He'd make her bleed! Maybe that would make Carter more *concerned*. Just then he heard a piercing scream coming from downstairs and immediately picked himself up and rushed to the basement.

The lights were back on, a video camera sat on a tripod by the bed aimed directly at Emily, and that fucker Calvin had his hand down her pants. Emily's shirt was ripped open, revealing a boring white cotton bra. She was thrashing and struggling against the ropes but to no avail.

"That's enough, Cal," Brody commanded. When Calvin ignored his order, Brody lost his cool composure. He walked over to Cal and yanked his hand out of Emily's pants and shoved the smaller man off to the side. Only then did Emily stop struggling.

"The fun's not over yet, princess," Brody sneered looking directly into her grateful eyes. She had absolutely nothing to be grateful for.

Brody took out the knife he kept holstered to his side. He watched as Emily's eyes had widened once again with fear, completely obliterating the tiny sliver of hope she must have felt. There was only one way out of this for her, but even if she made it out, it would not be unscathed.

"Oh God," she whispered zeroing in on the knife, tears streaming down her face.

"God can't help you now!" He paused for a moment, tilting his head to the side, remembering something she had blurted out when he held her against the SUV. "What did you mean earlier when you said 'I'm not that pretty'?"

She shook heard quickly as a response.

"I don't like repeating myself, Emily. I asked you a question."

"How do you know my—"

"I'm the one asking the questions here," he cut her off, growing impatient. She would not keep defying him. He placed the knife to her throat, the tip of it causing only a little sting, he imagined, but enough to see a small trickle of blood forming. Carter would not be privy to their conversation when he received the footage, but the footage would get the point across nicely.

"Do I need to ask you again, princess?"

She shook her head. "For your … for your sex slave ring?"

Brody couldn't help but laugh at that. Not only did her response come out as a question, but here she thought he was going to sell her into slavery and to top it all off, she didn't think she was pretty enough. "On the contrary, princess, you're quite pretty." She let out a small whimper when he pushed the tip of the knife further and added, "For now."

He felt his stomach churn when he remembered the video in his possession featuring another woman, tied to a bed, taunted about how pretty she was ... *for now*.

Brody pulled the knife away from Emily's throat and walked over to where Calvin stood by the camera. He powered it off and then with a smirk, he wiped off the small amount of blood on Cal's shirt. "I've had enough blood on my clothes for one day."

Brody removed the camera from the tripod and nudged Calvin forward to head up the stairs. When they reached the top, through gritted teeth Brody said, "She's mine to deal with. You get me?"

"I have just as much—"

"You can have Fallow." He handed him the camera before deadpanning, "Touch Fallow all you want."

"Fuck you!"

"No thanks," Brody replied with a chuckle. "Get this to Stephen." When Cal hesitated, Brody put his hand on the man's shoulder. "Focus, Cal. It'll be over soon." This time Cal nodded.

Brody turned from him and headed back downstairs. He wasn't finished with her yet. When he reached the bed, he sat down by her side. He didn't bother covering her up and unabashedly let his eyes roam down her scantily clad torso.

So she didn't think she was that pretty, huh? That certainly explained some things and confused him with others.

"Is it your turn now?" she asked him bitingly.

"Somehow I think you would enjoy it if it was *my turn*." The proof of his statement was given when with just the tips of his fingers, he brushed across her skin from between her breasts down to her belly button. Goosebumps appeared where he touched her, her pupils dilated, and her cheeks, which were ghostly pale before, bloomed a rosy blush.

"It's like you said ... you're pretty to look at," she retorted. "Doesn't mean I want you to touch me."

"This isn't about what you want, princess." He had to admit he liked her feistiness. He removed his hand from her stomach, but he could have sworn he saw a flicker of disappointment when he did so. "This is about what I want!"

"What do you want from me?"

"I want you to bleed," he began, watching as her face once again contorted in fear, "I want you to hurt," he continued as more tears stained her once again pale cheeks, "and most of all, I want Carter to see every moment of it."

"Louis?" His name came out as a whisper on her lips, but after she had said it, all traces of fear were wiped away, replaced by sheer disgust and hatred. And then she spat in his face.

He wrapped his hand around her throat, but she continued to stare at him with disgust instead of fear.

"Do that again, and your boyfriend won't get you back in one piece."

He removed his hand from her throat, wiped the spit from his face, and turned from her without a second glance. It was time to go check in with Stephen anyway. They had about forty-five minutes before the next video and things were going to get rougher for Miss Renard. He turned off the light again on his way up, plunging her back into darkness. He knew all too well how someone's own thoughts could be an enemy.

Chapter Four

It all made sense now. Two years and still she could not shake Louis. He may not have been the one to take her, but she was being used for ransom it seemed. She wondered if Shadow could be a rival drug lord and somehow learned of Louis's obsession for her. Payback, he had said. He wanted to use her, hurt her, make her bleed, as he had put it, and then after all of that, if she made it through alive, he was just going to hand her over. Louis would never let her go then. He'd convince himself she needed his protection, satisfying his pride, and she'd never be free of him. Maybe she'd be better off if Shadow ended up killing her after all.

And damn her Shadow for being right. Her body had responded to him from the moment he touched her. *What's wrong with me?* She felt a tightening in her belly from his touch, a touch so gentle and in complete contrast to his harshly spoken words and knife wielding ways.

The worst part of all of this was that she had no one to blame but herself. Out of pettiness she allowed Louis to pursue her, knowing full well that he had been heavily involved with something illegal. She just hadn't known how high up in the ranks he placed or that after a few months of being charming, he'd turn into a possessive control freak with an unhealthy obsession for her. He had hit her when she *misbehaved,* meaning when she had threatened to leave him. He had used up his last straw when he bent her over a table, hiked up her skirt, ripped of her panties, and forcibly took her in front of some of his men. All in the name of discipline, he had said.

She got help. She got out. Shadow, the bastard, had just dragged her back in.

Emily heard footsteps coming down the stairs. The other one, Cal, had let slip that they were going to be making a video every hour, so she deduced that roughly an hour must have passed. She immediately squinted her eyes when Shadow turned on the light and braced herself for another round of his sick game.

Emily did not have to wait too long to find out what would happen next. Wordlessly, he set up the small digital camera, like the other one had done, and came to sit beside her on the bed again. Her only consolation was that the short, strung-out-looking one with greasy hair and fish breath wasn't there with him this time. She still felt his cold slimy fingers inside of her anatomy and remembered tasting bile when he first shoved them inside of her.

"Let's test my theory, shall we?" Shadow asked cruelly. Once again, with only a feather light touch, he trailed his fingertips up and down her exposed flesh. Involuntarily, her hips lifted off the bed to receive more of his touch. She shivered and he laughed smugly.

His hands roamed further down until they reached the waistband of her dark blue slacks. He toyed with her, slipping his fingers inside her pants to just the very tip of her pubic hair and then back up, until finally, on his next pass, he spread her pussy lips with his ring and index finger and shoved his middle finger inside her core. He gave her another smug smile. "You're very wet, princess."

She was. She could sense it and she felt ashamed.

As if her Shadow became aware of her shame, his smile fell away and he removed his fingers and stopped touching her completely. He looked angry. He got up wordlessly and left the room again, taking the camera with him.

The next time he came downstairs, he resumed her pleasurable torture, and the next, and the next, each time playing her body more boldly and bringing her to the brink before leaving her unsatisfied. He massaged her bra-clad breasts in turn while his other hand flitted around her pussy, picking up quickly on all of her sweet spots. Two fingers massaged the front wall while his thumb drew small circles around her clit. His movements were masterful, relentless, like a good lover about to deliver an earth-shattering orgasm to his woman. It seemed he could sense when she was just moments away from achieving ecstasy despite Emily trying to stubbornly hold back and she would have come hard for him had he not immediately ceased his actions. After giving her a few minutes to cool off, he resumed the same torment. Over and over, impossibly bringing her to the brink each time, and then stopping right before she could climax.

"Stop it!" she cried out. "Please just stop it." The last plea was only a whisper, followed by more tears and whimpering. Truth be told, she wasn't sure if she was begging him to stop touching her, or to finally let her come.

Despite her outburst, Shadow, however, seemed less angry … more satisfied with what he had caught on camera this time she assumed. She had remained obstinate, giving no emotion away the last few rounds, so her breakdown would no doubt entice Louis to come *rescue* her.

Shadow took the camera and left the room again wordlessly. This time he left the light on for her. Whether by accident or on purpose, she could not be certain, though she concluded that he never did anything by accident. He had given her a small reward.

She finally took in her surroundings. It looked like a small studio apartment in a basement, minus a kitchen and it definitely had a hint of a feminine touch, particularly the design of the bed. She lay on a queen-sized bed with a metal head and foot board with some flowery design. The bedding was a dark plum with slightly lighter stripes going across it. To the left of her, she saw a small brown sofa and coffee table facing an entertainment unit with a large flat-screen television. A few nick knacks, books, and DVDs were haphazardly placed on it. She also noticed a video game console on the floor.

Emily wondered at which of the men, if either of them, had lived there and she couldn't help the sudden flash of jealousy that overtook her when the image of her Shadow shacking up with some woman entered her mind. She quashed that thought immediately. *Is there no end to my insanity?*

Another hour must have passed. The now familiar sound of Shadow's footsteps came barreling down the stairs. *Oh shit!* He was fuming this time. She had a sinking feeling in the pit of her stomach that this wasn't going to be like the last few times.

"He wants to fucking test me!" Shadow roared. "No more fucking games."

He set the camera up quickly. When he came over to the bed, he didn't sit this time. Instead, he loosened the bindings around her wrists, placed his large hand at the nape of her neck and lifted her into an almost seated position. He held the knife at her throat and pushed the tip in a little further than the last time, causing her to cry out in pain.

"Please, please."

"Please what, princess? Suddenly you're not a fan of knives?"

She didn't understand. "I don't … this is between you and Louis … I have nothing—" She cried out louder as he pushed the tip even further. It may have still only been a superficial wound, but it fucking hurt. She felt her blood trickling down her neck to her chest.

He shoved her down hard on the mattress and tightened her bindings. "The next time I leave scars."

He left the room, plunging her back into darkness, his threat lingering in her ears.

Chapter Five

The next time I leave scars. She changed her mind. He *was* as beautiful as he was cruel. He wanted payback for something, that part he made clear, but he wanted to hurt her too. And he got angry at himself whenever he showed signs of remorse about it. Why did he hate her so much? She may have partially gotten herself into this mess by being completely naïve and stupid, but whatever Louis had been guilty of doing to Shadow, she was innocent of.

"Oh God," she whispered when she heard Shadow's footsteps again. She braced herself for more pain.

"Time to go, princess."

Again, she felt confused. "Go?" He was letting her go?

He quickly undid the knots on her ankles and then freed her from the headboard, pulling her up to a seated position. The buttons of her shirt were haphazardly scattered around the room, making Emily wonder if her Shadow would take her out of there looking like that. Surprisingly, he undid the bindings around her wrists long enough to put on her coat. He even zipped it up before tying her wrists again, this time with her hands in front of her.

"Your boyfriend it seems has wised up. I am taking you back to him, only a little bit worse for wear, which is far better than you deserve."

"No!" she yelled in his face. Better than she deserved? "You cruel son of a bitch! What the fuck did I ever do to you?"

Now he seemed confused and then the anger returned. "That little miss innocent act may work on some, but it sure as fuck doesn't work on me. Sheila was my sister."

"I don't know your sister. I have nothing to do with—"

She flinched when it looked as if he was about to backhand her across the face. "I'd shut up now if I were you and count your blessings."

"Blessings?" Emily laughed sarcastically. "If you call Louis a blessing, I wonder what you would deem a curse."

She only had a few seconds to see confusion mar his features once again before he blindfolded her. And just like he had done before, Shadow threw her over his shoulder and carried her up the stairs and out of the house. This time when he put her in the back seat of what she assumed was the same SUV, he let her sit upright.

She had lost concept of time yet again. The Shadow commanded Cal to drive without telling him where to go. He also gave some clipped instructions to someone named Nowicki over the phone, none of which she could make sense of. None of it made any difference anyway. Wherever they were taking her, Louis would be at the destination waiting.

When the car finally pulled to a stop, Emily considered the possibility that her heart might beat out of her chest with how wildly it was thumping. Tears spilled out from underneath her blindfold. Shadow removed it suddenly and looked into her eyes. Wordlessly, he turned from her, opened the car door, and stepped outside, going around to let her out on the other side.

"Let's go," he ordered, his voice not as harsh as it had been in the basement.

Shadow tugged the ropes on her wrists, urging her out of the car. She complied and he expertly undid the ropes around her writs in a matter of seconds. When he finished, they remained standing a breath away from each other. She looked up at him and whispered, "It would have been kinder if you had just killed me."

For the first time since they had arrived, Emily took in their surroundings. She knew exactly where she was, one of Louis's warehouses in Downtown Brooklyn. He had made her wait in the car several times while they were dating whenever he needed to pop in to conduct some quick *business*.

She turned away from Shadow, not being able to stand the sight of his beautiful, cruel face any longer and began to walk toward the building, but he tugged her gently back. She turned to face him. "What? It's this way isn't it?"

"You would rather I killed you than delivered you to your boyfriend?"

He looked really taken aback by her earlier comment. "He's not my boyfriend. He's a drug lord, a thug, and one of the cruelest men I have ever known. Maybe second only to you."

"But I saw pictures of you with—"

Cal stepped out of the car just then, interrupting their conversation. She had seen Cal take a phone call when she and Shadow first stepped out of the car. "They're waiting. The team is in place."

Emily walked forward, but instead of stopping her again, Shadow kept pace beside her. When the three of them stepped inside the large open entryway of the building, only Louis and Fallow awaited them inside. She figured some of Louis's men were lurking close by—he certainly wasn't stupid enough to be without backup. Shadow's team was hidden as well.

Louis tilted his head to the side and came a little closer. When he stood only a few feet away, he clapped his hands together, threw his head back and laughed, startling Shadow and Cal in the process.

"It is you," Louis said after his laughter subsided. "Turning, to Shadow he added, "My apologies, Mr. Beckett. Had I known you had *her*, I would have made the trade immediately."

Then everything came out in a rush.

"I sent you videos," Shadow informed blandly.

At the same time, Emily wondered if Louis had been receiving the videos made of her in the basement, otherwise how could he not have known. *Unless ... It couldn't be...*

Meanwhile, Fallow had turned ghostly white. "Boss?" You said you were going to laugh in his face, tell him you didn't want her ... You were going to kill them all?"

More men started pouring in at Fallow's revelation, armed and dangerous men belonging to each side.

"He's all yours," Louis announced cheerfully and held out his hand toward Emily. "Come here, my love."

She turned to Shadow—though now he at least had a last name, Beckett—and with her eyes pleading, she begged her abductor to become her savior. His confused eyes stared back at her, yet he remained unmoving.

Fallow pleaded and cursed at the obvious betrayal. Louis's own men had handed him over to Shadow's men. He should have known he'd be expendable, right-hand man or not. Everyone was expendable to Louis, maybe save Emily, but then again, she was more possession than person to him. Fallow was forced down on his knees and held there by Shadow's men. Cal had a gun drawn to the man's temple. He was going to execute him.

"Come to me, Emily, or I shall come to you."

Emily feared what Louis's command entailed, worse still, what he would do to her in front of her Shadow if she disobeyed him. The shame she had felt the last time Louis punished her overwhelmed her now. She didn't want *him* of all people to see her like that. She turned from her Shadow and walked to Louis as he had ordered. He wrapped her tightly in a hug, his very scent producing even more painful memories.

When he released her from his suffocating embrace, he maintained a tight hold around her torso. "I will forgive the videos, Mr. Beckett as I am partially to blame for the delayed response. You have reunited me with my love, so today we shall part as friends."

She looked at her Shadow one last time as Louis steered her toward the front entrance, armed bodyguards in tow. "Monster." She had only whispered the word, but by his pained expression, he had heard her loud and clear.

"Oh, and for the record," Louis turned his head and spoke directly to Shadow before exiting the warehouse, "I did not order a hit on Mr. Dunne's brother or your sister, Mr. Beckett. Zeke had a personal vendetta against him and your sister was collateral damage. You have pleased me immensely today, so I'll even throw in the other one when I find her. I have no tolerance for whores who snitch."

"No!" Emily yelled. He simply rolled his eyes at her and escorted her out of the building—the sun had just started to rise—to what she knew would be a far worse fate than the one she had endured for the past ten hours.

Chapter Six

Monster. Her one simple whisper echoed loudly in his ears, continued to reverberate through his brain. A whisper which to him became loud and accusing, forcing him to overanalyze the word. He started out fighting monsters, justified his revenge because it would still be the monsters that paid his price. Only he had become one of them in the process. And if he was being honest with himself, he hadn't felt the slightest bit remorseful until accusing, haunting green eyes had made him examine, doubt, his own actions. Brody was about to stand idly by and watch the execution of an unarmed man. Granted, Fallow murdered Tyler, Cal's bother, and left Brody's sister Sheila to bleed to death, but this was not the way to dole out justice. It was cold-blooded murder.

And Brody realized in that moment what had been nagging at him since he had kidnapped Emily Renard. In his haste for justice he had missed, or had been led to miss, a huge piece of the puzzle. *I'll even throw in the other one.* Emily appeared terrified of Carter. She hadn't looked the part of doting girlfriend in person, not like she did in the photographs Cal had brought him. Doting girlfriends did not wish for death instead of being returned to their boyfriends, in one piece no less. Nothing added up … *she* did not add up.

"Wait!" Brody yelled in attempt to halt Fallow's execution, but it was too late. Cal had pulled the trigger simultaneously.

Fallow fell to the floor in a pool of blood and all Brody could do was stand there and stare at the dead man. His death did not bring Sheila back, nor did it make her passing any less painful. He grew a conscience way too late it seemed.

"Emily." Brody whispered her name while remaining frozen on the spot. How differently her name sounded now on his lips without the hatred he thought he felt for her. "Emily," he said louder, snapping himself out of his trance.

Cal and the others looked up at him. "What is it, Beckett?" Nowicki asked.

"I can't let him have her."

"It's too late, man. We made a deal."

"Don't tell me you're going all soft for a piece of ass?" Tanner, another one of his Navy Seal brothers, chimed in.

Brody didn't bother answering, prompting his brothers to return to the task at hand—taking care of the body and all the evidence that went with it. He did not hold Tanner's remark against him. After all, Tanner and the rest did this all for him, all to help him avenge his sister. He would have done the same for anyone of them, no questions asked, so he knew that they would understand what his next move would be, and that he would take the blame for it alone. He couldn't let his brothers become targets for Carter even though realistically, going after Emily meant taking Carter out and leaving his Navy Seal brothers with more blood on their hands. He would not ask that of them.

"Don't even think about it, Beckett." Crawford spoke up. Out of all of his brothers, Crawford always knew what Brody was thinking, sometimes even Brody himself knew his next move. "You can't take Carter alone."

Grunts of approval came from the rest. All but Calvin, who remained with his head bowed down. The man did just pull the trigger, ending someone's life, but he imagined that Cal felt much the same as Brody did. He didn't look like a man experiencing relief. Furthermore,

Cal *was* going to answer for the poor intel he brought Brody later. Now all Brody could think about was rescuing Emily.

He ran out of the building in time to see the direction Carter had sped off in. Brody jumped into Cal's SUV, while Nowicki hopped on his Duckati. Tanner and Crawford got in another SUV, while the rest stayed behind in the warehouse. They'd have to meet up later, if rescuing Emily proved successful, and discuss how to deal with Carter. After today, he would be after all of their blood. And as much as Brody wanted to tell them to stay out of it, Crawford was right. He couldn't get to Emily alone, no matter how good and efficient he was at retrievals.

They sped off in Carter's direction, turning on their com links. Keeping a healthy distance, they debated what the best approach would be, one of which was to cut them off on the road, force them to pull over, and grab Emily before Carter's other men, also in separate vehicles, had a chance to intervene. Brody and his men were heavily armed, but as of now they were outnumbered.

He had studied Carter for months, knew his patterns and that of his men. Grabbing Emily once they reached Carter's estate would prove even more difficult as it was heavily guarded at all times. Over the com, Brody brought up the optimal times to break into the estate. He and his men were in middle of formulating a plan to briefly disable the security system once Carter had gone to bed, even though the thought of Emily having to spend one night with Carter felt nauseating, when an opportunity presented itself.

"Car two is veering off," Nowicki informed, speeding ahead of them. Carter must have been pretty confident that matters had in fact been settled otherwise he never would have left himself so vulnerable.

"We got number one," came Tanner's voice. He and Crawford were about to cut off the other vehicle, leaving its passenger's blind to Brody's next move until it became too late for them to intervene. Retaliation would definitely be imminent, but they'd have time to plan once they got Emily to a safe house.

Brody waited for the signal.

"Go!" Tanner and Crawford had succeeded in cutting off the other vehicle. Now he just needed to wait for Nowicki's intel.

"Two armed up front," Nowicki notified. "Carter and the female in the backseat."

Nowicki would have to take the two armed men, leaving Brody to deal with Carter first before grabbing Emily. Brody sped up now as Nowicki's bike came dangerously close to the driver's side of their dark Lexus. It worked. The driver, distracted, veered off to the right.

"Shot out tires of car number one," came Tanner's voice.

"The fuckers were pissing us off," said Crawford. "Heading your way now. Keep 'em busy."

A few minutes later, Tanner and Sawyer cut off Carter's car then shot out more tires. The car swerved violently and ended up facing opposing traffic, but safely on the shoulder of the freeway. Nowicki was quick enough to get to the passenger side and knock out the other goon in the passenger seat before he had time to shoot him. Tanner quickly knocked out Carter—shooting him in broad daylight on a busy highway was not an option—while Brody grabbed Emily and basically shoved her in his car. The whole rescue may have been a lot messier than Brody would have liked, but damn if it wasn't quicker.

Once moving again, Brody said nothing at first and neither did Emily, but he saw in his peripheral vision that Emily had put on her seatbelt. Only after Tanner, Crawford, and Nowicki were safely away from the scene, did he speed up. He'd catch up with them all later at a different safe house, but for now, he needed to get Emily out of harm's way.

"Why did you do that?" Emily stared straight ahead as she asked. "He's going to come after you, you know."

"I can take care of myself," Brody replied, matter-of-factly. "But your concern is noted." Right now he needed answers from her, not the other way around. "What did Carter mean by the other one?"

"What difference does it make? You got the *right* one."

"I asked you a question, Emily. I don't like to ask things twice." She remained obstinate and said nothing so he decided on a different approach. He fished his phone out of his jacket pocket and easily found the video that had tortured him for months and set him on this crazy vengeful spiral.

"What's this?" she asked when he shoved the phone in her direction.

"Just press play."

She did as he asked and mere seconds into the footage gasped at what she saw. "Keep watching," he ordered when she looked ready to pass the phone back to him.

He already had the footage memorized. Sheila was tied to her own bed—the same bed he had tied Emily to in Calvin's basement—while a woman stood over her with a knife ... a woman who looked exactly like Emily.

"You're so very pretty, aren't you, Sheila?" the woman taunted. "You think you're prettier than me, don't you?"

Sheila shook her head fiercely, unable to speak due to the gag in her mouth.

"Louis thinks you're pretty. He thinks you're prettier than me. Maybe you are … for now." Sheila cried out in pain as the woman slid her knife slowly down the length of Sheila's left cheek.

"You have your own man, but that's not enough for you is it? You wanted mine?"

Again, Sheila fiercely shook her head as she sobbed prompting the woman to deliver a quick slash to her other cheek. This one looked deeper, the blood gushed faster, thicker. Then the woman placed the knife at Sheila's throat as she spoke her next threat. "The next time won't end well for you. You got me?"

Sheila nodded in understanding right before the door burst open and Tyler, Sheila's boyfriend and Cal's brother, came barreling down the stairs. He startled the woman who looked like Emily, causing her entire body to jerk. Brody didn't think the woman even realized that she had sunk the knife deeper into Sheila's throat as a result.

"Baby, we g—" Tyler had frozen in place due to the horrific scene before him.

Time would not have been on Tyler and Sheila's side to run anyway. Fallow had burst in seconds later and shot Tyler in the back of the head. Sheila let out a muffled cry at the same time the woman resembling Emily screamed. Fallow looked at her with disgust and said, "Let's go before I tell the boss what you were up to. Now!"

The woman hunched her shoulders and quickly scampered off after Fallow, leaving her digital camera behind. The video on his phone ended there since Brody didn't transfer the rest of the footage of his sister bleeding out to death.

Brody found her the next morning … dead, Tyler on the floor in a pool of his own blood next to the bed. That was the last memory he had of his sister, one that would be ingrained in him forever.

Chapter Seven

Emily had watched the footage in horror. By the end, tears were streaming down her face. It all made sense now why Shadow hated her so much, why he wanted payback. He thought she had been the one to do those things to his sister.

"That's not you in the video, is it?" Shadow asked.

"No." Emily shook her head repeatedly as she continued to cry. "No," she stated again firmly, still not believing that Enza could go that far. "But like I said before, you still took the right one."

"No," Shadow roared, slamming his fist on the steering wheel.

Despite his anger and outburst, the car remained steady. Emily couldn't help marvel at the man's total control.

She waited for him to calm down and when he finally did, he spoke more evenly. "You were innocent. I touched you … Cal … fuck!"

"Louis would have never come for her," she told him. And suddenly she was glad that he grabbed her instead of Enza. She shuddered to think about what her Shadow would have done to her sister. "I am not blameless here either, Shadow."

"What did you call me?"

"Oh." She hadn't meant to call him that aloud. "I didn't know your name, so …" she trailed off. She felt her cheeks redden.

Her Shadow chuckled. "It's Brody. Brody Beckett."

She supposed that suited him more now that he was real and not just lurking in the darkness. When he prompted her to continue to explain why she thought she wasn't blameless, she told him about how she stole Louis away from her twin sister.

Even though Emily and Enza looked nearly identical, save for the fact that Emily had an inch on her sister, and Enza had dark blue eyes instead of green, the two of them could not have been more different in personality. Emily, always the studious one, always the one who did the right thing, and constantly doted on by her parents, while Enza was a trouble maker, who hated school, had a new boyfriend almost every week, and snuck out of the house repeatedly. The strangest part was that in opposition to most twins, they were never close. They loved each other yes, but each girl had been jealous of the other.

Emily always had a hard time meeting men, especially around Enza whose flirtiness and outgoing personality overshadowed Emily's whenever they were together. Enza had once stolen Emily's boyfriend, something she never even felt any sort of remorse over. She had been crashing in Emily's dorm room under the guise of shopping for colleges when Emily walked in on her having sex with Devon, her college boyfriend. Enza's response at being caught was an "oops," followed by hysterical laughter.

Years later, Emily returned the favor by stealing Louis from her sister, the one and only man Enza claimed to ever love. Louis became infatuated with Emily even while still dating Enza. She would come to Emily in a rage, screaming about how once again Louis called out Emily's name in bed. He threw Enza to the curb when Emily finally agreed to go out with him and subsequently became his obsession.

"You may have been naïve about Carter, but none of this was your fault." Brody became angry again. He picked up his cell phone from the center console, where she had carefully laid it using her uninjured hand. "Put that fucker on the phone," he barked at someone. When whoever it was came on the line, in the same angry tone, he asked, "Did you know? Did you fucking know there were two of them?"

She couldn't make out what was being said on the other line, but she got the gist. Brody had been shouting at Cal who had withheld that important piece of information. After he ended the call, he told her about the recent photos he saw. Emily was shocked. She hadn't seen or spoken to her sister in almost two years, and had no idea that Louis had taken her back. She thought for sure that Enza wouldn't hesitate to rub it in her face if he had.

"I need to ask you one question," Emily stated. When he nodded, she proceeded. "Would you have still taken me if you knew that it was my sister in the video and not me?"

"No."

And that's why Cal had withheld the information from him, she concluded. Brody may have been out for revenge with questionable methods, but he still remained at least somewhat honorable. They rode in silence the rest of the way. What he had done to her clearly ate away at him.

An hour and a half later, Brody pulled into the driveway of a two story house somewhere in upstate New York. The neighboring houses were spaced far enough apart for privacy, but not to the point of being isolated. A thickly wooded area sat behind the house. Too bad she wasn't here under different circumstances where she could really admire the tranquil location. She loved the city, but sometimes it was nice to get away from all of the noise.

"Are you hungry?" Brody asked when they were inside the house.

A large open kitchen sat off to the right. All cherry wood with black marble countertops and a cozy looking breakfast nook. The place looked pristine, almost unlived in, but since he had offered her something to eat, she imagined the place came fully stocked. It was a safe house after all, she heard him mention on the phone. Chances are the luxury of grocery shopping was probably currently prohibited.

Emily couldn't remember the last time she had eaten, but found herself without an appetite. What she needed more was to wash the day away. "I'd like to just clean up first if you don't mind?"

"Come," he ordered gently, leading the way up the stairs, through the master bedroom, and right into the master bath. Emily stood inside the doorway. Brody stretched his hand out to her. "I need to look at your cuts."

"They don't hurt," she reassured.

He walked over to where she stood and gently took her hand, pulling her along with him over to the sink. Unyielding as ever, he would apparently have his way and she'd let him, not only to help appease his guilt, but because she suddenly wanted him to touch her. At least now it didn't feel wrong to admit it.

Brody helped her hop onto the counter and then he fished around in the cabinets for antiseptic and Band-Aids. He unzipped her coat to expose her neck and the top of her chest. The alcohol stung a little when he applied it, making her flinch. He surprised her by gently blowing on the area. "Sorry," he murmured. Emily knew his apology went deeper than causing her cuts to sting.

He applied bandages to the three small cuts he had given her, and wiped off all of the dried blood surrounding the exposed area. When he finished, he continued to stand a hair's breath away from her, his head bowed. "I'm so sorry." He then looked at her, his gaze penetrating and apologetic. "I'm so fucking sorry."

"I know." Emily whispered softly returning his gaze. She wanted to say that she forgave him. Her heart broke for him, for his loss, for what he had to witness and her anger toward him had dissipated somewhere between saving her to just now as he tenderly patched her up, but she still felt angry at what had been done to her.

"In my head, I tried to justify my actions." He took one step back and slid both hands in his hair, fisting his messy locks. "I convinced myself that since you seemed to be responding to me, that I wasn't really hurting you and it became an alternative to cutting you."

"I-I did…"

"You were ashamed that you enjoyed it," he finished for her.

Emily nodded and then it was her turn to bow her head. Brody stepped closer to her again and lifted her chin. "The only one who should be ashamed is me. You have nothing to be ashamed of."

"You responded to me, too," Emily whispered.

"Yes."

"That made you angrier."

He nodded. "I wanted to hate you, but I had blown up a photo of your face so I could get a good look at you and it haunted me for months. Your green eyes stared back at me every day, like they were pleading, accusing even. There were so many photographs though. I'm not even sure if that was you now."

"Enza's eyes are blue," she interjected. His lips curved into a slight smile. Unlike before, when had given her a cruel smile, this genuine one lit up his features and even made his eyes look kind. She reached out with her right hand, suddenly needing to touch his face, but immediately pulled back when she felt the sharp pain.

"What's wrong with your hand?" Apparently the movement did not go unnoticed. Brody lifted her chin up after she bowed her head again. "I think I have already made myself clear when I explained that I don't like to ask twice. That fucker hurt you?"

"He likes to *discipline*, especially in front of his men." Louis had grabbed hold of her wrist in the car, squeezing tightly and bending it back just enough to cause lasting pain without breaking it. *That's the last time you defy me*, he had said.

Brody tenderly took her hand to examine it.

"It's not broken," she quickly explained. "He's very precise. If he wanted it broken, he would have done it."

Funny how Brody's angry face no longer frightened her. In fact, it brought her comfort knowing that his anger was now on her behalf. Still, she worried about his future plans regarding Enza. "Brody, I know what Enza did was unforgivable. I have no objection to you taking the video to the police, but please … she's still my sister…"

"I won't touch her," he promised. "I recently learned that vengeance only does more harm and does not undo the sins of the past. He carefully laid her hand down on her lap. "I'm going to run downstairs to get you some ice. We need to get the swelling down."

"No," she said stubbornly. "I just need to take a shower now. Please just help me with my coat."

Brody hesitated briefly before he slowly slid the zipper of her coat the rest of the way down. They stared into each other's eyes as he spread the coat open and carefully removed it from her.

With her good hand, Emily reached out and brushed just the tips of her fingers against his cheek, mimicking the way that he had touched her bare skin for the first time. "What if I said I want you to touch me now?"

Brody closed his eyes. He seemed conflicted. "I don't have the right to touch you. I don't have the right to want you like I do."

She waited for him to open his eyes and look at her. "We're not the same people to each other that we were a few hours ago. I shouldn't have wanted you then, but I did. And I want you even more now. I need you." She finished on a breathy whisper. Her body shook from desire. Desire to forgive, to forget, to erase his mistake for him, but most of all to feel him all around her.

"If we met under different circumstances," she started to say, but Brody had pulled her close and pressed his lips firmly against hers.

He moaned into her mouth when she opened for him and allowed his tongue to twine with hers. She pulled herself even closer to him, wrapping her legs around his waist and her arms around his neck. She remembered how badly she wanted to feel his wild hair, so with her uninjured hand, she fisted his curls, eliciting another moan from him.

With one arm around her center, he lifted her off the counter, placing his other hand on her ass, and walked over to the shower with her. She kicked off her shoes, while Brody toed his off, and he stepped into the shower with both of them still dressed. The warm water soothed her overheated skin, despite the amount of clothes she still wore. When he placed her on her feet, the frenzy to divest each other of their clothes began. She could care less about her already torn white shirt, courtesy of the vile Cal. And the plain white cotton bra she wore seemed to offend Brody for some reason, so she definitely did not mind when he practically ripped it off of her. Her navy slacks and matching equally offensive panties came next, and finally her socks were gone, leaving her completely bare before him. She had managed to remove his sweater and undershirt thus far. While he took in the sight of her naked body, grunting appreciatively, she watched him remove his jeans and socks and smiled slyly that he had gone commando.

They simply stared at each other at first, she to admire the Adonis with a muscular chest, bulging biceps and six pack abs all the way down to his long, think cock and powerfully built legs, while he, though admiring her as well, seemed to want to be cautious. He must have seen the longing on her face, because suddenly she found herself wrapped up in him and he was kissing her passionately.

He hoisted her up again and she wrapped her legs around his waist. Emily cursed Louis for hurting her in the car, limiting her ability to touch Brody properly with both hands. She wanted to grab and feel every inch of him she could reach from her current position. While her bad hand rested on his shoulder, her other explored his steel frame that only yesterday had terrified her as he held her against it. Here, now in his muscular arms, with his hard cock pressed against her belly, she felt safe. She also felt bold. She licked his top lip swiftly before she bit down gently on his bottom one. He growled in response and bit her bottom lip back Her pussy spasmed from the pleasure and she began to rub herself against his cock. Her nipples ached for his touch, and hardened even more when he acquiesced to touching them.

Suddenly, she was on her feet again, her legs shaky, but before she could protest, she saw Brody go down on his knees and understood his purpose for putting her down. His soft lips were on her, first kissing her inflamed lips, and then he was parting them with his thumbs, giving him access to lick all around her clit. He threw one of her legs around his shoulder to get closer and she let out an embarrassingly loud moan when his whole mouth was on her, licking, sucking, kissing her. The vibrations of his chuckle only intensified her gratification.

He paused briefly to look up at her. "No teasing this time, Emily. Let me give you what I so cruelly withheld. Let go!"

Let go. His gentle command, his sincere desire to please her, and his mouth on her, followed by two, long and thick fingers inserted in her core, definitely did the trick. She threw her head back and completely let go as her orgasm ripped through her. Brody continued to lick and stroke her until her body had stopped shaking.

He stood, lifting her back up into her previous position. Their mouths collided fiercely. She tasted him and herself on his lips making her desire flare for him again. "I'm on the pill," she murmured against his lips, unwilling to lose contact with them for even a moment. He murmured back that he was clean and then he immediately impaled her.

They both froze. He touched his forehead to hers and held it there for several heart pounding beats. When he started to move with deep and steady strokes inside of her, he kissed her lips again—soft kisses that trailed down to her neck. She tilted her head to the side to give him better access. They continued slow and steady to the rhythm of the water running and their heavy breathing.

She felt another climax building as he stroked harder, faster, his hands supporting her ass, moving her in the direction he wanted her to go. She fisted her good hand in his hair again and fused her lips to his, tongues stroking then going in circles, then back to tasting each other's lips. Their heavy breathing turned to loud moans and he pounded faster, harder, his hard cock stroking every needy inch inside of her. When he shifted her just a little, lifting her higher, he hit a spot that made her lose control. She tightened around him, tilted her head back and screamed out her release while he simultaneously groaned out his, burying his head in the crook of her neck in the process.

He kept himself inside of her for a little while longer. Her legs were still shaky so she was beyond grateful that when he finally did pull out, he did not set her down to stand on them. Instead, he sat down with her under the now hotter spray of water, she still straddling him. He looked at her and smiled before hugging her close, skin against naked skin, one arm around her waist, the other, at the nape of her neck, holding her head against his chest. She heard his steady heart beat as the water washed away their tainted past.

Chapter Eight

Brody jerked awake to the annoying sound of his phone vibrating on the bedside table. Thankfully, Emily remained asleep in his arms. He knew that he should probably answer it given that it was most likely one of his brothers trying to coordinate a rendezvous point, but he ignored it.

After their shower earlier, Brody made breakfast—bacon, eggs, toast, and coffee. Neither of them had eaten anything since the night before. They had sat in virtual silence, save for the few complimentary grunts from Emily, wearing nothing but towels. Their heated stares were enough to fill the void of not speaking. He wanted her again ... badly. After they devoured everything on their plates and practically inhaled their coffees, he threw her over his shoulder and bolted up the stairs. He realized too late what he had done when he placed her on the bed, afraid it would remind her of her captivity.

She had sat up on her knees and touched his face. "I'm not afraid of you anymore." She then removed her towel and threw it on the floor.

Brody felt undeserving of her, but she wanted him, and he now seemed, would give her anything. He'd be kidding himself if he said it was solely due to guilt. He wanted her too, more than he ever wanted anything. So he took her, again and again, until they both fell into an exhausted sleep.

Now, in the quiet darkness of the room with her lying peacefully in his arms, he didn't think he could ever let her go. He only hoped she didn't want to leave him when this was all over. Regardless, he'd make sure that Carter never got his hands on her again.

His phone buzzed again. This time Emily opened her eyes. She had a breathtaking smile, an infectious one he could not help but return. "You gonna get that?" she asked. "The damn thing's just going to keep buzzing."

She was right of course. They had slept for far too long. Brody kept her snuggled against him as he reached for his cell phone. "Hello," he barked at Stephen.

"I'll remember that you're grumpy if woken up," Emily murmured into his chest.

Either Nowicki didn't hear her, or he was smart enough not to comment. He got right to the point instead. "We found her. The other one."

"Where? Is she safe?" Brody knew his concern for Enza stemmed from wanting to spare Emily any more pain. Hearing Emily speak of Enza made him understand her better. He already knew she hadn't meant to kill his sister, but still, her cruelty, shallowness, insecurity, and selfishness made her responsible. He had no idea how someone like her could possibly be related to someone like Emily, let alone be her twin. He'd never forget what she did or forgive her for it, but he wouldn't be the one doling out justice to her either.

"We got her," Nowicki reassured.

Emily picked her head up and rested her elbows on his chest. She must have understood they were talking about her sister. Brody nodded to let her know that Enza was indeed safe.

"Get this. She was on her way to meet Carter wearing a wire. We need to play it cool. The Feds are all over this." Nowicki went on to explain that Enza had no problem spilling her guts to them—while also flirting with each and every one of his Seal brothers once they disabled her wire. The cops had busted her for possession with intent to sell, and in exchange for immunity, she agreed to give up Carter and Fallow, having witnessed the latter commit murder, and obviously not knowing yet that Fallow was dead. Somehow Carter must have found out about her extracurricular activities. That's what he had apparently meant earlier when he had made the "whores who snitch" comment.

By the time Brody ended the call, a plan was set in motion. His brothers, Cal, and Enza were on their way to their safe house and would arrive in just under two hours. First thing in the morning, he and Nowicki would escort both girls and Cal to safe house number two, further up north, while the rest of his brothers figured out a way to neutralize Carter. They had contacts in the FBI. Perhaps they could take care of things without further bloodshed.

"Cal will be there?" Emily asked with trepidation.

"That fucker will never lay another hand on you. He's also going to answer for his deceit, I assure you." Brody cupped her face. "Hey, I'll keep you safe. I promise."

"I don't want you to feel like you have to—"

"Believe me, Emily, I am not doing anything because I *have* to. You got me?"

She nodded and gave him another one of her breathtaking smiles. It was enough to end any further conversation for a while.

"We should probably get dressed before your motley crew arrives," Emily said some time later as she lay sprawled out on top of him, her back to his chest. Her injured right hand rested on the pillow by his head, while her left hand played with his hair. Brody's hands were busy massaging her breasts. He couldn't remember the last time he felt this content.

He contemplated on going one more round before scrounging up some clean dry clothes for them when something suddenly seemed off to him. "Get up."

"What's the matter?" she asked sliding off of him and positioning herself seated on the bed.

"Shhh." He sat up too and listened intently. He heard the sound of a twig snapping outside. Wordlessly he got up and walked over to the side of the window, making sure to stay out of sight. He saw several figures creeping closer to the house. He turned to Emily and held one finger to his lips, indicating she should remain quiet. She nodded quickly.

He walked over to the dresser on the other side of the room and pulled out clothes for the both of them. Thankfully he had several sizes in sweatpants, sweaters, and pullovers, though all of them would still be big on Emily.

They dressed quickly. When they were done, Brody led Emily out of the room and down the stairs of the darkened house. They ended up in a den, where Brody began loading up on weapons stored in various cabinets. Moonlight filtered in from the double window, allowing them to see the room and each other.

"Do you know how to shoot?" he whispered to her

"No, I've never even held a gun."

Brody quickly showed her how to toggle the safety then stated, "Someone comes at you, point and shoot! And if I tell you to run, you run."

Emily looked hesitant. "What about you?"

He cupped her face. "I will take care of the both of us." He had already informed her earlier a little about his past as a Navy Seal.

Meanwhile, he had never once lost sight of the shadows moving toward the house. He counted four. He'd bet his life that these were Carter's men and that Carter himself was not among them at the moment. Waiting in the car until the dirty work was completed sounded more like his style. Brody also assessed that Carter would have a bodyguard with him, maybe two, therefore he'd be dealing with six or seven men in total. He texted Nowicki with the new development. If he could find a way to somehow stall them for twenty minutes, the cavalry would arrive.

"How did he find us?"

"Good question. One we will have to deal with later."

The silent alarm had been triggered and Brody realized that stalling would not be an option. He had to try and incapacitate as many of them as possible without them knowing he'd caught on to them.

"Listen carefully, Emily," Brody pointed to the clock on the wall, "in exactly five minutes, I want you to crawl out that window and run to the wooded area. Once you're out of sight, run that way," he pointed to the left. "It's the second house. Climb over the small fence and knock on the back door. A guy named Shawn lives there. Ex army. Tell him I sent you."

"But you can't—"

"Please, Emily. Do as I say."

"Okay," she whispered.

He cupped her face and kissed her hard on the mouth. All too quickly, he ended the kiss, and walked out of the room. Carter and his men were about to get a lesson on what it meant to fuck with him and those he cared about.

Chapter Nine

Emily raced through the woods. She didn't want to leave Brody, but she trusted him. His sincerity about keeping her safe had her convinced that his survival was crucial to that goal. The gun in her left hand felt heavy and foreign to her, but she vowed to herself to use it if she had to. She would never be someone's victim again.

She spotted the house, the moon and neighboring houses lighting her way. Just as she was about to exit the woods, she heard a noise behind her.

She spun around. "Brody?"

It wasn't Brody. A sneering Louis and one of his bodyguards stepped out from behind the trees instead. "Well, aren't you the little whore. Just like your sister. I'm not sure if I could forgive you for this one."

"I don't want your forgiveness, Louis," she spat. "All I want is to finally be free of you."

"That could be arranged, my love, but first I am taking you back to the house so that you can watch as I gut your boyfriend. Tell me, did you plan the whole thing with hi—"

Emily raised her gun before Louis had a chance to finish his sentence. His eyes widened in shock. He must not have seen her holding the gun at her side when he had been speaking to her. Despite how shaky her hand felt, and the fact that it wasn't her dominant one, she managed to toggle the safety off as Brody had shown her and pointed it straight at Louis.

Louis stopped his goon from charging her. "Put that thing down, Emily. You're not a killer."

"No, but you are. I won't let you hurt him." She steadied her hand. "If he makes one more move," she said, referring to the goon who tried reaching into his jacket, "I shoot you, Louis." Louis held up his hand, making the said goon lower his.

Emily could barely remember what happened next, as if time had sped up and slowed all at once. Shots were fired from every direction. She fell to the ground landing on her outstretched left arm. Her right shoulder stung at first before the pain became almost blinding. She'd been shot. More bullets whizzed by her head and shouts echoed in the forest. She thought she heard a male's anguished cry followed by a female's scream.

She tried to stand, but the pain made it hard to even breathe. She looked over at where Louis and his goon had stood to find their two dead bodies lying on the ground. Louis's cold dead eyes seemed to be staring back at her. Through her peripheral vision, she spotted a shadowy figure running toward her. When the figure came closer, she realized it was Brody.

"Oh God, you're hit." Brody fell to his knees beside her. "Emily, please talk to me." She closed her eyes briefly, though he continued to speak to her. Everything seemed muffled now. "…your shoulder?"

Brody gently prodded her, examining her injuries. Thankfully, the pain seemed to have been subsiding and turning into numbness. "Cold." Her teeth chattered as she spoke. Her eyes closed again briefly, and she when she opened them, she felt pressure being applied to her shoulder.

She had no idea how long the process of opening and then closing her eyes again carried on, but the next time she opened them, she thought she saw another figure approaching them. "Cal."

"Shh, princess, don't try to talk. That fucker ran off like the weasel that he is."

"No, he—"

Brody shushed her again. "I'll deal with him. He'll regret giving us up to Carter."

She hadn't imagined it and couldn't get the words out to warn Brody that Cal stood behind him, a gun aimed at his head.

"You're a disgrace, Brody," Cal sputtered with disgust. "That bitch cut up your sister, left her to bleed to death."

"Emily is innocent." Brody remained calm, though Emily could see his anger boiling underneath the surface.

"Fuck that! She shacked up with Carter, too. How innocent could she be? Carter promised me the other one after he was done with her. Where is she?"

"Why did you shoot him then before he could deliver her?" Emily knew that Brody kept him talking so he could formulate a plan.

"I shot Emily. Carter was about to shoot me. Now where is she?"

Brody growled low, his face looked murderous over Cal's confession that Emily had been his intentional target, but he remained in control. "You got Fallow. Let me deal with her sister."

Cal laughed maniacally. "You'll probably end up fucking her, too."

Lightning fast, Brody spun around to face the vile man, but now the barrel of Cal's gun touched Brody's forehead.

"My brother never loved Sheila the way I did," Cal announced. Emily thought he looked high. "I'll have justice for them both, even if it means going through you and your little piece of ass to get it."

Cal wasn't in his right mind, and Emily, even through her own not completely coherent state, knew that he wasn't bluffing. She felt the cold steel in her left hand.

Point and shoot, Brody had instructed earlier. So she did. Cal fell to the ground and then everything went black.

Chapter Ten

It took Emily almost four months to convince him. Afraid to dredge up old memories for her, Brody constantly refused … until today. "Please, let's just try it," she had pleaded with him. It was pointless to deny them both what they had craved when the past had already been buried.

It's not like she could entirely forget the past, especially not on the days she would visit Enza in prison. With Louis and Fallow dead, Enza lost her bargaining chips. Emily managed to get her a good lawyer though, who helped her plea down to a lesser sentence. Brody decided to withhold the recording she had made, lest it implicate his Navy Seal brothers in Fallow's death. She hoped that Enza would come out of prison a better person than she went in, especially now that they were both free of Louis.

Enza would have been by her side that night in the forest, she later learned, had Nowicki not whisked her away to safety. Some of Louis's men had still been out there, and Cal had thirsted for her blood. Through some moments of clarity, Emily had recalled how Enza had begged her not to die. "I'm so sorry. I'm so sorry for everything," she had cried. Emily actually thought she *had* died and that hell had frozen over, since she never once recalled Enza ever apologizing for anything. But that night, she had put her and her sister's past behind them too. The only hurdle left to get over, was her boyfriend's aversion to tying her up.

She found herself now, fully able to experience the pleasure of Brody's expertise in the art of Kinbaku. He sat back against the headboard in their bedroom and ordered Emily to remove her clothing slowly. She complied, feeling confident in her newfound love for sexy lingerie. When all that remained were her bra and panties, he told her to stop.

"Come and kneel on the bed in front of me."

She walked over to the foot of the bed and climbed on top. Like a stealth panther, she crawled forward to him, stopping right in front of his outstretched legs, and she gave him a sly little smile. He moved quickly then, tying her ankles and calves together in intricate knots. Her hands came next, tied behind her back in reverse hand prayer position and then she leaned her torso forward, leaving herself completely at his mercy.

Brody circled her on the bed as he removed his own clothing, both of them breathing heavily. He tugged the cups of her bra down freeing her breasts, and moved her panties over to the side, leaving her trussed up and fully exposed. She moaned at the sensation of the ropes against her skin and felt herself becoming even wetter, knowing what Brody could see when he stood behind her. Her ass in the air, and her wet pussy completely open and on display for him. She became even greedier for his touch.

He circled around to the front of her, positioning himself on his knees, his cock angled toward her. "Take me into your mouth," he commanded, his voice low and husky.

She licked just the tip of his mushroomed head and savored the flavor of his salty pre-cum before sucking hard on the entire head. He took charge from there. With one hand, he swept up her hair into a makeshift ponytail, while the other tenderly cupped her face as he fed her his cock. Emily looked up and met his eyes. They were glazed over with desire. His mouth slightly ajar, his breaths heavy.

"Enough," he breathed, swiftly pulling out of her. "I want to come in your pussy. Fill you up and mark what's mine."

"Yes. Please, Brody." As much as she loved pleasuring him with her mouth, she needed to be filled by him. To be as he had said, marked, taken in a way that he had not taken her yet. And then she would be completely his.

Brody positioned himself behind her. He swept her hair to the side so that he could trail kisses from her neck all the way down her spine. She tried not to giggle when he placed a few soft kisses on her ass. Then, with his arms balanced on either side of her and his torso flush against hers, he entered her, filling her completely in one long stroke. His next movements were slow, pulling almost all the way out, and then pushing hard all the way in, jerking her body forward each time. Over and over, he stroked her inner walls this way, his grunts getting louder, her moans growing more desperate with each pass. She felt his hard stomach against the sides of her hands.

He nuzzled the side of her head with his before delivering kisses to her cheek, her neck, and she nearly convulsed when he bit down on the tender flesh between her neck and shoulder, bracing herself for the earth-shattering orgasm he was about to deliver. He lifted himself up enough to free her hands and place them out in front of her. That's when he really let loose. He picked up the pace and pounded into her, twining their outstretched hands together. The headboard banged into the wall from the force of his movements. Emily squeezed his hands tighter as her climax built to its peak. And then she came … loud and hard, taking Brody with her.

After Brody pulled out of her, he undid the rest of her bindings and massaged her ankles and calves. He massaged her wrists next while lying down with her resting in his arms.

"You really enjoyed that, didn't you?"

"Yes." Emily looked up and smiled at him. "Very much. Did you?"

"Very much."

"Does that mean we get to do it again?"

"Don't you worry," Brody promised with a chuckle. "I have a lot more patterns to show you with the ropes." he paused for a moment before adding, "I love you, Emily." He'd implied it many times before, but this was the first time he had said it outright.

"And I love you."

He had come out of nowhere, her Shadow, carrying her into the darkness with him, until they were both safe enough to step back into the light.

The End

www.elenakincaid.com

GODSEND

Jocelyn Dex

Copyright© 2016

Chapter One

Gia tromped through the woods of the Mark Twain National Forest, her heavy backpack weighing her down. She probably shouldn't have taken so many supplies, but the tiny store in the podunk town had just been too easy to rob. And the more supplies she gathered, the longer it would be until she had to make another trip to another town and do it all over again.

A felled tree in her path seemed like as good a place as any to take a break and rest her aching feet. She slid the backpack off her shoulders and let it drop to the ground. The canned goods inside were packed so tight they didn't even clank.

She stretched her arms, back, and legs before plopping down on the rough bark of the oak tree, pulled a bottle of water from her pack, and tried not to suck the entire thing down in one sitting. Careful rationing kept her in the woods, where she preferred to be. Away from people. People sucked.

After quenching her thirst, she stuffed the half bottle of water back in the bag and pulled out a small notebook and pen. She flipped to an empty page and wrote "Earl's Grocery, 5-15, $50" and then put the notebook and pen away.

The urge to set up her small tent right there and take a long nap was tempting, but she had a lot of daylight left and wanted to cover more ground before stopping. Plus, according to her map, there was a lake about four or five miles south and she really wanted to bathe. It'd been a couple days since she'd had the luxury, and she was pretty sure she could smell herself.

She inhaled the fresh air of nature as she trudged on. Rays of sunshine filtered through the dense canopy of trees, and fallen leaves and acorns crunched beneath her boots. The occasional bird sang to her, and she always smiled when the squirrels chattered at her.

By the time she reached the lake, she was about to pass out. She'd pushed it extra hard that day, and she didn't even know why. It wasn't like she had anywhere to be.

She found a sandy embankment, ditched her pack, shucked out of her clothes, and waded into the water. She shivered as the cold water lapped at her skin but sank down into it anyway.

She scrubbed her body and hair with one of the fruity bars of soap she'd pocketed earlier that day and made quick work of rinsing herself clean before jumping out and standing in the sun, willing it to hurry and dry her enough to get dressed. She'd kill for a big, fluffy towel, but they took up too much space she needed for more important things.

When her skin was sufficiently dry, she twisted as much water from her hair as possible, shook it out like a dog, then combed it straight. She washed her shorts and t-shirt in the lake, set them out to dry, and then dressed.

Just as she decided to make her camp there, a glint in the distance caught her attention. Her best guess was that it was about a mile away. It could be nothing, but it could be something. If there were people that close by, she didn't want to camp there. Never knew what kind of asshole you might come across. And she'd dealt with quite enough assholes in her lifetime.

She sighed, gathered her things, and hiked toward the glint hoping it wasn't something that would force her to keep walking.

The closer she got, the quieter and more cautiously she listened and scanned the area. Then she saw it. A dilapidated old shack. One of the windows was cracked, and several of the boards were rotted. She stood there a long while watching, listening, waiting, but saw no signs of life. No vehicles. Nothing.

Over the last several months, she'd come across a few deserted old one-room shacks that had probably been thrown up by hunters or trappers. A couple had had old, rusty wood burning stoves in them—a luxury for her. She'd pretended they were her homes, had even fashioned brooms out of sticks and brush, and had swept the floors, dusted away the cobwebs. But each time she'd run out of supplies and move on.

She waited another fifteen minutes before sneaking up to the shack. She tried peeking into the windows but dark coverings blocked her view. Surely no one lived there. Up close, it looked to be in worse condition than she'd originally thought. She wasn't even sure if it was safe for her.

She sneaked around to the back and got a glimpse inside a small dusty room with busted up floorboards. Sketchy, but it convinced her no one was living there.

The back door was locked but gave in with a little jimmying and force. Her face scrunched up in confusion as she stepped inside. The hardwood floor shined as if new, and the place was furnished. Uh oh. Definitely not deserted. Just as she was about to get the hell out of there, something slammed into her from behind. Her forehead banged against the doorjamb and everything went black.

Chapter Two

Gia's head ached, but when she reached up to assess the damage, she couldn't move her right hand, so she tried her left and her fingers came into contact with a bandage. She forced her eyelids open and blinked rapidly trying to adjust to the dim light. Where the hell was she and why was her right wrist tied to a … bed?

The memory flooded back to her. Someone had attacked her. Oh shit. What if it was some crazy hillbilly who wanted to slice her up, maybe eat her, like she'd seen in a movie one time?

She jerked her wrist and tried to work out the complicated knot with her left hand, but it wouldn't budge. Panic shot through her system, her heart beating so hard she feared it would explode. When she heard footsteps, she kind of wished it would explode. Better dead than eaten alive by some deranged psycho.

When a large silhouette appeared in the doorway, she tried to swallow the scream in her throat, to be strong, confident, but she couldn't. It tore from her like a bullet, loud, piercing, and reverberating off the walls.

The silhouette didn't move, just stood there. When she finally stopped screaming, she yelled at him. "What the fuck do you want from me?"

Suddenly, he flicked a switch on the wall, the bright light temporarily blinding her. She scrubbed at her eyes with her free hand, scared to see but needing to see what terror awaited her.

"What the fuck do *I* want?" a deep voice asked. "You're the one who broke into my house. I'd say the question is…What the fuck do *you* want?"

When her vision finally cleared, she blinked hard not sure whether to still be scared or to drool. His muscular, tattooed frame had to be over six feet tall. His dark hair was cropped close to his scalp, and a totally inappropriate desire to run her fingertips across the stubble to see if it was soft or prickly swept through her. When she realized he might likely be her worst nightmare, she abandoned such ridiculous thoughts.

"I'm s-sorry," she stammered. "I was hiking and didn't think anyone lived here. It looks like a deserted shack from the outside."

He crossed his arms that were both completely sleeved with tattoos—intricate designs of color mixed with black and gray—across a sculpted chest and leaned nonchalantly against the door frame. "You break in, get caught, and then insult my home. You're not very bright, are you?"

Even in her frightened state, that comment raised her ire. "I'm not stupid. It was a mistake. Just untie me and you'll never see me again."

He looked her up and down and ran his tongue slowly across cruel lips. "Maybe I like *seeing* you. Besides, how do I know you weren't planning to rob me? Maybe I let you go and you come back with reinforcements. Maybe the Martins sent you in as bait."

"Bait? I don't know any Martins. I don't know anyone. And I swear I wasn't trying to rob you." Although, had he not been home and she'd found supplies worth stealing, she totally would have. He didn't need to know that though.

"Let's see about that," he said ominously and hauled her pack up from the floor. He detached her knife and tomahawk from their outer riggings, then unzipped every compartment, turned it upside down and shook out the contents on the bed at her feet. She winced as some of the canned goods rolled off the bed and hit the wood floor. Everything she owned was in that pack, and every bit of it was precious to her.

He carelessly tossed her first aid kit, her damp clothes, and other items to the floor. "Please," she said. "That's everything I own. Don't ruin it."

His piercing blue eyes pinned her in an intense stare. "What makes you think you'll be alive to use any of it?"

She flinched and shrank back as far from him as possible.

He held up her notebook, an "aha" look on his face. "What do we have here? What truths will be revealed when I open this? Tell me now. Admit your real reason for breaking into my home and maybe, just maybe, I'll kill you quick instead of dragging it out."

She gulped. "Nothing in there has anything to do with you. I swear. It's personal."

He scowled. "You had your chance." He flipped through the notebook one page at a time, slowly, reading every word. He frowned more with every page. By the time he got to the end, he looked truly confused. "What is all this?"

Shit. She didn't want to tell him. It would just confirm his initial accusation that she was a thief. She went for vague, hoping it would suffice. "It's a list of debts. That's all."

"Why would you owe grocery stores and thrift stores and gas stations?"

She stuck out her chin. "I just do."

He dug through the rest of her items, her cringing the entire time at his carelessness. "Where's your wallet?"

"I don't have one."

"Purse, wallet, pocketbook, plastic bag," he snarled. "Whatever the fuck you keep your ID and money in."

She blanched at his tone. "I don't have any of that. I lost my ID months ago and never got it replaced."

"Bullshit."

She tried to curl into a ball as he stomped toward her, but he grabbed her legs and pulled her so she was laid out flat on her back. When he let go of one leg and grabbed at her shorts, she kicked at him, a lucky shot catching him in the chin. Hard. His head snapped back, but he didn't loosen his hold.

"Stop. Now." He ground out between gritted teeth, his dark-blue eyes flashing ominously. "I'm not going to hurt you … yet."

She stopped struggling, praying his words were true, and really, kicking him in the face wasn't going to get her anywhere. It was only going to piss him off more. He didn't look like the kind of man you wanted to have pissed off at you.

She protested when he snaked a hand into her front pocket and then the other. When he flipped her over, instinct kicked in and she kicked despite her earlier thought. He straddled the backs of her knees, pinning her to the bed as he checked her back pockets.

"Not in your pack, not in your pockets. In your bra then?" he asked.

She was about to tell him she wasn't wearing a bra when his hands slipped beneath her shirt. Chills stole down her spine when his rough hands cupped her breasts. A loud hiss escaped him, a deep, rumbling moan accompanying it.

She clenched her teeth, waiting for him to realize she really didn't have any ID or money and to get off of her, to stop touching her, but he didn't move for a full minute. Seemed to be frozen, and she froze with him. She gasped when his fingers twitched and he pinched her nipples and rolled them between thumb and forefinger.

"Fuck," he whispered so quietly she barely heard him.

He kicked her legs apart with his knees and settled between her thighs, pressing an obvious erection against her ass.

"Wh-what are you doing?" she stammered. Her stomach clenched painfully, fear of his intentions paralyzing her.

"Quiet," he growled in her ear. He ground against her over and over, his hands still gripping her breasts, but he never made a move to remove her shorts or his jeans. His breathing sped up, his grunts coming in pants, his hips jerking wildly against her.

"Fuck!" He bellowed this time, going rigid, fingers squeezing her nipples almost painfully. Finally, he sagged against her, his heart beating into her back, breathing hot breath against her ear.

Had he just dry humped her? Come in his pants? Was her pussy tingling? What the hell had she gotten herself into? What would he do next?

She sucked in a relieved breath when his weight lifted off her. He didn't say a word, and she didn't flip back over until his footsteps told her he'd left the room. She struggled with the knot at her wrist again. She had to get out of there. He had to be a paranoid schizophrenic, coupled with sexual deviant, and she wanted no part of that. She cursed herself for not being more careful but damnit the place had looked empty.

"You're not getting out of that knot, so you might as well relax."

She jumped. She had been so consumed that she hadn't heard him return. She immediately noticed that he'd changed his pants. "You know I wasn't lying about the ID and money. Will you let me go now?"

"Either you're here on behalf of the Martins, you're a thief, or you're just damn unlucky. What's your name, woman?"

"I told you," she said through gritted teeth, "I don't know any Martins or anyone else. My name is Gia."

"Maybe, maybe not." He shrugged. "But if not, you must be a thief. No money, but a pack full of food, and a notebook with debts to stores that sell the items filling your pack."

She sagged, feeling defeated. Maybe if she admitted it, he'd be satisfied and let her go. "I'm going to pay them back. One day." It was why she kept a tally. Even though she had no idea when or how she'd ever pay them all back, she liked to tell herself that she would. Just because other people sucked, didn't mean she had to.

She continued when he smirked at her admission. "But I swear I wasn't intending to steal from you. I thought it was a deserted shack that I could spend a few days in. That maybe it'd have a useable wood stove."

"Why are you out here all alone? I'm just outside the boundary of the forest, so it isn't on your map. And the closest hiking trail is several miles away."

It was none of his damn business, but she had to tell him something. "I prefer the woods to towns, and I make my own trails so I rarely run into anyone."

His eyes bugged. "Are you saying you *live* in the woods?"

"I have for months," she admitted.

"Why?"

"*You* live in the woods." She pointed out the obvious.

"In a cabin. I don't wander around, steal, and"—
he pointed to her tent that he'd thrown to the floor—"live
in a tent and break into people's houses." He considered
her a moment, and she thought maybe he was thinking of
letting her go, but he shook his head. "Sit tight," he said
and closed the door behind him.

Chapter Three

Bane rested his forehead against the door a moment before heading to the kitchen. From a distance, he'd seen her sneaking around and had assumed she was with a group of a punk teenagers looking for mischief. Up close it was clear she was no teenager. In the years he'd lived out there, he'd only encountered three groups of people. One group was teenagers, and two others were twenty-somethings who couldn't read a map to save their lives.

When he scouted and didn't see anyone else hiding in the bushes, he wondered if the Martins had found him, but he couldn't figure out why'd they'd send a sexy woman in. Maybe for the element of surprise, thinking he wouldn't suspect.

The younger brother of the man he'd killed had sworn to hunt him down and kill him no matter how long it took. After three years, he had mostly quit believing it would ever happen. People said dramatic things in the heat of the moment, but rarely followed through. Especially with murder. It took more than most could imagine to take a life.

He couldn't be certain, but after searching her things, he didn't think she was involved with the Martins. He did, however, believe she would have robbed him blind if he hadn't caught her. But, it was a reason for him to rationalize keeping her. And he did want to keep her. She was like a sexy gift dropped at his doorstep and who was he to turn such a gift down?

He couldn't believe he'd lost control, had fondled her tits, dry-humped her ass, and come in his pants. It'd been so long since he'd touched a woman. It'd been longer since he'd seen one who looked like her. He'd wanted those athletic legs wrapped around his waist or his face at first sight. Wanted to wrap that silky blonde hair around his hand and tug her to her knees. And when she'd first turned those brilliant hazel eyes on him, it'd rendered him momentarily speechless.

He'd been so close to tearing those ass-hugging shorts down and filling her with every inch he had to give, but he'd exercised every bit of restraint he had inside him. He might be a killer, he might be damaged, but he wasn't *that*. Yet. If he didn't get her out of there... That tight little body definitely tested his resolve. But damnit, he wasn't ready for her to leave. No. He'd keep her a while and enjoy the scenery while she was there.

He opened a can of beans and a can of beef broth and mixed them together with random spices in a bowl and put it in the microwave. It wasn't much, but it was quick, simple, and easy. Then he hurried back to his sexy captive, eager for more interaction.

He quietly opened the bedroom door and found her picking at the knot again. "How many times do I have to tell you you're not getting out of that?"

"Arrrrg!" She banged her feet on the bed.

"While your temper tantrum is amusing, the food is getting cold. Hungry?"

She immediately stilled and licked her lips. "Food?"

"Yeah, ya know..." He mimed holding a plate and spooning food into his mouth, and then rubbed his stomach.

She rolled her eyes, but he'd definitely caught her attention.

"I'm starving," she admitted.

He moved to her side and blocked her view while he unlatched the part of the rope that was tied to the bed.

"Thank you," she said. "Finally."

He raised an eyebrow at her and bound both of her wrists together in front of her. She struggled, and she was strong, he'd give her that, but she was no match for him.

"Arrrrg!" She yelled again. "Why?"

When he only smirked at her, she hauled off and kicked him in the shin. Shit. That hurt, but damned if he'd let her see it. He tugged her by the rope binding her wrists, and she had no choice but to follow him or to fall on her face.

When they got to the kitchen table, he kicked out a chair. "Sit," he commanded.

"I'm not a dog," she grumbled under her breath. But she sat anyway.

He grabbed the bowl from the microwave, spooned out a large helping, and set it in front of her. Then he buttered a piece of leftover cornbread and tossed it on a napkin next to her bowl.

"Lovely service," she sneered.

He sneered back, but had to hold back a laugh. In her position, she should be scared and being as nice as possible, but she obviously had too much fire for that. It was admirable if not a little stupid.

"I don't have to feed you at all. I could make you sit here and watch me eat just because I can."

She spooned up some soup and brought it to her mouth the best she could in her bound condition. Half of it spilled down her chin. Her face scrunched up, and he assumed it was because she was refraining from bitching at him. He was wrong.

"Ew." She dabbed at her fuckable lips with the napkin. "What *is* that crap?"

He blinked at her and dunked his bread in the soup and took a bite before answering. "Soup. What the hell does it look like?"

She shook her head, her blonde hair swishing around her shoulders with the motion. "No. It looks like soup, but it tastes like … like dirty ass."

Shocked, he blinked at her while his mind warred with whether or not to be offended and tell her to fuck off, or to laugh at her boldness and choice of words. He opted for a combination of the two.

"Well then, you can eat dirty ass or you can starve. It's no skin off my nuts."

"Where'd you learn to cook?" she taunted. "Prison?"

He looked her dead in the eyes. "Yes."

Her eyes bugged and she muttered, "Of course you did."

She closed her eyes and grimaced as she bent over and tilted the bowl so she could slurp the dirty-ass soup into her mouth.

His dicked twitched when he imagined how he'd like to have her bound, on her knees in front of him. Him gripping her hair as he forced his cock to the back of her throat, fucking her face until she slurped up his cum like she slurped the soup. *Shit.* He had to rearrange his dick and take several deep breaths before resuming eating.

After finishing her meal, she cocked her head to the side, perusing him. "Am I allowed to know the name of my captor?"

He eyed her, shoved the last bite of bread in his mouth, and swallowed. "Bane."

"So, Bane, why were you in prison?"

He didn't hesitate or bat an eyelash as he said, "I shot a man between the eyes and watched his brains blow out the back of his head."

She blanched, her skin going ashen. Her voice was quiet when she asked, "Why?"

"He deserved it."

"For breaking into your home?" she asked.

He could tell she was trying for a light tone, trying to make a joke to ease her fear, but her voice wavered and cracked.

"No." It wasn't something he liked to think about much less talk about, but even though part of him wanted her to fear him, part of him wanted her to know he wasn't a cold-blooded killer. Well, okay, he was, but not without reason. At least he hadn't been. After prison, he wasn't sure what kind of man he was anymore. "He killed my little sister. Got off on a technicality. Since the system failed to punish him, I took care of it."

"That's awful." She looked truly horrified and he assumed it was because of him blowing a man's brains out, but she surprised him. "I never had a real brother or sister, but I guess I might do the same thing." She looked thoughtful a moment and then grimaced. "No. I'm not sure I could handle the brain explosion. I probably would have gone with poisoning or hiring a hitman. How long were you in prison?"

"Ten years."

She winced. "That must've been awful."

"You have no idea." It felt strange as if she actually felt sorry for him. He'd tied her up, dry humped her ass, thrown her things all over the floor, threatened her, and she felt sorry for him. It had to be an act. She was playing him, trying to soften him so he'd let her go.

"How long have you been out?"

Her pretty hazel gaze oozed sympathy and he wanted to revel in it, soak it in, but it was bullshit. He scowled at her, dumped his bowl in the sink with a loud clang, and leaned back against the counter. "Enough questions."

"Um." She worked her lower lip between her teeth. "I have to pee."

He quirked an eyebrow at her. "What's stopping you?"

Her luscious mouth dropped open exposing the pink tongue that he wanted to see licking the head of his dick. "You can't be serious."

He let her sweat for a few seconds. He liked getting her fired up, even scaring her. It was mean. He was mean. He hadn't always been mean. "Fine." He moved around the table, grabbed onto the rope, and led her to the bathroom.

When he made no move to leave, she said, "Are you gonna stand there and watch?"

"Yes."

"Please." She danced around. "I really gotta go."

She tried to back away when he reached to unbutton and unzip her shorts, but there was nowhere for her to go. She squealed and sat in attempt to cover herself when he jerked the shorts to her knees.

He'd intended to watch her, not because he got off on the bathroom scene, but because, well maybe because he was a bastard. Because she'd broken into his home. Because he felt like it. Because getting under her skin was the most fun he'd had in thirteen years. But one glimpse of the sweet pussy between her legs had him ready to either jack off right in her face or throw her down and fuck her until she passed out. So, he turned his back.

He couldn't get the image out of his mind, and if he didn't take the edge off, there were going to be consequences. His dick was so hard it hurt, throbbed, demanded relief. His brain was want to agree. To touch her, taste her, fuck her, and to *make* her want him…

He shook his head, trying to clear it, but the urges overwhelmed him. By the time she finished, his fists were tight at his sides, his teeth were gritted, and pre-cum soaked the front of his shorts. He spun around to face her, pulled her shorts the rest of the way off, and set her bare ass on the countertop next to the sink.

"What are you doing?" she cried. "Please, don't."

"Be quiet. Do what I say and I won't hurt you."

"Please."

"Shut the fuck up." He freed his aching dick and spread her legs so he had a great view of her pink slit. She closed her legs as soon as he let go of them. He growled and got in her face, his voice low and ominous when he said, "I have a thin thread of control. It's about to snap. Let me see that sweet cunt if you don't want this to get painful."

She gulped, moisture flooding her eyes, but this time when he spread her wide, she stayed that way. He grabbed his dick and stroked fast and hard, his eyes never leaving her pretty slit. He imagined he was thrusting into that sweet hole instead of his hand.

He coated his hand with pre-cum and stroked faster. He moved in right between her legs, his cock so close to her slit, it'd be easy to slide right in. His balls pulled tight against his body, liquid fire rushing through his groin. "Fuck," he bellowed. "Fuckin' fuck." Cum burst from the head of his dick, thick ropey jets shooting onto her pussy. The sight would be burned into his brain for eternity.

Spent, he slumped forward, his forehead resting on her shoulder. Goddamn, he hadn't come that hard in what seemed like forever. None of the porn he'd watched had revved him up as much as seeing her glistening cunt up close and personal.

Coming back to reality, he noticed her breaths were harsh. He pushed away from her and saw her eyes were closed, her face strained. Jesus, he'd probably scared the shit out of her and disgusted her. Well, too bad. He hadn't violated her the way he'd longed to. And she'd gotten herself into this mess and would just have to deal with the consequences.

He washed his hands, pulled a wash cloth and towel from the closet and tossed them on the sink next to her before walking out and closing the door behind him. The window wasn't big enough for an escape, and he needed a moment away from her. He'd damn sure bet she could use a minute to compose herself too.

Chapter Four

Gia's eyes flew open when the door closed. She looked down at the mess between her legs and tried not to be affected by what had just happened. At first, she'd assumed the worst and she'd been terrified, horrified, disgusted. When she'd figured out his intention, she was still freaked out, but as he'd stroked himself while staring hungrily between her legs, her body had reacted against her brain's will.

How could her body betray her like that? Getting turned on by the maniac holding her captive for no good reason? And now her brain was betraying her by balking at the term "maniac." If what he'd told her was true, it was hard to blame him for killing that man.

She couldn't imagine spending ten years in a prison cell. She knew without a doubt that she'd have lost her mind. Which made her contemplate him further. What kind of man had he been before the incident? Had he been kind, caring? Had prison changed him at his core? It would have to. If the movies got it even half right, he must've suffered horrors she couldn't imagine. Maybe that's why he'd done what he'd done. Maybe he'd had similar experiences. Maybe after ten years of such treatment, it was all he knew. Could he find peace? Be redeemed?

It wasn't an excuse for what he'd done to her, but in reality he hadn't hurt her, hadn't taken his advances as far as he could have.

A knock sounded on the door, startling her out of her thoughts. "Just a second," she said. She slid off the counter, ran the water and even though her hands were tied, she managed to clean herself up and pull her shorts back on.

She cast her gaze downward when he opened the door. Saying she was embarrassed by what'd occurred, was a massive understatement. The fact that some part of her had been turned on by it was even more embarrassing, disturbing. She didn't really want to think about what that said about her. He opened a small closet and pulled out a box of bandages and a clean cloth before stepping to her.

"Does it still hurt?" he asked.

She winced when he pulled the old bandage from her forehead then wet the cloth and dabbed at the cut. "Ow."

He inspected it a second and shrugged. "You'll live." He untied one of her hands and she was grateful for the reprieve, but he left the other tied then dumped a couple ibuprofen in her free hand. She popped them in her mouth and drank from the faucet to wash them down.

His eyes burned when she licked water droplets from her lips, but he only grabbed the rope, tugged her along behind him to the bedroom, and secured the loose end to the bed post.

"Get some sleep," was all he said before walking out the door.

She picked at the rope for what seemed like hours until giving into sleep. It'd been a helluva long day, and she'd need her strength for tomorrow.

****

Gia groaned when Bane's gruff voice woke her and reminded her of the predicament she was in. She kept her eyes closed, hoping he'd go away and leave her to sleep awhile longer because she wasn't ready to deal with the craziness yet.

"Ow!" Gia yelped as pain exploded in one of her ass cheeks. "What the hell?" She opened her eyes, shot him the shittiest glare she could manage, and then rubbed her stinging backside with her free hand.

"I said, wake up."

"Well, I'm awake now."

He untied her from the bedpost and led her to the bathroom. Memories of what'd happened in there yesterday flooded her mind. Her stomach clenched at the idea it was about to happen again, but he only told her to take more ibuprofen and then stepped out of the room and closed the door.

She used the facilities and took her time splashing cold water on her face, combing her hair, and wondering what torture was in store for her today. At least her head didn't hurt much anymore.

When he retrieved her, he shoved two peanut butter crackers into her hand. "Eat it. We have work to do."

She made a face at the crackers then gawked at him. "Work? We?"

He tugged her along behind him and when he didn't tie her wrists together when he took her outside, she almost jumped for joy. It was her chance to escape. The minute he turned his back, she'd run. But her pack, everything she owned was inside. Not that it was much, but it was hers, and she didn't know how far she'd make it with zero supplies. She needed to decide whether getting away from him without anything to survive or waiting for an opportunity to escape with all of her things was the riskier but better choice.

After following him down a short path, turned out the choice was taken out of her hands when he stopped and tied her to a tree.

"Seriously?" She huffed as she sat with her ass planted on the grass, the rope tied around her midsection and the tree.

"Eat the crackers." He pulled a bottle of water out of a small blue cooler, opened it, and handed it to her.

She snatched it from him, shoved a cracker into her mouth, and chewed angrily.

Bane pulled an axe out of a stump next to a tree he'd obviously chopped down at an earlier date and started hacking away at the trunk. She gulped when he whipped his tank top over his head and carelessly tossed it to the ground. Was he doing that for her benefit? Did he know how much the sight of his muscled form made her squirm?

He swung the axe with force, his back and shoulder muscles rippling while he split each round into fours. She forced her gaze away before she started drooling.

The sun was hot, and watching him was making it much hotter. Sweat rolled down his body, his tattoos glistening. The small grunts and heavy breathing coming from him made her start to sweat. Psycho or not, the man exuded sex.

He stopped, wiped the sweat from his forehead with the back of his hand, popped a bottle of water, and drank half of it in one long gulp. "Why are you living in the woods?" he asked before swinging the axe again.

"What's it to you?" She knew it was a childish response, but didn't care. Watching him, fantasizing about him was pissing her off, making her twitchy.

He stopped swinging and moved to a foot in front of her, axe held menacingly as though he might chop her into little pieces. "You can tell me, possibly make me believe you and live, or…" He sneered and spun the axe around.

She barely suppressed a shudder. Would he really kill her? He'd threatened as much more than once. Her voice wavered as she said, "It's the only place I feel free."

He considered her a moment before moving back to his chore, but before he started, he said, "Explain."

She pressed her lips together defiantly, but decided to talk. Maybe it would keep her mind off his sweaty body. Maybe it would make him feel bad for her and give her an edge. "I grew up in foster care. I was shuffled around from home to home, each a little worse than the last. The homes were always crowded, felt claustrophobic. The last family I was with took me and their two other foster kids on a week-long camping trip. It was the best week of my life. I hiked for hours, never running out of space."

She stopped, figuring that was a good enough explanation, and he didn't seem to be listening to her anyway. Wrong.

He peered over his shoulder at her. "And?"

"And what?"

"Keep talking."

She leaned her head back against the tree and stared at the sky. "Once I turned eighteen, I drifted, had a string of bad relationships, crappy jobs, and crappy apartments. Then, I thought I'd found a good guy. I had a decent job … for someone like me."

He shot her another over-the-shoulder gaze. "Someone like you?"

She sighed. "You know. No stability. Product of the system. No formal education. Blah, blah."

A curt nod was all he offered. "Go on."

"Long story less long. I was wrong about the guy, but I was living in his apartment. When I realized I needed to get away from him as soon as possible, I started saving every penny I could to get out of there. After a few months, I had enough stowed away and even had a tiny but cute apartment picked out. The day I planned to pack my stuff and tell him, he wasn't there. And neither was my money. He came home late that night drunk and high and let me know he knew what I'd been planning, and was so proud of himself when he told me he'd spent every last dime I'd saved."

She paused. Thinking about it still burned her insides, still made her furious, emotional. Tears stung her eyes but she blinked them away. She wouldn't waste another tear on him.

Bane kept chopping when he said, "And?"

She rolled her eyes and flipped off his back. She was baring her shitty memories to him and all he could say was "and?" Jerk. But she reminded herself he had the upper hand and continued.

"And… In the early hours of the morning while he was sleeping it off, I filled my pack with whatever would fit, hitched a ride as close as I could get to the forest, and here I am."

He stopped now and turned to her. "But you had a job."

"Yes and nowhere to live. I couldn't stay with him a minute longer after that. I just couldn't. I hated him. Wanted to … kill him."

A slight softening of his facial features, understanding, and maybe even sympathy in his eyes surprised her. Then he nodded and went back to chopping wood without a word.

Thirty minutes later, he poured a bottle of water over his head and she couldn't look away as it ran down his face, his body. She flushed when he caught her staring, a cocky smirk turning up the corners of his lips. She rolled her eyes and averted her gaze. The last thing she needed was for him to know how much he affected her.

"Your turn," he said. He untied her from the tree but tied the end of the rope around his wrist with plenty of slack between them. "Grab as much as you can."

"You're making me carry your firewood?"

"Gotta earn your keep."

"If you wouldn't keep me…"

He just stared at her menacingly until she huffed and picked up as much as she could carry. He did the same.

"Why are you chopping wood now anyway? It's so hot."

"So, you would wait until you're freezing your ass off to chop the wood?"

Well, no. It made sense to get it done ahead of time, but she wasn't going to admit that.

They made several more trips until all the wood was stacked at the back of his cabin. She was hungry and sweaty and stinky. Jesus. She could totally smell herself, and whereas she shouldn't care, should be glad for it, hoping she'd stink bad enough to keep him from advancing on her again, she was kind of embarrassed. The sweat and stink on him made him somehow hotter. Her, not so much.

Once inside, he tugged her along to the bathroom, untied the rope from his wrist, and stripped.

"What're you doing?" she practically squeaked. He was all rock hard man and if he wasn't a crazy asshole, she'd jump him in a second.

"Showering. Now, strip," he commanded her.

"I'm not showering with you." She tried to back away.

He advanced on her, grabbed the hem of her shirt and jerked it over her head even though she flailed and fought him. She didn't stop fighting after he'd successfully bared her chest and she landed a punch on his nose. His face contorted into a mask of rage as he wiped the blood from his face, but then he laughed. A laugh that chilled her to her bones.

"I endured ten years of hell in prison. You're no match for me, Gia." He practically spat her name. "Now take off your fucking shorts and shoes. If I have to do it for you, you'll pay."

She had to get away from him. Somehow. Someway. There had to be a way. With shaking hands, she removed her shoes and her shorts. Fear pooled in the pit of her stomach as he eyed her as though he wanted to devour her. Then he grabbed her arms and she thought that was it, he was going to show her just how much of a psycho he was, but he spun her around and tied her arms behind her back, then turned on the shower.

"Get in," he said.

Her legs shook as she stepped in, and even though fear ate at her, the hot water felt like heaven on her tired, aching body. She almost cried when he got in and pushed her to the back so he could hog the heavenly spray.

Bane soaped and scrubbed his face, arms, legs, and had no shame when he soaped up his dick and balls before washing his hair. She tried not to watch, but the scene mesmerized her. His soap smelled manly and earthy with a hint of spice. He smelled delicious and if the situation had been different, she'd have laughed at her stomach choosing that moment to growl loud and long.

"Hungry?" he asked as he rinsed his hair.

Throat dry from watching his bathing show, she simply nodded.

He switched places with her, the glorious flow sluicing over her body again and she wished her hands were free. She jumped when he gripped her hair but relaxed as he worked shampoo through it.

His fingers were magic as he kneaded her scalp, her shoulders, her back, and then down her legs, but humiliation shot through her as he soaped her crack. Her entire body flushed from embarrassment. No one had ever done that to her before.

She tensed when he spun her around. The unadulterated lust in his eyes both frightened her and somewhere deep in the recesses of her mind, turned her on as he filled his palm with fresh soap and caressed her breasts. Her stomach quivered as his hands moved lower. Was he going to wash her there? Was he going to violate her?

She squeezed her eyes closed as he cupped her, massaged her. She told herself he was only cleaning her, it wasn't so bad, but when a finger slipped between her lips and stroked slowly, sensually, she pleaded. "Please." The word was a quiet, breathy whisper. "Please don't." And *she* didn't even believe her plea.

He circled her clit with slow strokes at first, slowly building the pressure and friction. As much as she tried, she couldn't control her body's reaction. Her pussy tingled, wanted, and grew wetter.

"That's it," he said, his voice low. He slicked two fingers through her wetness then resumed flicking and rubbing her clit until she thought she would burst. His breathing sped up, little grunts escaping him. When she opened her eyes, he was pumping his cock while watching his fingers work her. And damnit, her hips bucked.

He looked up, his eyes glazed. "You want to come." It wasn't a question.

She squeezed her eyes shut again. She wouldn't admit it, but a few more strokes and she'd come apart, wanted to come apart, wanted the release even if it was *him* touching her.

He removed his hand from between her legs and she whimpered, her body all raw nerves and needy.

He wrapped his arms around her and pressed his erection against her stomach. His warm breath puffed in her ear. "Suck me off," he said. "Suck me off, and I'll make you come."

She stood there frozen, aroused, ready to hump his leg to get off, but she couldn't do that. Not to him. Not to someone holding her hostage. Could she? Would it be so bad? She must be going insane to even consider it, so she said nothing.

He grabbed his cock and slicked it around her clit. He growled now, clearly determined to get what he wanted. He gripped her neck, his voice rough and almost desperate as he said, "Suck me off or I'll bend you over and fuck you."

Her entire body shook, fear and desire warring with one another. What the fuck was wrong with her? "N-no. Please."

His eyes squeezed closed as his grip tightened around her neck, but then he let go and spun her around so that her ass was facing him. Oh God. He was going to do it. Was going to do what he said. She screamed when his erection pressed against her ass. He clamped a hand over her mouth, and then reached the other hand around between her legs to stroke her clit again. It took only seconds to bring her back to the brink. Her traitorous body burning for that release.

"It's just your mouth, sweetheart. Suck me off and I'll let you go."

Would he really? She couldn't think straight with his fingers between her legs. "Oh God," she moaned, the words muffled beneath his hand.

Her body tensed, shook, ecstasy erupting between her legs. Her mind blanked from the pleasure making her momentarily forget her situation. When she slumped, her knees giving out, he held her tight against him.

When she was able to hold herself upright, he spun her around to face him. He grabbed his dick and stroked slowly while imploring her with his dark gaze.

She told herself that she sank to her knees and took him in her mouth because she believed he'd let her go. When "liar" whispered through her mind, she shut it out.

Her pussy still tingling from climax, she closed her eyes and parted her lips as his fingers twisted in her hair and he pressed his thick cock into her mouth. She sucked him in, took him as deep as she could.

"That's it." He moaned as he stared down at her. "So good."

He fucked her mouth slowly at first, purposefully, watching with clear lust and fascination as his cock slipped in and out of her mouth. Quickly, guttural moans and grunts burst from him as he pushed harder, faster, deeper. She closed her eyes concentrating and somehow reveling in the pleasure he found in her.

When he stilled and an animalistic roar tore from him, she sucked and licked as cum shot to the back of her throat. She opened her eyes to find him looking down at her, his face a picture of adoration, awe, and worship. No one had ever looked at her like that after a blowjob, and she couldn't stop the warm feeling that spread through her chest.

They stared at each other, something she couldn't name passing between them until he finally pulled from her mouth. He staggered, but then steeled himself and helped her stand before turning the shower off and getting out. In silence, he toweled them both dry, untied her wrists, and handed her a toothbrush.

Chapter Five

"Are you letting me go now?" she asked as she pulled on the large t-shirt he'd tossed at her.

He pulled on a pair of black workout shorts before turning to her. "No."

"But, you said—"

"I didn't say *when*. Come on."

She wanted to scream, to rip his lying fucking tongue out of his mouth. She'd given him what he wanted, had lowered herself. She shivered as images bombarded her mind. His taste, his enjoyment. She'd wanted it, had craved it. She obviously needed a shrink.

When they arrived in the kitchen, he motioned to the fridge and the pantry. "Make lunch," he said and sat at the table.

"What?" she asked, wondering what the catch was. He'd removed her ties, and he was giving her free reign in his kitchen? The blowjob must have done at least some good. Leaving her unbound was definitely a slip up.

"You insulted my cooking, so you make lunch."

Her stomach rumbled again, reminding her how hungry she was. She gave him a leery look but shrugged and opened the fridge. "What do you want?"

"Whatever."

The temptation to make something disgusting was strong, but she really wanted to eat.

The refrigerated items were sparse, so she checked the pantry and marveled at the size of it and how many items were available. If she could carry it with her, she'd be able to avoid towns for the next six months.

Her gaze lit on a package of mac and cheese and she practically drooled as she snatched it up. Next she chose a can of tuna, canned diced tomatoes and chilies and set them on the counter. She looked over at Bane. He was sitting and watching her intently.

"I need a pot and a casserole dish," she said.

"Bottom left."

It was nerve-racking knowing he was only a few feet away watching her every move, but the more she got into her task, the more she relaxed and even enjoyed herself. She hadn't had access to a real kitchen since taking to the woods.

After the mac and cheese was cooked, she dumped it into the casserole dish and stirred in the tuna and tomatoes and chilies.

"Cheese grater?"

"Top right."

Man of few words. She pulled the block of cheese from the fridge and grated some on top of the mixture. It would be good, but it needed something else. She went back to the pantry and grabbed some crackers to crumble on top.

"I'm hungry," he said.

She jumped when she realized he was standing right behind her. She hadn't heard him walk over. "It'll only take about fifteen minutes," she said nervously.

He opened the fridge and pulled out two cans of beer, handing her one. Surprised, it took her a full fifteen seconds to reach out her hand and accept it. When he went back and sat at the table, she did the same.

The silence as they sipped at their beer was making her anxious. "Um," she stumbled for something to say. "Why does the outside of this place look like such a dump but the inside is so nice?"

He raised an eyebrow at her use of the word "dump" but didn't seem pissed. "The inside used to match the outside. I fixed it up but left the outside alone as much as I could. Didn't want any passersby to think it was worth breaking into." He eyed her. "Apparently, that didn't work."

Her face heated at that. "What about that room in the back?"

"Haven't gotten to it yet."

"Oh." She took another swig of beer and looked around awkwardly.

By the time the oven timer dinged, she was about to jump out of her skin.

She practically ran to the oven, relieved for the break in the tension.

"Bowls?"

"Top left."

Instead of asking this time, she opened one of the only two drawers looking for utensils. Her eyes widened when they lit on the steak knives next to the spoons. Couldn't believe she hadn't thought of that. Her hand hovered over a knife. Could she do it? Could she sink it into his flesh and twist and turn it?

"Do you really think you can take me down?" he asked calmly as if reading her thoughts.

She stared at the knife another few seconds before grabbing a spoon and two forks, filling the bowls and carrying them to the table. It wasn't the right time. Catching him unaware was key.

He leaned over the bowl and inhaled before forking up a hefty bite, and scarfed down the rest of the bowl before speaking.

"Not bad," he said.

"Thanks." It wasn't much of a compliment. It might not have been a gourmet meal, but it was damn tasty and one hundred times better than the slop he'd cooked. She wasn't finished, and it was difficult to eat with him staring at her so she tried to distract him. "Who are the Martins?"

He scowled and she damned herself for opening her mouth, but the scowl eventually faded. "Family of the man I killed."

She swallowed a mouthful of mac and cheese and the lump that had suddenly formed in her throat. "Oh. Are you expecting them to come after you?"

He shrugged. "I was. But after being out three years ... maybe they can't find me. Maybe they don't have the balls. Maybe after thirteen years, it just isn't important to them anymore. People move on."

"Is that why you moved out here? To hide?"

"I don't need to hide. They show up, they die. I moved out here because I needed ... space, privacy, to be left the hell alone."

She found herself nodding and sighing. "I completely understand. I'm sorry I invaded your space." And she truly was sorry. Not just because her invasion had gotten her into trouble, but because she understood that need. Felt it down to her core.

She couldn't read the expression that crossed his face as he studied her intently, but finally he shrugged and leaned back in the chair. "You've proved to be ... entertaining."

Her face heated. Hell, her whole body flushed as she thought of how she'd taken him into her mouth. How he'd played her body until he'd had her wanting him even though rationally she knew it was stupid and wrong.

Uncomfortable, she gathered the dishes and carried them to the sink. She eyed the drawer with the knives but forced her gaze away. If she kept playing nice, he'd let her go. He had to. At least she had to believe that.

Strong arms wrapped around her before she could turn around. His muscled body pressed against her. "Still want to stab me?"

"W-what?" She feigned ignorance.

His hand slid lower slowly until he was stroking lightly between her legs. She shuddered but fought the urge to spread her legs to give him better access. Was she seriously so fucked up in the head that she burned for this psycho? Did Stockholm Syndrome set in that fast?

"Go clean up your stuff," he said gruffly as he pulled away from her. The action was so abrupt, she almost fell backward. She steadied herself and shot him a silent question, not sure she understood.

"The bedroom. Clean up your stuff."

She walked toward the bedroom on shaky legs. Was that it? Was he letting her go now? Her knife was in there. He hadn't taken it. Oh hell. This was it. He wasn't even following her, just leaving her to her own devices. She kept her steps calm until she turned the corner then she ran on tiptoes into the room. She grabbed her knife first and held it to her like a lifeline while sloppily shoving the other items into her pack.

If she could just get past him, hold the knife on him, and get to the door, she was pretty sure she could outrun him. Maybe. She hoped. She pulled on her shorts and tucked the knife into the waistband. If he was about to let her go, she didn't want to pull it on him and piss him off and make him change his mind.

She steeled herself and made her way out of the room, pack on her back. He was standing in the living area staring her way.

He quirked an eyebrow at her. "Going somewhere?"

"I-uh. I thought…"

"I only asked you to *clean up* the mess."

Her hand instinctively grabbed at the knife on her waist as he advanced on her. He stopped short and held out his hand. "Give it to me. You can have it back when you leave."

Her fingers trembled as she pulled the knife from under the baggy t-shirt and pulled it from its sheath. "Just let me leave, Bane. I don't want to hurt you."

The smile that pulled at his lips left her cold inside. "Hurt," he mused. "You have no idea the hurt I've endured." He took another step forward. "You ... the only time I feel relief from the torment I've endured is when I'm touching you. I'm not ready to let go of that yet."

Another step put him just in reach if she slashed out at him. She told herself to do it. Her mind screamed for her to do it and run but her feet stayed planted.

"Am I really so bad?" he asked. "Do you know how much I've wanted to plow into every hole in your tight little body? To feel the brief relief that comes with it?" He reached out and stroked her wrist. The knife trembled in her hand.

"But you ... in the shower," she accused with less heat than she should have.

"I gave you a choice. I even made you come first. You didn't have to do it. Admit it. You wanted me."

She shook her head fiercely in denial. "No. I only did it so you'd let me go."

A hurt look that quickly turned to anger crossed his face. "Liar. You want me now." His grip tightened on her wrist, the knife slipping from her grasp and clanking on the hardwood floor. "Ease a little more of my pain, Gia. Make me feel like a man again."

It took her three tries to swallow the lump in her throat. His eyes projected a sadness, a pain that made her heart ache for him when she shouldn't. It wasn't her fault he'd suffered in prison. It wasn't her fault his sister had died. But it was *his* fault that he'd tied her up and kept her against her will and forced unwanted sexual advances on her. Unwanted. She thought of how he'd made her crave his touch and *unwanted* felt like a lie.

He kicked the knife across the floor and cupped her cheek, stroking his thumb lightly across her bottom lip. Her mouth parted, the tenderness of his touch surprising her. She cringed as the possibilities of what had happened to him in prison to make him not feel like a man entailed.

She didn't stop him as he slid her pack off her shoulders and dropped it to the floor. She was frozen in a whirlwind of confusion, indecision. When his lips met hers in a gentle but passionate kiss, she melted into him. The kiss was so soft and tender and his body trembled against her as if the tenderness frightened him. It was nice, sweet, but something inside her craved the other side of him. The harsh, forceful side.

Without thinking, she wrapped her arms around him and pulled him close, deepening the kiss. That was all the encouragement he needed. Maybe that's exactly what he needed. Needed someone to want him. He moaned and ground his erection against her, his tongue delving deep into her mouth, taking charge, now demanding her response and she gave it.

How long had it been since someone wanted her with a desperation that made her head spin? How long had it been since someone made her want a man's touch the way he did?

She'd been so caught up in the kiss, she hadn't noticed he'd been walking her backwards until she hit the wall.

His fingers fumbled with the button on her shorts. "Tell me you want me. Not because I promise to let you go. Not because you're scared. Tell me you want me because you mean it. Just let me hear it one time. Make me feel it and I *will* let you go."

His gaze implored hers with need, pain, and she couldn't deny him in that moment. She slid her hands across his rock hard abs and up his chest and neck, and then cupped his face. "I want you, Bane. I don't know what it is, but I do." She looked down at his hands gripping the button of her shorts. "*Feel* how bad I want you."

Bane squeezed his eyes shut before opening them again. He popped the button and unzipped her shorts, letting them slip to the floor before slowly sliding his hand between her legs and fingering her juices. Something like a growl rumbled deep in his chest as he shoved a finger inside her. She gasped, her hips jutting forward searching for more.

He pushed her t-shirt up with his free hand. She took the hint and whipped it over her head. He licked and nipped at her nipples until they were tight and raw as he pumped a finger in and out of her.

"I want to fuck you hard, rough," he said through gritted teeth, seeming to have only a thread of control. "To fuck away all the memories eating at my soul." He picked her up and sat her on the arm of the couch, grabbed her knees and roughly jerked them apart so she was completely open to him.

Her stomach clenched, goose bumps broke out over every inch of her skin as he stood in front of her looking as though he wanted to break her. His muscles bunched as he shucked off his shorts. His cock stood high and hard and she yearned to know how it'd feel deep inside her.

Suddenly he dropped to his knees, shoved a thumb inside her, and latched onto her clit with his lips. He sucked her, lapped at her, moaning and grunting as if she was his last meal.

Her nails dug into the leather of the couch arm as she fought to keep from falling backward. Sensations rocked from her pussy through her stomach and out every limb. Her nerves sizzled as the pressure built and finally exploded, her juices squirting. He slurped at them, rubbed his stubble around in them, and seemed to revel in it.

When her body started jerking uncontrollably from too much stimulation, he shot to his feet, pulled her to him and fed her her own orgasm before flipping her around and pressing her face down ass up over the arm of the couch. He rammed into her, not sparing an inch.

She gasped and cried out.

His fingers dug into her hips. "Fucking Christ almighty," he said in a strained tone. His breaths hissed in and out of his lungs, but he stayed still, buried deep. "I want to fucking hurt you." His fingers dug deeper into her hips and she bit back a squeal. "But I don't want to."

****

The urge to fuck her like a goddamn wild animal beat inside his heart, his soul, hammered in his brain. He'd suffered unthinkable injustices in prison and wanted to wipe it away inside her. Wanted to punish her for all those wrongdoings, but another part of him didn't want to. She was beautiful, gorgeous, a godsend that demanded to be treated with care and respect, but that wasn't him anymore.

His cock pulsed, demanding to be satisfied, to pound, to batter, to ram.

She looked over her shoulder at him. Her eyes half lidded, mouth parted seductively, and breathing coming in sweet pants. "Fuck me, Bane. Use me. I want it."

Yes, a godsend. He spread her ass cheeks, that pink pucker calling to him, but not this time. Her juicy pussy was a heavenly sheath sucking at him, clenching around him, and it would take the first round of his wrath, his pain, his fucking need.

He pulled back and slammed into her unmercifully. She cried out but said "yes." Over and over he slammed into her. Smacking sounds reverberated in the room. Juicy suction noises and the feminine smell of her filled his head, and all he could think about was that this was his reward. His reward for righting an injustice. His reward for ten years of suffering the penalties of righting that injustice. Her perfect pussy was his, his prize, his godsend.

His legs shook, his balls pulling tight against his body as liquid fire ran the length of his cock. At the last second, he pulled free and stroked his load onto that pink asshole. Spurt after spurt of cum coated her delectable crack. He staggered from the powerful sensation but gripped her plump ass cheek with one hand, his still hard dick in the other.

He pressed the head against her impossibly tight hole and pushed forward. She squealed and the sound spurred him on. "I want in this hole too, Gia. Let me in."

When she raised her ass as much as she could in her restricted position, he almost fell to his knees and wept. She wanted it. She was giving herself to him in whatever way he wanted and goddamn he was going to take it.

He flicked her swollen clit with a fingertip while rubbing the head of his cock against her asshole. The more she bucked and moaned, the more pressure he put on her ass. When the head popped inside, she screamed his name and he almost came right then. Her body jerked and twitched and he didn't stop flicking her clit until she calmed.

Slowly, he pushed farther inside. So tight, almost too tight. A sheen of sweat covered her gorgeous skin. He wanted to ram into her, the urge to hurt her hard to fight, but he did. He eased himself all the way in. It'd been so long since he'd experienced this kind of want and acquiescence from a woman, he wanted to treasure it, savor it, brand it into his being.

He leaned forward and wrapped her hair around his wrist, tugging firmly.

"Who's fucking your ass, Gia?" He needed to know she wasn't daydreaming, fantasizing that she was with someone else.

With her head tilted back and him rocking his cock in her ass, her words came out in choked huffs. "You. Bane."

"Say it louder," he demanded. "Mean it."

"You. Are. Fucking my ass. Bane."

"Tell me you like it. No. Tell me you fucking love it."

"Love it. More."

Jesus Christ. That ecstasy wrapped around his balls, his dick, and he was about to fucking shoot off again. "Tell me you want me to come in your ass. Tell me now."

He let go of her hair, grabbed handfuls of her ass cheeks, and thrust a little harder.

With her face smashed into the couch cushions, her words came out in muffled pants. "Come in my ass."

That was it. He roared like a wild fucking beast, the sound something he didn't recognize as his own and his cock unleashed torrents of cum into her sweet ass. Sweat ran down his face, his chest, his heart pounding like a fucking jackhammer in his chest. When the sensation grew too much he pulled from her with a "pop" and slumped over her back.

They lay there like that for long moments. No words, just heavy breathing and a slick of sweat between their bodies. When he felt as though he could stand, he pulled her up and carried her to the bathroom. They cleaned up in silence, and then he took her to bed.

He curled around her and stroked the soft skin of her stomach. She sighed sweetly and relaxed against him, the sound and action softening the hard barrier around his heart. He couldn't remember ever feeling so content, so sated, the anger and pain of the past receded into the background and all he wanted was to hold on to that feeling, stay right there with her forever.

Chapter Six

Sunlight streamed through a small split in the curtains and cut right through Bane's eyelids. He blinked and jerked upright. It was morning? Shit. That was the longest and most restful sleep he'd had in thirteen years. He stretched and harsh reality hit him. He was alone.

He ran to the bathroom. She wasn't there. He checked the kitchen and living room. She wasn't there and neither was her pack. He ran all around the outside of the cabin. No sign of her. She'd left. His gut clenched and his heart ached. He still needed her. Why had she left him?

He threw his fists into the air and yelled at the sky. Rage at himself, his life, and her poured out of him. Of course she'd left. He'd tied her up, he'd terrified her, and he'd forced his advances on her. She'd played him yesterday. Played along with his animalistic fucking in the hopes she'd be able to get away. And he'd bought it because he'd wanted it so desperately. God, he was a fucking bastard. A fucking bastard and an idiot.

He sank to the grass and wept. The pain and memories were back in full force and the loss of her was the icing on his shit cake. He wished he could see her one more time. He'd apologize and then he'd beg her, pay her, give her everything he had for just one more time inside her sweet salvation. He'd be gentle, caring like she deserved. If she said no, he'd tie her up and make her want him for real. *Bastard.*

"Bane?"

His head snapped up at the most beautiful sound. A voice. *Her* voice. He wiped the moisture from his eyes and watched in disbelief as her athletic body ran down the path toward him. The backlight from the sun formed a sort of halo around her making her look even more like the angel of salvation she was. He had to be hallucinating. She wouldn't come back. Not for him.

She sank to her knees beside him and slipped her pack off. An electric jolt shot through him when her delicate hand gripped his shoulder.

"Bane? Are you okay?"

He reached out and touched her face. "Are you real?"

She looked at him oddly then smiled. "Um. Are you high?"

High? She was making a joke. Teasing him. He grabbed her and crushed her to him as he burst out laughing. The relief made him giddy, stupid, dizzy. "I am now," he choked out.

He didn't know how long they stayed like that, but she didn't pull away, just let him hold onto her. When he finally did pull back she smiled at him again and the sight left him awestruck.

"You came back," he said.

She brightened even more. "I brought you breakfast."

"Breakfast?" he asked stupidly.

"Well, I mean, I need to make it for you. If you want."

"Yes." Breakfast. Such a normal idea never sounded so awesome. He jumped up, grabbed her pack, and then took her hand to help her up.

"Careful with that," she said as they went to the kitchen.

She took it from him, set it on the table, unzipped it, and pulled out the t-shirt he'd given her. It was all rolled in a ball. Then she unwrapped the cargo inside. Four brown eggs.

"Where did you get those?"

"Well, I woke up super early and you were still out. I wasn't sure…" She fidgeted with the eggs. "I wasn't sure if I should stick around or leave or what. So, I went for a hike to clear my mind. I must've been walking for an hour when I heard a rooster. Not too long after, I came across a small house that had a chicken coup out back." She grinned. "I couldn't resist."

"Little thief."

"Well, that's when I decided to come back. You only have that powdered egg stuff in your pantry." She frowned, a little crease splitting her forehead, and slipped onto a chair. "Why do I want to make you breakfast?"

He swallowed hard. "Tell me."

She gazed at him, her frown deepening. "I don't know. I kept telling myself to keep moving. To get far away. You could tie me up again, keep me against my will."

"I won't," he quickly reassured her. "Never again, Gia. Unless…" He couldn't hold back the shudder as he remembered her on her knees, hands tied behind her back, sucking him off. "Unless you want me to."

Her eyes darkened, a light dusting of blush coloring her cheeks and he knew she was remembering the same thing. She squirmed in her seat. "Beneath the scary asshole, you're…" She frowned again. "Vulnerable. Sweet even. And the way you touch me…" She closed her eyes and shivered. "I feel like you need me. No one's ever needed me before. I like it."

"I do." He kneeled between her legs on the hard floor. "When I touch you I feel in control, like I've gotten back a part of myself that was lost. Stay awhile. Come and go as you please, but don't disappear without saying good-bye."

He traced the insides of her thighs with light strokes of his fingers. He'd hardened at first sight of her running down the path toward him. She shivered and licked her lips as his touch neared her pussy, and he wanted inside her now. Needed the connection. Needed to know she would stay for at least a little while.

He had to tread carefully, lightly, not be too demanding and scare her away. Wanted to show her he could be good even if what he really wanted to do was rip her clothes off and fuck her with rough abandon.

"Can breakfast wait?" He had to force the question out. Asking politely for what he wanted wasn't an easy task. Not anymore. "I need to touch you."

Her brow furrowed as she looked down at him. "I don't know. Can it?"

Her voice was sharp, annoyed. What was that about?

He gritted his teeth and bit back the anger and need to demand what he wanted. "Yes," he barely managed the word. "I'll wait."

A hard slap across his face shocked the shit out of him and then pissed him off. "What the fuck?" he bellowed as he jumped to his feet and pulled her off the chair with a hard jerk of her arm.

"I want *you*," she said.

The urge to strangle her warred with the urge to kiss her. Had she lost her mind? "I want you too."

"Then take me," she whispered.

When he only stood there staring at her and trying to figure out what the hell game she was playing, she slapped him again. He snapped and grabbed her throat.

"You want me angry, Gia?" He shoved a hand down her pants, his dick jerking when he found her already wet. Fucking Christ. She wanted him. The way he was. The way he'd taken her before. And goddamn if that didn't make him insane with lust.

He shoved two fingers inside her. Her hips bucked and her raspy breathing due to his hand around her throat brought him back to life. "You want to come?"

"Yes," she choked out.

"Me first," he said. "Strip. Then suck me off. Right here. Right now. I want to come on your pretty lips." He gave her neck a little squeeze before releasing her. Her entire body shook as she hurriedly stripped out of her clothes then sank to her knees before him. He fisted his dick in one hand and fisted her hair in the other. He swiped his throbbing head across her lips, smearing his pre-cum across them.

"Lick it off," he demanded. When her pink tongue darted out and did as he'd ordered, he pressed into her warm, wet mouth. *Godsend.* The word drifted through his mind as she bobbed before him. She sucked his dick like she was starving for it. She moaned and hummed as she sucked him to the back of her throat, the vibrations reverberating to his balls.

She was good. Too good. She was his godsend, and he couldn't hold back, didn't want to hold back.

Every muscle in his body tensed, contracted to the point of pain until a wave of utter euphoria crashed through him. He jerked back, palmed his dick and stroked, watching as he coated her pretty lips and chin with his cum. Never had he seen such an erotic sight as she licked her lips and gazed up at him with lust-drugged eyes.

He reached down, wiped her chin, and watched as she licked it from his fingers. "What do you want, Gia?"

"To come."

He left her kneeling on the floor and took a seat a few feet away and crooked a finger at her. "Then come."

She crawled to him on hands and knees looking like a hungry tigress.

"Turn around."

She did, putting that luscious ass in the air right in front of him. Juices coated the insides of her thighs. Her body jerked and she cried out when he leaned forward and shoved two fingers inside her, fucking her rough and hard.

"More," she pleaded when he removed his fingers.

Seeing her like that, wanton, needy, juicy, had his cock hard again. He kneeled behind her and bit each of her ass cheeks before ramming inside her. His fingers found her swollen clit and frigged it fast, furious.

He smacked her ass as he plowed into her. Smacked it until it was bright red and she cried out. "Don't disappear on me again."

"I won't." She whimpered and rocked backward taking his abusive fucking as if she couldn't get enough. "Bane!" His name tore from her throat as her sweet cunt convulsed around his dick.

"That's it. Say my name."

He grabbed hold of her hips and pumped inside her frantically, hard, deep, rough. He wanted to come inside her sweet salvation while her muscles still spasmed, to join her in ecstasy.

"Fuck, Gia!" He yelled as liquid fire shot from his balls and out the tip of his cock. Bright lights flickered in his gaze partially blinding him and he thought he might actually pass out from the all-consuming pleasure pouring from his body as he shot off inside her.

When they collapsed, he rolled to the side, lay back on the cool hardwood floor, and pulled her on top of him. He traced circles on her back as she lay there limp, her heart hammering against his chest.

He didn't know how long they lay there and didn't care. He felt like a man again because of her. "That was … nice."

Her soft body shook against his. "Only nice?"

"Mmm. I might give it a fucking-amazing rating if I had some breakfast in my stomach."

She lifted her head, her mouth dropping open. "Did you just make a joke?"

He had to fight back the smile pulling at his lips. "No joke. I'm starving."

"Well, you're going to have to help me up. Not sure I can stand after that."

He wrapped his arms tight around her. "You'll stay awhile. I'm not finished with you yet."

A little smirk twisted her lips as she shrugged. "It's not like I have anywhere else to be."

Bane returned her smirk and gave her a light smack on the ass before turning serious. He brushed a lock of hair out of her face and tucked it behind her ear. Emotion welled in his chest and formed a lump in his throat. It took a full minute of swallowing hard before he could speak, and his voice still came out rough and choked up. "Tell me you *want* to stay."

Gia's hazel gaze met his, her smirk replaced with a tender smile. Instead of answering, she pressed her lips to his and kissed him with more emotion than any words could ever express.

Godsend.

The End

www.jocelyndex.com

EVERNIGHT PUBLISHING ®

www.evernightpublishing.com